He had his arm round her before Genevra could realize what he was doing. She could feel his breath on her face. She turned her head to one side, but Francis wrenched it round and his mouth was on hers, hot and wet. Genevra struggled, but he only held her more tightly, until at last his hold slackened and she was able to push him away. With only one thought in her mind – to keep him at arm's length – she brought up her riding crop and struck out wildly . . .

By the same author

The London Linnet

TANIA LANGLEY

Genevra

GRAFTON BOOKS
A Division of the Collins Publishing Group

LONDON GLASGOW
TORONTO SYDNEY AUCKLAND

Grafton Books
A Division of the Collins Publishing Group
8 Grafton Street, London W1X 3LA

A Grafton Paperback Original 1987

ISBN 0-586-07008-7

Printed and bound in Great Britain by
Collins, Glasgow

Set in Times

1

Four people were seated in the library of Leylands House, all attired in deepest black. A silence had settled on the room, the silence of profound shock. Outside, the weak March sunlight shone on a few early daffodils, tossing in a cold wind under trees whose bare branches framed a vista of the Surrey hills.

At last Genevra Kerslake roused herself to speak.

'Am I to understand, Mr Ryman, that there is *nothing* left in my father's estate?'

The lawyer bowed his head in sad acknowledgment.

'But this house . . . the land . . .'

'Heavily mortgaged.'

To the hilt, he might have said, and the interest unpaid; but he was trying to spare her, as far as he could.

'My mother's jointure . . .'

'Re-settled during her lifetime – with her consent, of course.'

'She would have done anything for my father,' Genevra sighed.

She was taking it quietly, better than Mr Ryman had expected; but suddenly a realization of her position seemed to come to her and she asked, in total bewilderment, 'What am I to do?'

The other woman in the room roused herself to answer.

'You will come to us, of course. You must have done that in any case, since it would be quite out of the question for you to live at Leylands alone.' She smoothed her hand over her black silk skirt. 'I must say it comes as

5

no great surprise. Uncle Ludovic's affairs have been in a desperate state for as long as I remember.'

'He always said so,' Genevra agreed. 'But I never took him seriously. There always seemed to be money . . .'

'Uncle Ludo usually managed to find the means to pay for his pleasures,' her cousin, Leonora Hamden, replied, with just enough of a sneer in her voice to make Genevra wince.

Leonora glanced at her husband, lounging on the sofa with a look on his face which she recognized as concealing a profound distaste for the situation. They had already agreed that it would be proper for Leonora to offer a home to her orphaned cousin, the only child of her own mother's sister, but neither of them had anticipated that the girl would be a complete pauper. Sir Francis was well able to support an extra dependant, but how were they ever to get the girl off their hands if she hadn't a penny to her name?

Genevra Kerslake, only daughter of Ludovic and Miranda Kerslake, of Leylands House, Charleigh, in the County of Surrey, was twenty-one years old. Her mother had died some eight years earlier. It had been anticipated that Mr Kerslake would marry again and Ludovic himself, in the first flush of early middle age, vigorous and good-looking, had had the idea in his head ever since emerging from the first year of mourning for his wife; but he had set his sights too high for an obscure country gentleman loaded with debt. His first application, to a woman of wealth and title some twenty years his junior, had been courteously discouraged by the lady's family; his subsequent pursuit of a widow, even richer but less well connected, had seemed to promise both a stepmother of a suitable age for his young daughter and a speedy settlement of his money worries – until the lady had

6

disappointed all her friends by betrothing herself to a clerk in her late husband's business.

Ludovic Kerslake had retired to his country estate to restore his wounded pride and to try, by desperate measures of economy, to recoup the cost of his wooing. This had proved so boring that it had surprised no one when he had been forced by his ennui to return to London. Unfortunately, he had celebrated his return to the metropolis by falling victim to an actress who had cost him a pretty penny, first and last, until she had informed him that if the dibs weren't in tune then neither was she, and sent him off to Surrey once more.

A neglected head-cold had descended to his chest, an obstinate decision to ride out in a pelting rainstorm had brought on pneumonia, and Ludovic Kerslake, to his own immense surprise and his daughter's despairing grief, had been called to face the disapproval of his ancestors. For who could doubt their displeasure? He was the last of a long line, some of them as profligate, none of them as improvident as Ludovic had proved himself to be. They had left their estates encumbered, but this was the first time a Kerslake daughter had been left a penniless orphan.

Her cousin thought bitterly that Genevra was a pretty girl and if she had been properly presented might already have been suitably settled. But Ludovic's affairs had not permitted the expense of a London season for his daughter, while his pride had jibbed at escorting her to minor local festivities in Surrey. The result was that Genevra had lived a retired life and although not without a certain quiet assurance, which came from having had the running of Leylands in her hands since she was little more than a child, she had few of the social arts.

She was slightly over middle height, but not too tall, with a charming, neat figure. Her colouring was delightful

7

– a fair complexion with a delicate flush of colour in her cheeks, eyes of a soft hue between grey and mauve, and a mass of pale gold hair. 'His flower girl', Ludovic had called her in a poetical moment; but his pride in her looks had not inspired him to put himself to the trouble of seeing her suitably established in life.

Properly dressed, given a little polish, encouraged to overcome her natural diffidence, she might have achieved a success in London Society. As it was, her cousin Leonora foresaw with gloom that Genevra was destined to remain an inmate of her household for many years to come, and possibly die a spinster unless some country curate offered for her.

'There are bills outstanding to local tradesmen which must be settled,' Genevra said.

'I have everything of that sort in hand.' Mr Ryman answered with what he intended to be sympathetic reassurance. 'No need to worry your head about such things, Miss Kerslake.'

He missed the look of ironic impatience which passed over Genevra's face. Did he imagine that she had not been in the habit of dealing with household affairs, scraping and saving to ensure that small businesses did not suffer because of her father's improvidence? She had always known, even though she loved him, that he was not to be trusted with money: but Genevra had imagined that with her father's death the resources of the estate (which she had to admit he had drained severely) would soon recover, and it would be possible by careful contrivance to keep the house and land together.

She had foreseen that her relations would think her too young to live at home alone, though she had spent long periods on her own during her father's lifetime. She had decided to give in to their wishes, but always with the intention of returning to Leylands one day . . . When she

8

was married, she had thought vaguely. with no one in mind as a possible husband, only a lonely girl's romantic dream of a loving companion to share her beautiful home . . .

'If the house were let to a tenant?' Genevra asked, following her train of thought.

'I'm sorry, that will not be sufficient,' the lawyer said. 'The person who holds the mortgages requires them to be redeemed.'

He was reluctant to mention the word 'foreclose', but that was what it amounted to; and considering the arrears of interest he could not bring himself to blame the mortgagor.

'So Leylands must be sold,' Sir Francis said. 'Where are you going to find anyone willing to buy it?'

'I know of a party who may be interested,' Mr Ryman replied.

He hesitated and then decided not to reveal that the prospective purchaser already owned the estate in everything but name. Mr Pyrritt had shown exemplary patience in his dealings with Ludovic Kerslake, rather more than one would have expected from such a hard-headed businessman, and he might not wish to have it known that his acquisition of this desirable property owed more to the repayment of debt than to hard cash changing hands.

'Someone acceptable to the neighbourhood, I hope,' Leonora said sharply. 'Such odd people seem to get hold of money these days.'

'Mr Matthew Pyrritt,' the lawyer stated.

For a moment Leonora looked blank then she asked incredulously, 'The *shopkeeper*?'

'You can hardly call him a shopkeeper, not in the ordinary sense,' her husband pointed out. 'Pyrritt's must be one of the largest new stores in the West End. No expense spared, I believe. Marble pillars, mahogany counters, even electric light.'

'Oh, it's all very splendid as a *shop*, no doubt,' Leonora said. 'But here, at Leylands – really, one wonders what the world's coming to! We shan't visit, of course.'

'He's a bachelor, so you wouldn't have called on him in any case,' Sir Francis remarked. 'I wonder what a chap like that wants with such a property? Is he about to get married?'

'As to that, I couldn't say,' Mr Ryman said.

'Will he – look after Leylands?' asked Genevra, her voice strained with the effort of self-control.

'I believe he'll be prepared to spend money in restoring it to its former good order,' Mr Ryman said.

He was afraid that he had been tactless in implying that the house was shabby and the estate in shocking disarray, but Genevra seemed more relieved than offended.

'Then I think he ought to have it,' she replied. 'But the furniture . . . the pictures . . .?'

'I have not had time to discuss the details with Mr Pyrritt, but I believe he would wish to take the house as it stands. Indeed, I believe it to be essential if you are to be left free of debt, Miss Kerslake. You will, of course, remove anything which belongs to you personally.'

'I have few possessions,' Genevra said. 'My clothes, some small pieces of jewellery, my piano . . .'

'We have a piano at Perry Court,' Leonora interrupted. 'You will hardly need two.'

'My horse . . .'

'By Jove, yes, that beautiful mare,' Francis said. 'You won't deprive her of that, Mr Ryman?'

'Papa gave her to me for my last birthday,' Genevra said in a voice that was not quite steady.

And failed to pay for her, Mr Ryman thought grimly:

10

but he was deeply sympathetic to his young client, and had no doubt that debt could be accommodated out of the estate, once he was sure that Matthew Pyrritt would take over Leylands.

Genevra drove back to Perry Court with her cousins in a state of exhaustion brought about by strain, grief and shock. They had gone to Leylands for Ludovic's funeral. Although neither of the two ladies had attended the committal Genevra had wished to be in the house when her father had been carried out of it to his last resting-place and Leonora had thought it proper to agree. The meeting with the lawyer immediately after the funeral had been arranged by Sir Francis, with a degree of insensitivity which his wife thought typical, although to do him justice he had not expected it to lead to such a shocking revelation.

Something about Genevra's still, white face made Leonora say abruptly, as they bowled along in the carriage on the three-mile road between Leylands and Perry Court, 'It's all very unfortunate, but of course you will always have a home with us, Genevra.'

Genevra bowed her head in acknowledgment, unable to bring herself to speak. Francis and Leonora had been kind, but she detected a degree of impatience behind Leonora's generosity. It was natural for Genevra to go and live with her only surviving relations, she accepted that, but it was bitter to know that she was dependent on their charity.

They were not particularly compatible with one another. Leonora, handsome, worldly, some nine years Genevra's senior, had married early and with more of an eye to Sir Francis Hamden's possessions than his charac-ter. Having presented her husband with two sons in the first four years of their marriage she felt that she had done her duty and might follow her own inclinations.

11

They both spent more time in London than in Surrey and neither of them enquired too closely into the other's affairs. Leonora was discreet. No breath of scandal had ever touched her. An occasional raised eyebrow perhaps, but only from the most rigid of dowagers. Sir Francis, rich, indolent, and as pleasure-loving as his wife, meandered along his own path and was not dissatisfied with the bargain he had made.

Leonora and her husband were at one in agreeing that it was a bore to have to go into mourning for her uncle-by-marriage; but Ludovic had been a figure in Society, for all his poverty, and it would never do to be seen to be lax in the outward observances. Fortunately, black was becoming to Leonora, with her chestnut hair and high complexion, and she was not averse to wearing it; but she had no intention of allowing the bereavement to interfere with her amusements. At the end of a month of meticulous mourning in the country Leonora announced that she and Francis were leaving for London, as they always did in April.

Genevra accepted her cousin's decision with a feeling that she would not be altogether sorry to be left alone.

'Another time perhaps you can accompany us,' Leonora said vaguely. 'This year, I think, it's far too soon.'

Genevra agreed quietly. She had come to know Leonora well enough to doubt whether she would ever be invited to join in her London pleasures. As for Francis, she found his cousinly attentions irksome. Sir Francis was a man who could never pass a woman without brushing against her. The simplest action entailed a gentle squeeze of her hand, the unnecessary support of his arm, a would-be avuncular pat on the cheek. He would have been astonished to learn that what Genevra thought of as his 'dabbing ways' were resented; but Genevra, seeing

12

the way he ran his tongue over his full moist lips, the way his eyes glistened, and the satisfied amorous expression on his face as he placed a footstool for her and lifted her feet onto it, felt an instinctive recoil.

When she was left alone at Perry Court she was at a loss to know how to fill her days, something that had never been a problem at Leylands. There she had seemed always to be busy, conferring with the housekeeper, settling menus, keeping accounts and juggling such money as was available; overseeing the gardener, arranging flowers in the house, darning the fine damask napkins with tiny stitches, visiting old servants and sick people in the village, taking a Sunday School class. None of these occupations was available to her at Perry Court. She rode out, accompanied by a groom, practised her music and walked in the grounds. It was not enough to keep her mind occupied, and her thoughts were not happy ones.

The books in Sir Francis's library were not of a nature to interest her, nor did Genevra have a high opinion of Leonora's selection of music for the pianoforte. She regretted having left so much of her own music behind at Leylands and at last, towards the end of April, on a day which promised brilliant Spring sunshine, Genevra gave in to the temptation to ride over to Leylands to retrieve the sheets of music she wanted.

The process of transferring the estate to Matthew Pyrritt had begun, but he was not yet in residence. So far, all the old servants had been kept on and Genevra knew that she would get a warm welcome from Mrs Bertram, the housekeeper.

It was not a happy experience, riding up to her old home and knowing that she no longer had any right to enter it. Leylands was looking its best, mellow and glowing in the fitful April sunlight, the wide lawns fresh with new grass, the trees bursting into leaf.

Genevra rode round to the stable yard and entered the house by the kitchen entrance. As she had anticipated, she was received ecstatically by the staff.

'Miss Jenny, it does my heart good to see you,' the housekeeper exclaimed, bustling into the kitchen.

'Oh, Bertie, no one calls me "Miss Jenny" now except you,' Genevra said.

She bent and kissed the cheek of the woman she had known since she was a baby and got a quick hug in response. There was no need for words: they both knew the heartache this visit entailed.

There was a deep tie of affection between Genevra and Mrs Bertram. The housekeeper had taken the thirteen-year-old girl to her heart when her sweet ailing mother had faded out of life. There had been some talk then of sending Genevra to live with her cousin, but Leonora had been newly married and pregnant and had not found it convenient to take on another responsibility. Genevra had been left at Leylands, to the uncertain attention of her father, with a governess to provide female companionship.

The governess had been a poor creature in Mrs Bertram's opinion. She might be capable of instructing Genevra in the rivers of Europe and how to reply to a letter from a bishop; but Mrs Bertram saw few signs of her giving the girl any guidance about her approach to womanhood, so she had taken it upon herself to supply the lack.

Mrs Bertram, widowed young, had reared two daughters, placed them in good service and seen them sensibly married. She lacked the graces required from a woman in a similar post in one of the grander or more fashionable establishments, but she knew all about the practical side of running a house and was adept at supervising a staff of young girls.

Not that she would have compared Genevra with the ignorant country girls who came to her to be licked into shape. Still, a young woman was a young woman, no matter what her station: Mrs Bertram, the daughter of a farmer, with a sturdy commonsensical view of the facts of life, had taken it upon herself to talk to Genevra in a straightforward way about matters which were certainly not touched on by anyone else in Genevra's restricted circle.

The governess was dismissed when Genevra was sixteen, an economy which Ludovic Kerslake had seized on with relief. Genevra, being of a naturally thoughtful turn of mind, had continued to read widely and to practise her music, but more and more of her time had been spent in learning the skills which her housekeeper was able to pass on to her.

Mrs Bertram deplored the quiet life her young mistress led and would almost have welcomed the change in her circumstances after her father's death if she had thought that the Hamden household would be congenial to the girl. On this, Genevra's first visit since her removal to Perry Court, Mrs Bertram took one look at her pale quiet face and told herself that Miss Jenny was being left too much to her own unhappy thoughts and needed taking out of herself.

'You'll take a cup of tea with me in my room,' she said. 'This is a pleasant surprise, and no mistake.'

Genevra hung back. 'There's no risk of Mr Pyrritt coming in, is there?' she asked.

'Not him. He's not moved in yet and in any case he's busy on a weekday with that shop of his. He's been round, more than once, but Leylands doesn't belong to him yet and so I let him understand.'

'I hope you weren't too haughty with him.'

'Not me. I know my place, whether I'm dealing with a duke or a jumped-up counter clerk.'

'Bertie, you mustn't talk about him like that!'

'Neither would I, not to anyone but you, Miss Jenny, but he's not a gentleman, and no amount of money will make him one. Still, I have to admit he spoke pleasant enough and seems to be ready to lay out money on the place.'

'I hope he doesn't change it too much,' Genevra said wistfully. She sighed and then made a determined effort to speak more cheerfully. 'I will sit down and have a chat with you, Bertie, and I'd love a cup of tea before I go, but first I want to collect the music I left behind. May I go into the drawing room?'

'Of course you can, Miss Jenny, and I'm sure I don't know why you think you have to ask. If I know Mrs Hobbs she'll already have the kettle on, but I'll just go and make sure.'

The drawing room faced southwest and the afternoon sun was flooding in through the long windows overlooking the garden. Even in the short time that Genevra had been away the room had taken on an unfamiliar look and it was shabby, undeniably shabby, far more so than she had realized before spending a few weeks in Leonora's well-appointed house.

Genevra opened the piano and touched the keys with regretful fingers. To her mind it had a mellower tone than the newer instrument she now played. She took out the albums and sheets of music which were jumbled together in a stand by the side of the piano and began sorting through them. She heard voices in the hallway and half expected the old butler to come in and reproach her for not having used the front door. When the drawing room door opened she looked up with a smile, but instead of a familiar friend she saw a complete stranger.

16

He was a tall man, in his mid-thirties, very dark. His thick black eyebrows gave him a frowning, almost menacing look, especially when, as now, they were drawn together, not so much in annoyance as in puzzlement.

'And who may you be?' he asked, and the very way he put the question, as one having the right to know, told Genevra who he was himself.

'I'm Genevra Kerslake,' she said. 'And you . . .'

'Matthew Pyrritt.'

Genevra shuffled the loose sheets of music together, but her agitation made her nervous and they fluttered out of her hands and on to the floor.

'Mr Pyrritt, I really must apologize,' she said. 'I have no right to be here, but I wanted my music and I was told I might take anything that was my personal property, and it *is* mine, paid for out of my own money.'

'No need to get in a fuss,' Matthew Pyrritt said, advancing further into the room. 'As for having no right to be here – nonsense! I know no one with a better right; and if you're thinking *I* have then you're quite out because the deeds aren't signed yet and can't be until the lawyers get probate. So you might say I'm the one who's trespassing.'

'It's very kind of you to say so,' Genevra said.

He picked up the loose sheets she had dropped, put them together and handed them to her.

'You're fond of music?' he asked.

'Very. And I play a great deal now.' With a slight deprecating smile she added, 'The truth is, time hangs heavily on my hands after having always been so busy at Leylands.'

'I can understand that. I like a nice tune myself. Play for me.'

He seemed to realize from her startled expression that

17

he had been too abrupt and said, more gently, 'I'd take it very kindly if you would.'

Half a dozen chaotic thoughts chased through Genevra's mind, but in the end it seemed simplest to do as he asked. She chose at random a Chopin nocturne and managed to get through it without stumbling.

'Very pretty,' Mr Pyrritt said. 'Yes, I liked that.'

He looked over his shoulder and saw Mrs Bertram hovering in the doorway.

'Ah, there you are,' he said. 'Miss Kerslake and I will take tea.' He turned to Genevra. 'You will, won't you?'

'I was going to have tea with Bertie in the house-keeper's room,' Genevra said helplessly.

'You belong in the drawing room. Besides, there's things I want to ask you.'

It did not seem to occur to him that it was unconventional, even improper, for a young girl in her circumstances to be visiting – or should it be accepting a visit – from a solitary unmarried man. It was all too much for Genevra to untangle and she had an instinctive feeling that to bring it to his notice would be to introduce into the encounter an embarrassment that was lacking at the moment, at least on his side.

'Ask Maud to bring tea in here,' she said to Mrs Bertram and her unconscious authority both dismissed the disapproving housekeeper and made Matthew Pyrritt look at her with sharp attention.

Because she could think of no subject of conversation which would not be difficult to sustain, Genevra played again until the tea appeared. Mr Pyrritt listened with every appearance of enjoyment, lounging in one of the armchairs as if he belonged there – which, of course, Genevra reminded herself, he did. All the same, he looked out of place in that elegant room. It was not so much that he was unpolished as that he seemed to be made out of an entirely different material to the men she was used to.

At least pouring out the tea gave her something to do.

'Beautiful china,' Mr Pyrritt said approvingly.

'It was one of my mother's wedding presents,' Genevra said.

'It seems I have to watch every word for fear of upsetting you,' Matthew Pyrritt commented. 'Well, I'll say it once and not again: it must be hard for you, giving up everything you've grown up with. I feel for you. Now, having got that out of the way, I'd like to ask your advice.'

For one moment Genevra hardly knew whether to laugh or cry, then she decided to accept his brief speech in the spirit in which it was intended.

'Anything I can do to help . . .' she said.

'This house needs putting to rights, as you must know better than anyone.' He looked round disparagingly at the faded walls and yellowing paintwork. 'I've put the man who decorated Pyrritt's Department Store on to it, but to my mind his ideas are a bit heavy-handed for a gentleman's residence. I was pleased with the effect in the shop, and the customers like it, but I don't think he quite understands what I want at Leylands. Here, take a look at these samples of wallpaper he's given me and tell me what you think.'

Genevra leafed through the samples with growing dismay.

'Oh, no!' she said, looking at a square of heavily flocked crimson.

'He says it's bang up-to-date and what all the best people are hanging on their walls.'

Genevra sought for tact. 'Perhaps if you were decorating a *modern* house . . .' she began.

'Just my own thought!' Matthew Pyrritt interrupted

her. 'I could have bought a piece of land and built a spanking new mansion, no expense spared, if that had been what I wanted, but it was Leylands I'd a fancy for. Now, you don't need me to tell you, Miss Kerslake, that this house is a hundred and twenty years old, and what may be right for a house built in 1885 won't do for one built in 1760.'

'No, indeed,' Genevra interrupted in her turn, since there seemed no other way of stopping him. 'Leylands has always been decorated in a light and elegant fashion. If you change it you will make all the furniture look out of place.'

'And I'm not set on buying new, though I can't say I find this chair particularly comfortable. Still, the arm-chairs in the library are made right and I dare say I'll sit in there as much as anywhere. I'm glad to know you agree with me, though it leaves me with a problem to know where to turn for a decorator.'

'I could give you the name of the firm we've always dealt with,' Genevra suggested.

'Local people,' Mr Pyrritt responded with a frown. 'I want the best and I was looking to get it from London.'

'It will be very well received if you deal with local tradesmen. Crocksley & Son have been in business for nearly as long as Leylands has been standing and they know the house.' She paused and added with difficulty, 'They've been very good about doing small repairs in an emergency. They deserve to be rewarded for faithful service.'

'Maybe, but it's a question of *taste*, you see.'

'Follow your own judgment. It's already led you to see that your shop decorator's suggestions are wrong.'

'I'd trust myself to know what'll look right in a big store, and I could see the same style wouldn't do here, but I'd be in a puzzle to get it right when it came to choosing curtains and such like. I can get everything made in our own Soft Furnishing Department, and nowhere will make them better, but I don't know that I want any of my supervisors telling me what I'm to have at my windows.'

He gave Genevra a sudden piercing look.

'You were saying time hung heavy for you. Will you give me the benefit of your advice? See these Crocksley people for me, tell them what you think is suitable?'

'Mr Pyrritt! You must see I can't do that!'

'Why not?'

'It would be quite, quite improper.'

'It might be painful for you, I admit that. Still, I'd think it would please you to see the place being perked up.'

'It would be a pleasure, in one way. No one knows better than I do how much Leylands needs refurbishing. Yes, it would be hurtful as well, but I could overcome that if it were really something I could undertake. Only it isn't.'

'I'm sure I don't see why.'

Genevra looked at him helplessly. If he was really unable to see that it was a question of propriety, then she could think of no way of explaining it to him.

'I'll pay you for your time and trouble,' Mr Pyrritt said, as if that would settle the question.

'No! I couldn't possibly take money from you. Oh, dear! Why can't you see that it's out of the question?'

'Because it isn't.'

His air of calm reasonableness suddenly awoke in Genevra a sense of humour she had thought almost dead.

'I can understand why you're so successful in business – you never take no for an answer! I'll make one concession. If you'll send to Crocksley's for samples I'll come

21

over and visit Mrs Bertram and select the ones I think most suitable.'

Genevra left shortly after that, none too sure why she had capitulated to his strange request. It would be a bitter-sweet pleasure to have a hand in restoring Leylands, but that was not what had influenced her. She had quite simply not been able to withstand the force of Matthew Pyrritt's determination. Strange man! Not at all the ogre of her imagination, and yet she would not like to get on the wrong side of him.

As for Matthew Pyrritt, he was left with an impression that lingered a long time in his mind – of a girl, tall and slim in her close-fitting riding habit, who had turned enormous startled eyes on him. A girl who was too pale, with shadows under her violet eyes; a girl who had lent an added grace to the elegant drawing room of the house he had acquired through her father's folly.

2

Genevra went twice more to Leylands and on the second occasion she met Mr Pyrritt again. She had seen Mrs Bertram, had left messages to be passed on to Mr Pyrritt about Crocksley's proposals, and had been tempted by the fineness of the day to walk to the end of the garden, to look out over the ha-ha that divided the lawn from the fields towards the view that stretched away to the distant hills. As she turned to go she saw Matthew Pyrritt coming towards her.

'I'm glad to have caught you,' he said. 'I want to thank you for the time you've spent on the task I set you.'

'I'm afraid I haven't spared your pocket, Mr Pyrritt.'

'No need to worry about that. Quality was what I wanted and what you've seen to it that I'll get. The thing is, I'm puzzled to know how to repay you.'

'I told you I wanted nothing,' Genevra said with heightened colour.

'It goes against the grain for me to be beholden to anyone, especially a young lady in your circumstances. You ought to have charged me for your time.'

'That is quite out of the question,' Genevra answered firmly.

Since he still looked unconvinced it was fortunate that she had a flash of inspiration.

'I'll accept a bunch of flowers to take back to Perry Court, and think myself amply repaid,' she said.

'Has Sir Francis got no flowers of his own?'

'Yes, but he also has a very fierce gardener, and with

Sir Francis and cousin Leonora away I daren't pick a bud!'

'I should have thought you could have put him in his place. Still, if it's flowers you want we've got plenty. Help yourself.'

It seemed that he meant to stand by and watch her. Genevra busied herself gathering a handful of daffodils which were now blooming in profusion under the trees.

'Was your shop designer upset when you told him you weren't using his ideas for Leylands?' she asked.

'Upset? Why should he be? I told him I wasn't suited and was looking elsewhere and that was the end of the matter.'

'You make everything sound so simple!'

'So it is if you deal straightforwardly. It's the way I do business and everyone knows it.'

'I've been wondering, Mr Pyrritt, why you want to live at Leylands? Wouldn't a house in London have been more suitable?'

'I've kept a suite of rooms over the store that I can use for three or four nights a week, but I'd a fancy for a place in the country. This district suited me. There's a good train service not three miles distant and I can be at my office within the hour. Besides, I wanted to be near Epsom. I've a couple of horses in training there.'

'I didn't know that.' Genevra bent to pick another golden daffodil, her face averted. Almost under her breath she said, 'I've no great love of horse racing.'

'I can well believe it. You don't have to tell me that your father lost a packet on the turf. But I'm not a betting man. Five to ten pounds is the most I've ever put on a horse. It's the breeding that interests me. That, and the race itself. Is that all you're going to take, just a handful of daffs, growing like weeds?'

'Mr Pyrritt, I put a great deal of thought into the

24

placing of these daffodil bulbs! Growing like weeds, indeed!'

'I thought they came up natural. It shows how little I know.'

They strolled towards the stable yard. When Genevra's thoroughbred mare, Marietta, was led out, Matthew Pyrritt patted her neck approvingly.

'Now there's a fine lady!' he said. 'Ah, you're a pretty girl, aren't you, my lass?'

It made Genevra laugh to see Marietta coquetting with him.

'She'll accept any amount of admiration,' she said.

She handed her bunch of flowers to the groom, but it was Matthew who stepped forward to help her into the saddle. With heightened colour Genevra adjusted her reins and whip.

'This will be the last time I shall trespass at Leylands,' she said. 'Goodbye, Mr Pyrritt. I hope . . . I hope you will be happy here.'

The transfer of Leylands was completed. Genevra heard through the country grapevine that Mr Pyrritt had moved in and was employing an army of builders and decorators to carry out the alterations he required. She tried to turn the subject when anyone spoke to her about it.

At the end of May she had a brief note from Leonora to say that she and Francis and a party of friends would be returning to Perry Court in time for the Derby on the third of June.

'And would you believe that the Pyrritt man is having a houseparty for Derby Week?' Leonora demanded when she and Francis had arrived. She looked round with a dissatisfied air. 'They say he's tearing Leylands to pieces and making it all new.'

'Hardly that.' Genevra protested. 'He's had two bath-rooms installed, which will be very useful, and a new stove in the kitchen and the rooms redecorated.'

'You keep up to date with the gossip,' her cousin remarked.

'I am . . . I have become slightly acquainted with Mr Pyrritt,' Genevra said.

'My dear! The creature didn't have the gall to come here, surely?'

'I went to Leylands, to fetch some music I'd left behind, and met him by accident.'

'And he told you all his plans for the house.'

'He asked my advice.'

'Did he indeed!'

There was a touch of malicious amusement in Leonora's manner which Genevra did not understand until she went on. 'Well, he's a good catch as far as money is concerned, if you can stand being ostracized by everyone who matters. I didn't know you had it in you to be so enterprising.'

'Leonora, you know there is nothing like that in the situation.'

'If you say so,' Leonora agreed obligingly. 'Tell me, what is he like? I suppose it's too much to hope that he's presentable?'

'His manner is a little abrupt,' Genevra said carefully. 'I believe his intentions are good and he's behaving well towards the old servants.'

'But what does he *look* like?'

Genevra found herself at a loss, unable to describe Matthew Pyrritt except as an irresistible force with a deep voice and very black eyebrows.

'He's big,' she said lamely. 'And dark.'

'A rough diamond?'

'Well . . . he's certainly not polished,' Genevra admitted.

'The reason I'm interested is that I've been surprised to hear the names of one or two people who've accepted an invitation to stay with him. I mean, if he's going to be taken up one may as well be in the know.'

'He owns a couple of racehorses and one of them will be running at Epsom during Derby Week.'

'You're a fount of information! I suppose that accounts for it. Some of the people from the Shires are so horse mad they'll stay with anyone who has an interest in their obsession. He only needs to invest in a yacht and the Prince of Wales will make a friend of him. Oh, dear, what a bore! I may have to make Francis call on him after all.'

Genevra had thought that it would be pleasant to have Perry Court full of people, after the dreary routine of her empty days; but she had little in common with Francis and Leonora's friends, and her presence, quiet and serious and dressed all in black, seemed to make them uncomfortable.

There were undercurrents amongst the party which Genevra did not wholly understand. She saw that the married women flirted with the men in a way that she thought unbecoming, but she did not grasp that during the course of the week Sir Francis quarrelled not only with his wife but also with his current mistress, with the result that when the guests fluttered away Leonora went with them and her husband stayed behind, sulky and disgruntled.

Left alone, Genevra and Francis dined together every night, but she saw little of him during the day until one rainy afternoon when she offered to play billiards with him and, to Francis's astonishment, beat him soundly.

'Papa taught me,' Genevra explained.

She gave no thought to the charming picture she presented, bending over the table, her hair slightly ruffled and gleaming like gold in the overhead light. She did realize that Francis was looking amused and lively for the first time for days and was relieved that he had come out of his fit of sulks.

The following day, out of a perverse idea that it would annoy Leonora, Francis rode over to Leylands and called on Matthew Pyrritt. He had not expected to find him at home, but he did – and their interview gave Francis a shock that sent him back to Perry Court in a state of outrage.

He stormed into the sitting room in search of Genevra and her heart sank as she saw his flushed furious face and the glitter of temper in his eyes.

'Just how have you been employing your time while you've been at Perry Court?' Francis demanded.

'Riding, playing the piano, amusing the children and sewing,' Genevra replied.

'And getting on terms with our new neighbour,' Francis accused her.

'I told Leonora that I had become acquainted with Mr Pyrritt,' Genevra said.

'Did you! A fine way for a young girl to behave! You've been riding over there, taking tea with him, advising him about doing up the house . . .'

'It was all harmless.'

'Other people won't think so, as you'll find out if you carry these manners out into the world. It comes of having no mother, I suppose. Leonora ought to be here to tell you about it, but as she's not I have to take it upon myself.'

'Very well, you have told me. I'm sorry if I have offended, but I think you exaggerate. I'm sure I've done nothing Papa would have disliked.'

'Ludovic was too easygoing, but even he would have

28

discouraged his young daughter from striking up a friendship with a jumped-up counter clerk. No, more than friendship! I haven't told you yet what your conduct has led to. The man asked my permission to pay his addresses to you! He actually had the effrontery to think he might marry you. What passed between you to give him that notion, I'd like to know?'

'Nothing.'

Genevra had gone very white. She felt completely confounded. What could she have done, or said, to put such an idea into Matthew Pyrritt's head?

'It's out of the question, of course,' she said.

'I'm glad you think so! It's what I told the man, and in no uncertain terms. I left him in no doubt what I thought about it. There won't be any more contact between Perry Court and Leylands.'

'Mr Pyrritt seems to have behaved very correctly,' Genevra said wearily. 'He asked your permission, which was not strictly necessary. I am of age. He could have approached me in person.'

'I dare say you would have accepted him!'

'No, I would have refused him. Francis, please don't be so angry. It must have been a great surprise when he brought up such a subject immediately on becoming acquainted with you. It was just like him; he's a most abrupt man. But it was not my fault. Nothing he ever said – and we have only met *twice* – could have prepared me for such an offer. Truly, you do me an injustice in thinking that I . . . that I encouraged him.'

She got nothing but an angry mutter out of Francis in response to that defence. He blundered out of the room, leaving Genevra with her head spinning. She had been offered the chance to return to Leylands as its mistress. For one moment she contemplated the possibility with longing; then she remembered Matthew Pyrritt – dark,

29

frowning, strongminded, uncompromisingly masculine, and she knew, in spite of her ignorance of the married state, that she could not be his wife. To sell herself to such a man for the sake of an establishment would be to enter into slavery. She had no affection for him; he could hardly have any for her after such a short acquaintance; it was unthinkable.

Two days later, with Francis still in a state of offended huffiness, Genevra rode out with her groom and met Matthew Pyrritt.

She had ridden up the rise behind Perry Court, to a point where the ground levelled out and a grove of trees crowned the hill. Mr Pyrritt rode towards her from the opposite direction on a fine black horse which Genevra recognized with a pang as coming from her father's stables. As they drew level she felt her cheeks burning. She could scarcely look him in the face, but she managed to meet his eye and got, in response to her embarrassed 'Good morning', no more than the curtest of nods.

They had passed one another when Genevra, on an impulse she could not explain, turned her horse's head and called, 'Mr Pyrritt! I would like to speak to you.'

He was frowning as she walked her horse towards him, but when he saw that she meant to dismount he got out of the saddle and came to help her. Leading their horses behind them they walked slowly towards the trees.

'Sir Francis told me about his conversation with you,' Genevra said. 'I think . . . I am afraid that your . . . your request was treated with less courtesy than it deserved.'

'Aye, he didn't spare me. He's a fine opinion of his place in the world, that gentleman. Seemed to think I'd be dragging you down to my level if I made you my wife.'

'I'm sorry. You took him by surprise and Francis doesn't have a very flexible mind.'

'He gave no thought to the benefit to you if I took you on, a penniless girl whose father frittered away a fortune.'

'If you put it to him in those terms I'm not surprised he became annoyed!'

'I didn't say it out loud, but if he'd anything in his head but snobbery and foolishness he would have seen it that way.'

'What I can't understand is what made you think of me,' Genevra said helplessly.

Mr Pyrritt took his time about answering. He looked thoughtfully into the distance, over the plain on the far side of the hill, to where amidst the beech trees the chimneys of Leylands could just be seen.

'Leylands needs a mistress,' he said. 'And you're the best person for the job.'

In spite of herself Genevra could not suppress a momentary feeling of wild amusement.

'A housekeeper!' she said. 'Yes, that's something I could do well. But a wife . . . no, Mr Pyrritt!'

'So your answer would have been the same as your cousin's if I'd addressed you direct?'

'I would have had to refuse you, but I hope with a greater sense of . . . of the honour you have done me.'

For the first time since they had dismounted Mr Pyrritt turned his head to look at her directly.

'I don't know what you're going to do with your life,' he said. 'A pretty girl like you won't dwindle into an old maid, but I hope when you're driven to accepting the curate or the doctor's assistant you won't regret turning down a far better offer.'

'Poverty with a man I loved would be more honourable than accepting someone just for the fine position he could offer me.'

'I wonder if Lady Hamden would agree with you,' Mr

Pyrritt murmured, but Genevra thought it better not to hear that remark.

'Come along, let's get you back on your horse,' he said.

She let him toss her up into the saddle, in spite of the old groom's disapproving stare, but when she was installed Matthew Pyrritt did not move away.

'If there's ever a time when you need a friend, then you can look to me,' he said. 'You've had a hard deal, in my opinion. I would have made it up to you if I could, but since you don't see it my way we'll say no more on that score. If you ever get tired of being the poor relation in your cousin's house come to me and I'll give you a job.'

'In your shop?' Genevra asked in disbelief.

'You might do worse. There's plenty of young women earning a living in Pyrritt's Department Store. Keep it in mind.'

'I will – if I find the curate insupportable,' Genevra said gravely. She held out her hand. 'Goodbye, Mr Pyrritt.'

He took her hand and stood for a moment looking at her with a frowning enigmatic look that puzzled her.

'You think it's a joke,' he said. 'But there's worse things than gainful employment. Good-day to you, Miss Kerslake.'

Genevra rode back to Perry Court with a muddled feeling that she would have done a great deal better not to have stopped Mr Pyrritt, while at the same time knowing that she would have felt dissatisfied with herself if she had not seized the opportunity of speaking to him.

Francis met her in the hall, still, she saw regretfully, in a blazing temper.

'Come into the library,' he said.

She followed him, her riding habit looped over her arm, carrying her gloves and crop.

'If I were your father I'd take that whip and lay it about you,' Francis said. 'Fine behaviour! You never encouraged Mr Pyrritt, oh no! At the first opportunity you rode out to meet him, strolled about with him, shook hands. Don't deny it. I saw it all.

'You have good eyesight,' Genevra said.

Without saying anything more she stared hard at the field glasses lying on the desk near the window. Francis saw the direction of her gaze and flushed uncomfortably.

'I'm not accustomed to being spied on,' Genevra said. 'Once again, I can only say that my meeting with Mr Pyrritt was entirely innocent. We met by accident and I spoke because I wanted to apologize for the discourtesy with which I believed you had treated him.'

'*You* apologized to *him*, and on my behalf? Damn it, girl, have you no sense of the fitness of things.'

'Rather more than you have, I think.'

'I suppose he renewed his filthy proposal?'

'He asked me if my answer would have been different if he had approached me direct and I said it would not. As for "filthy" that is a disgusting way to describe an honourable proposal of marriage.'

'Honourable! You walked into the trees with him. What happened? Did he kiss you?'

Genevra's face was flooded with colour. 'How dare you!' she whispered. 'We were never out of Brown's sight, nor of yours either it seems. There was no impropriety – no thoughts of kissing or . . . or lovemaking – oh, I'm so angry that I can't make sense!'

'*You* may not have thought of it, but I'll be bound it was in his mind. A man does think of such things with a girl like you. If you weren't such an innocent you would have seen . . .'

33

He had his arm round her before Genevra could realize what he was doing; she could feel his breath on her face. She turned her head to one side, but Francis wrenched it round and his mouth was on hers, hot and wet. Genevra struggled, but he only held her more tightly, until at last his hold slackened and she was able to push him away. With only one thought in her mind – to keep him at arm's length – she brought up her riding crop and struck out wildly, catching him across the face. She heard Francis exclaim in pain, and then she was across the room, her hand grappling desperately with the door knob, out of the library and into the hall.

No man had ever kissed her before. She had scarcely known that such things could happen. He was *married*! More than that, he was married to her own cousin. And she was his helpless dependant, a girl without other friends, who should have been able to rely on his chivalry to protect her from such advances. Alone in her bedroom Genevra buried her face in her hands as she relived those moments in the library, overcome by shame and disgust.

At last she sat up and began to think more rationally. Francis had behaved outrageously; but for a man, even a married man, to try to steal a kiss was not the end of the world. With an insight she had not known she possessed she saw that there was some trouble between Francis and Leonora, that he was in a disturbed mood because he had been left behind when his wife went off with her friends.

More than that, Matthew Pyrritt's proposal had upset him because it was a challenge to the established order of things as Francis understood them. Mr Pyrritt was one of the new men, wealthy without inherited land, in trade but no longer excluded from Society, able to buy an ancient estate, to raise his eyes to the daughter of some-one in Francis's world. And there had been an element

34

of jealousy behind Francis's resentment. She had been foolish not to realize that he had begun to look at her with covetous eyes himself, but the thought had never entered her head. She would be more careful in future. Perhaps it was a lesson she had needed to learn.

All the same, she could not bring herself to face Francis over the dinner table that evening.

'I'm indisposed,' she told the maid who came to help her out of her riding habit. 'I shall not leave my room again today. Ask cook to send me up something on a tray.'

The maid dropped a respectful curtsy, but the thought in her head was that Miss Kerslake gave her orders with a high hand, considering she was nothing but a poor relation. Still, she might be ill: there was a funny look about her, blazing colour in her cheeks and her eyes hard with determination.

Genevra would have done better to have gone down and dined with Francis, and frozen him with the icy disdain she felt for him. Left alone, conscious of the weal across his cheek, knowing he had behaved badly, he lashed himself into a state of justification and solaced his sense of injury with the brandy bottle. She had led him on, just as she had encouraged the Pyrritt upstart. Damned little hypocrite, full of false modesty. A girl didn't live with a father like Ludo without learning what was what. By the time he lurched upstairs to bed Francis had made up his mind to face Genevra and make her admit that it was she who had been in the wrong.

Genevra was asleep when her bedroom door crashed open. She raised herself on one elbow, vaguely alarmed but not sure what had woken her, and saw the wavering light of the candle Francis had carried upstairs.

'Who is it? What has happened? Is something wrong!' she demanded.

'Yesh . . . *yes*,' Francis mumbled. 'Said I'd take a whip to you, that didn't give you the right to take one to me. Apologize, that's what you're going to do, my girl. Go down on your knees and ask my pardon!'

She had the presence of mind to get out of bed on the side furthest from where he was standing. With trembling hands she felt for her dressing gown and pulled it round her.

'Francis, you're drunk,' she said. 'How dare you come to my room! You must leave immediately.'

'Drunk, am I? That's another insh . . . insult. Wait till I get my hands on you.'

If she could get to the door she could escape him. Cautiously, Genevra edged round the end of the bed, but with a wild lunge Francis caught a loose fold of her dressing gown and pulled her towards him.

'Francis, you can't behave like this,' Genevra said in a frightened rush. 'Please, please let me go. If I've offended you then . . . I'm sorry. We'll talk about it tomorrow.'

With his hands fumbling awkwardly at the soft silken folds of her nightclothes Francis seemed to have forgotten about the need for an apology from her.

'I'll tell Leonora!' Genevra cried despairingly.

'Much she'll care!'

'This is unbelievable!' Genevra pushed desperately at the hand that was clasped over her breast. 'Do try to remember that you are supposed to be a gentleman.'

'A gentleman! That's not what you like. Men like Pyrritt, that's what you prefer. We're all the same in the end, you know. I'll show you, shall I? Show you what it's like to have a man, any man?'

'No!'

Up to that moment Genevra had been annoyed, disgusted and uneasy. Now she was really frightened. The bell was out of reach, and in any case the servants must surely be in bed. From a state of maudlin indignation Francis had switched to an uglier mood. For all her inexperience she knew that he was wildly excited by her nearness and her state of undress. He was dangerous, really dangerous, with his better instincts blunted by the drink he had taken, enjoying the sense of power her helplessness gave him.

It was the dressing gown that gave her a chance of escape. She slipped her arms out of it and left it in Francis's hands while she darted to the other side of the room. An ewer of water stood on her washstand. Genevra seized it and swung it wildly, with the idea that a thorough drenching might bring Francis to his senses. Instead, she caught him on the side of the head, broke the ewer and felled him to the ground.

For one terrified moment Genevra stood frozen in horror at what she had done, then Francis stirred and she realized that he had suffered no lasting harm. All the same, she would need help in getting rid of him. Once again Genevra rescued her wet bedraggled dressing gown, clutched it round her and went down the corridor to Francis's own room.

As she had hoped, his valet was still waiting up to put his master to bed.

'Sanders, I need your help,' Genevra said.

With her chin in the air and looking the man straight in the eye, she went on. 'Sir Francis appears to have taken too much drink. He mistook my room for his, blundered about in the dark and has had a fall. Please come with me.'

Francis had just succeeded in sitting up. By the dim light of the guttering candle he looked dazed and sick. Without comment Sanders took in the details of the shattered water jug and sopping carpet. As he bent over his master, Francis snarled, 'Damn you, I don't need your help.'

'As you wish, sir.'

All the same, as he got to his feet Francis was glad to clutch at his valet's supporting arm. He stood unsteadily for a moment and then shook himself free. He looked towards Genevra and a spasm contorted his face.

'You little bitch,' he muttered.

'You are not yourself,' Genevra said, with an apparent calm that astonished her. 'Let Sanders get you to bed.'

As Francis blundered out of the room Genevra looked again very steadily at the valet.

'Would you like a cloth from the kitchen for your carpet, miss, or shall I fetch one of the maids?' he asked.

'It can be dealt with in the morning. Sanders, I want no talk about this.'

'I'm sure I wouldn't demean myself,' the valet said loftily.

Genevra stripped off her wet dressing gown and then, because she could not bear to remember the way Francis's hands had pawed at it, took off her nightdress and found a clean one in a drawer. She climbed wearily into bed, and there was only one thought in her head: at all costs she must leave her cousins' house.

The valet had said he would not talk, but of course he would. He would not be able to resist dropping a confidential word into the ear of his crony the butler; and the butler would keep it entirely to himself, except for telling the housekeeper, who would be the soul of discretion, but would hint of what she knew to the cook.

Tossing and turning, Genevra tried to think of a way of escaping from a house that had become intolerable to her. She could complain to Leonora, but she would still have to go on living at Perry Court. Unless . . . unless she did what Mr Pyrritt had suggested and found employment.

There was little enough scope for a young lady who needed work. She could become a governess, but Genevra thought that she had few qualifications for such a post. She could apply to Mr Pyrritt for a job in his shop, but that would put an end to all pretensions of being a lady. Would that be so very bad? She had been brought up to think of herself as a Kerslake of Leylands and to be proud of her family's long connection with the land; but Leylands was already lost to her. Moreover, her earliest ancestors had been no more than yeoman farmers: why should she not go back to the beginning and start again, earn her own living and hold her head up high in the knowledge that she was independent of charity?

Leonora would drop her. At that moment Genevra thought she could well support that. She would be free from the hypocrisy of having to be thankful to people she did not really like for every mouthful she ate. Greater independence for women was in the air now: Genevra felt a thrill of excitement at the idea of being one of the pioneers.

3

Genevra's brief stiffly-worded note to Matthew Pyrritt took him wholly by surprise. He sat frowning over it for a long time. What could have brought about this change of mind? When he had spoken to her on the hill Genevra had treated his suggestion as something of a joke, which perhaps it had been in a way. He had not really expected her to take it up. Girls of her sort preferred to sacrifice their pride and retain their gentility even if it did mean living off other people. He had formed a good opinion of Genevra, but he had not expected her to go against the conventions of her class.

So she preferred being one of his shop girls to becoming his wife! For a moment a gleam of amusement lit up his face, a touch of humour which would have surprised his subordinates. Had the chit considered what a slap in the face that was for him? No, obviously she had not: because she had taken his proposal no more seriously than she had originally taken his offer of a job.

Mr Pyrritt looked round his newly decorated breakfast room in dissatisfaction. He was pleased with Leylands, but he was very conscious that there was something missing. As he had said, the house needed a mistress. Come to that, he needed a wife. He would never achieve the position he wanted for himself without a settled domestic background and Genevra would have supplied exactly the right touch, besides being a pretty girl who appealed to him quite forcefully.

The truth was, he ought to have married years since; but his father's early death (with their plans for moving

Pyrritt's from Holborn to Oxford Street only half formulated) had left Matthew with little time for courtship. The transfer of the shop his grandfather had started had been carried out just as Matthew's father had intended, but the immediate rapid expansion had been all Matthew's doing. The new store was far larger and more diversified than Jonah Pyrritt had ever foreseen. It was a great achievement and now Matthew felt entitled to some reward for his hardheaded enterprise. He had bought Leylands and he wanted a wife to go with it: someone suitable who would be an asset to him and put him right on social questions.

He was past the age of believing in romantic love, though he suspected that Genevra still dreamt of a lover who would rescue her from poverty and humiliation. He kept a mistress in a discreet house in North London, a comfortable down-to-earth woman, not one of the highflyers who had battened on Ludovic Kerslake. Rose knew her place, understood what he wanted from her, made him welcome when he chose to visit her and did not run up bills which would have put her position in jeopardy.

It was an arrangement which had worked well enough until he had been unsettled by moving into Leylands. Now Matthew wanted something more than the physical satisfaction Rose could provide, a great deal more than the limited companionship she offered. He wanted a wife who would grace his lovely home; he wanted a son to inherit the fortune he had amassed. It was a piece of foolishness for which he had no patience to find himself haunted by the memory of a slim sad girl in black, standing by the piano in his drawing room.

The smile faded from his lips as he sat thinking, and his eyes narrowed. He had a shrewd suspicion that Genevra had not the slightest idea of what she was letting herself in for by offering to work as a shop assistant. He believed he treated his staff fairly, but it was not an easy life. It would come as a shock to a pampered young lady to find herself on her feet from early morning to late evening, at the beck and call of capricious customers. Perhaps it was unworthy to want to give her that experience; on the other hand it might make her realize what she had lost when she turned him down; it might even make her more amenable if he chose to renew his proposal. Would it diminish her value if she worked in a menial post instead of coming to him as the untouched daughter of a gentleman? Mr Pyrritt considered the matter and decided that on the whole he admired her independence: he would not let her departure from convention stand in his way if he failed to get over his present obstinate preference for her.

Matthew Pyrritt spoke about the matter to his General Manager that same morning, taking care to refer to Genevra as 'the orphaned relation of a neighbour', a description which gave him a certain inward satisfaction.

'Twenty-one and no previous experience,' he said. 'I'd like to give the girl a chance, but where the devil are we to place her?'

'Could she be trained for the telephone exchange?' the General Manager suggested dubiously.

'N-no, I think not. It's more genteel than serving behind a counter, but I'd like her to be somewhere where she can rise up if she's got anything in her.'

'The Gown Department?'

'It'll cause jealousy if she goes straight into a plum job. How about Haberdashery? Does Miss Littlejohn need an assistant?'

The General Manager pursed his lips. 'Miss Littlejohn is always in need of an assistant.'

'She's a cantankerous old devil,' Mr Pyrritt agreed. 'But she's been with me ever since I was serving in my grandfather's shop and her knowledge of the trade is second to none. Perhaps this young lady will get on better with her than the usual run of juniors.'

'It's a vacancy for a fourteen-year-old,' the General Manager protested.

'Miss Kerslake probably knows less about shops and shopping than most fourteen-year-olds we take on. Start her there and keep an eye on her progress. Time enough for her to move to Model Gowns when we see if she's going to stay the course.'

'Do you want me to write to the girl?'

'No, I'll do that myself.' The General Manager did not appreciate the irony behind Mr Pyrritt's smile. 'I owe it to her cousin,' he said.

On a hot still day in July Genevra entered into her employment at Pyrritt's Department Store. She was nervous but determined, screwed up to sticking-point by the words which had passed between her and Leonora when she had announced her plans. Leonora had abandoned a highly enjoyable visit and had come back to Perry Court in a tearing rage in response to a letter from Genevra.

'It passes all belief,' she said. 'I merely turn my back for a moment and you get into a worse scrape than anything Uncle Ludo ever dreamt up. Of course it's out of the question for you to work in that man Pyrritt's shop.'

The reference to her father infuriated Genevra and goaded her into an unwise speech.

'I would rather earn a living for myself than be kept by you and raped by your husband.'

'Rape!' Leonora's shocked response made Genevra realize that she had spoken the unforgivable. 'A girl of your age shouldn't know the meaning of the word. Francis

43

has told me he had reason to reprove you for your conduct towards Mr Pyrritt . . .'

'After midnight, in my bedroom?'

Leonora looked shaken, but only for a moment.

'Unwise perhaps, but he meant it for the best. It's only your disordered imagination that saw anything improper in his . . . his attempt to guide you. He has been very much hurt by your attitude.'

'Yes, his head must have been sore after I broke the water jug over it,' Genevra agreed. 'Come now, Leonora, we both know what really happened. Francis was drunk. I'm prepared to believe that he didn't come with the intention of molesting me, but it was very frightening and I have no intention of allowing it to happen again.'

There was a short dissatisfied silence and then Leonora said, 'Francis is a fool.'

'I agree, though it is unbecoming of his wife to say so.'

'How dare you criticize me after all I've done for you!'

'You've given me a home and I know that you are prepared to go on keeping me here, but this life doesn't suit me. I'm bored and lonely and it goes against the grain to know that I'm beholden to you for every mouthful I eat. Far, far better for me to take a job and make my own life.'

'But in a *shop*! I can't agree to it.'

'I'm of age. You can't stop me.'

'I shall write to the Pyrritt man and forbid him to employ you.'

'I doubt if he'll take any notice.'

'Have you wondered why he's prepared to take such an interest in you? You've accused Francis of something unmentionable. Perhaps it will become a reality when Mr Pyrritt has you in his power.'

'Oh, Leonora, this is the language of melodrama! Mr Pyrritt made me an honourable proposal of marriage,

44

which I refused. When he suggested a position in his shop as an alternative he never thought I'd take it up. Well, I have, and if I understand him as I think I do, that puts me outside the pale for him as well as for you.'

'If you persist in this perversity I'll never speak to you again. Don't imagine you'll come back to Perry Court if you find the life insupportable, because I won't have you.'

'I won't ask to come back,' Genevra replied. 'I know that I've got to succeed and I will, Leonora, I will!'

After that, nothing would have made Genevra give in and return to Perry Court, not even the shock of seeing the accommodation provided for Pyrritt's shop assitants.

It had been a relief to be told that she would be required to live in, since Genevra had no idea of how to go about finding suitable lodgings. She had suspected that being housed in the Ladies' Hostel would involve sharing a room; but nothing had prepared her for the sight of a stark bedroom containing six narrow beds. Beside each bed there was a washstand with a basin and ewer.

'There's space behind the curtain at the end of the room for hanging clothes,' the housekeeper told her. 'I see you have a trunk. You'll have to keep it under the bed. You make your own bed each morning and empty your wash basin. Apart from that, cleaning is provided.'

Genevra looked round and thought that if the house had been under her supervision she would have seen that the cleaning was more thoroughly carried out.

'You take your breakfast and supper here and have a dinner break at the shop,' the housekeeper went on. 'Breakfast is at seven and supper at eight o'clock. Punctuality is essential. I have a hundred and twenty girls to cater for and I can't be expected to keep food hanging about for latecomers.'

She was a thin pale woman with a tight-lipped mouth. There was an air of mousy respectability about her, but Genevra noticed that she wore a gown of good quality black silk, and a long gold chain looped several times round her neck. She had introduced herself as Mrs Thredgold.

'I'll give you a copy of the rules of the house,' Mrs Thredgold went on. 'Study them, please, and make up your mind to abide by them. If I appear to be watching your conduct for the first few weeks it's only because I'm responsible for the tone of this establishment. Pyrritt's is extremely careful about the kind of girl it employs. One report from me about rowdy behaviour and you'll find yourself in trouble.'

'I don't think I'm likely to be rowdy,' Genevra said mildly. 'Thank you very much, Mrs Thredgold. I'll unpack now.'

Without realizing it, she had spoken in the voice she would have used to dismiss a talkative servant. She even opened the door with a polite smile and before she well knew what was happening Mrs Thredgold found herself outside.

Genevra looked round. The floor was covered by plain brown linoleum; each of the narrow beds had a white cotton counterpane. She tested her bed and grimaced. It felt uncomfortably hard. Only one pillow, and that apparently filled with brickbats. The sheets seemed to be clean and the fact that they were coarser than she was accustomed to was not important. One blanket of reasonable quality, and an eiderdown which in the thick heat of midsummer was surely superfluous.

The hanging-space at the end of the room was covered by a cretonne curtain which needed washing, as did the curtains at the one sash window. Genevra, well accustomed to overseeing the cleaning of a house and encouraged by Mrs Bertram to take an interest in even the most mundane details, looked round with experienced eyes and diagnosed that the room had been swept regularly, but nothing had been moved, and it was a long time since the linoleum had been washed, let alone polished. The windows, too, were grimy.

The heat, high up under the eaves of the house, was unbearable. She tried to open the window and discovered that it was screwed down. The only reason she could think of was that it overlooked a lower expanse of roof and might perhaps offer a means of entry, though Genevra could hardly imagine that the poverty of this establishment would be a temptation to any burglar.

She leaned against the sooty window and closed her eyes. A wave of nostalgia for Leylands swept over her as she remembered the spacious rooms, sweet-smelling and full of charm, for all their shabbiness; the wide sweep of the lawns and the hills beyond; the freedom she had enjoyed, and the privacy. But that was all foolishness! Leylands had been lost to her before she had uprooted herself and come to this slovenly lodging-house. All the same, she felt the first stirrings of indignation as she contrasted what Mr Pyrritt was enjoying with the surroundings he provided for his shop girls.

She had brought with her some of the dresses which had formed her wardrobe before her father's death, but they were not suitable for her present circumstances and she left them in her trunk. She had two black gowns, one of which she was wearing. She hung up the other, piled her underclothes in the cupboard of her washstand, put out her brush and comb and began to feel, for good or ill, that she was installed.

There was a rush of feet on the stairs, the sound of

highpitched voices and then the door was flung open. Two girls ran in, one short, plump and fair and the other taller and darker. Genevra stood in the middle of the room, struck dumb by the realization that these were her new companions and there were three more to come.

'Are you our new girl? I say, what's your name? I'm Sally and this is Ruth,' the fair girl said. 'Genevra? Did you say Genevra? Cor, what a name! Aren't you ever called anything else?'

'Sometimes . . . Jenny,' Genevra stammered.

'That's more like it! Jenny! I can get my tongue round that. Come on, look lively, Jenny. Old Thredgold only needs half an excuse to starve us to death. "Those that don't come to the table on time don't deserve to eat".'

Her mimicry was wickedly exact, so was the way she minced across the room. Genevra began to smile.

'That's better,' Sally said. 'It's a shocking life, but we have to grin and bear it. Oo, my feet! They're killing me.'

'So're mine,' Ruth agreed, the first time she had managed to get a word in edgeways. 'Still, we had the fans going in Millinery today and it did make a difference. I do think electricity's marvellous. Where are you starting, Jenny?'

'I have to report to Miss Littlejohn in Haberdashery.'

'Gawd help you!' Sally exclaimed. 'Littlejohn's a real Tartar.' She looked at Genevra curiously. 'Not much of a job for you, is it? What experience have you had?'

'None.' Genevra admitted. 'I . . . kept house for my father. He. . . he died.'

'Oh, hard lines! Poor thing, that's rough. How old are you?'

'Twenty-one,' Genevra said, suppressing her surprise at the direct question.

'Three years older than me and starting in Haberdashery,' Sally said sympathetically. 'Never mind, you look the bright sort, I 'spect you'll soon get into something better. Well, I certainly hope so because if you don't you'll either go mad or murder old Littlejohn.'

'We'd better go down,' Ruth intervened.

'That's right. I hope you like Lancashire hot-pot, Jenny, because it's Monday and that's hot-pot day.'

'Not what I would have chosen for a stifling summer's day,' Genevra commented as she followed the other two girls downstairs.

'You'll be glad to eat anything after twelve hours at work,' Ruth said. 'Which is just as well because otherwise we'd none of us have much appetite for the cooking in this establishment.'

Since Genevra had not been working and was less ravenous than the other girls she made a poor meal from the dish of fatty mutton that was served up to her. There was very little meat on the bones that floated in a thin liquid with golden spots of grease swimming on the surface. The rest of the meal consisted of sago pudding with a dab of red jam, and a hot strong cup of tea.

'It's not good, but it's filling,' Ruth commented afterwards. 'I don't half miss my Mum's cooking. Have you lost your Mum as well as your Dad, Jenny?'

'Yes, some years ago. My only relative is a cousin.'

'That's hard. Never mind, you'll soon make friends at Pyrritt's.'

'What do you say to a stroll round the park?' Sally asked. 'Are you game, Jenny?'

'I'd give anything for a breath of air,' Genevra said.

'You're a country girl, aren't you? I'm a proper London sparrow and so's Ruth. You latch on to us. We know all the wheezes. Come on, half an hour in Hyde Park before it gets dark. You do know old Thredgold closes the door on us at ten o'clock, don't you?'

'And ten-thirty on Saturdays,' Genevra said. 'I've read the rules. I must say I think they're a bit extreme. After all, we're not children.'

'Some of us are,' Ruth said as they went out into the airless street. 'You haven't met Letty, for instance, who's in our room. She's only sixteen and as scatty as they come. Ten o'clock's quite late enough for her to be out and about.'

The park was an oasis of green and peace. Genevra would have liked to stroll quietly under the trees, but the other two girls sank down on the first seat they reached.

'That's as far as I can go,' Sally said. She pulled up her skirt in an uninhibited gesture and stared at her ankles.

'Look at them! Swollen like footballs. Let's just sit here and talk. How did you come to get taken on at Pyrritt's, Jenny?'

'I applied to Mr Pyrritt.'

The two girls stared at her as if she had fallen from the moon.

'To Mr *Matthew* Pyrritt? Himself, in person?' Sally demanded.

'Do you mean you *know* him?' Ruth added.

'I . . . I've met him a few times.'

'Saints above!' Sally murmured. 'D'you think we ought to go down on our knees, Ru? She knows Mr Pyrritt – and she's sharing our room! Talk about going up in the world! I can feel my head swelling already.'

'Makes a change from your feet,' Ruth said.

They both stared at Genevra and she looked back, nonplussed by their amazement and by another quality in the way they were regarding her – a touch of uneasiness, a suspicion that she was 'in' with the management.

''Course I saw straight away you was a touch above the

rest of us,' Sally said slowly. 'You not having had to work before and the way you talk an' all that. Still, I didn't think you would have been mixing with the nobs to that extent.'

'I've spoken to Mr Pyrritt about three times,' Genevra protested.

It was true, as far as it went. She had met him three times and he had asked her to marry him. How would the girls have reacted if they had known about that? They would have thought her mad to refuse, and perhaps, in view of the revelations that day had brought her, they were right.

'Tell us about him. What's he like?' Sally asked.

'He seems hard, but underneath I think he's got quite a kind heart,' Genevra said. 'When I asked him to help me he did it without hesitating.'

'It's like a fairy story,' Sally said dreamily. 'One of those musical comedies at the Gaiety. Lovely girl – you're ever so pretty, Jenny, better than either of us – befriended by the wealthiest man in the world, works in his shop . . .'

'Turns out to be a duchess in disguise,' Ruth supplied helpfully.

'Ends up marrying the boss, though I can't say I'd fancy him myself, not with those black eyebrows. I should think he's got ever such a temper.'

'Still . . . all that money,' Ruth pointed out. 'I could swallow the eyebrows for the sake of the bank balance.'

'There is absolutely *nothing* like that between Mr Pyrritt and me,' Genevra said.

She was so agitated that she stood up, ready to leave them, even though she had only the haziest idea of how to get back to their hostel.

'If you say so, dearie,' Sally agreed.

'Look . . . better if we don't tell anyone else,' Ruth

said abruptly. 'I mean, we're only joking, but it'd be a bit hard on Jenny if anyone else got hold of the wrong end of the stick.'

'True enough. Sit down, Jenny. Our lips are sealed. I say, do you know that house he's just bought? They say it's a real show-place.'

'I know it well. I . . . come from there.'

'And is it a really fine house.'

'It's beautiful!'

Genevra's voice wavered. She looked down at her tightly clasped hands, biting her lips to keep back the tears.

'Poor Jenny, you're homesick,' Ruth said. 'Never mind, love, you'll get over it. Come on, time to go back.'

'Cheer up,' Sally exhorted her. 'No use being a sensitive plant in this world. Tomorrow's another day – and you've got to face Miss Eliza Littlejohn, Gawd help you!'

4

Miss Littlejohn was a small woman of unimaginable age. Her hair was still black, but her face was as wrinkled as a dried apple. She held her body ramrod straight, but her head was bent forward and she had a way of turning it sideways and looking up out of the corners of her eyes as if in the hope of catching sight of something she was not meant to see.

She was not pleased at being saddled with an inexperienced assitant of Genevra's age.

'Twenty-one and never worked! A fine state of affairs! What I want is a fourteen-year-old I can train up, not a fine lady who won't listen to a word I say.'

The other condition attaching to Genevra's employment reduced Miss Littlejohn almost, but not quite, to speechlessness.

'Not to be dismissed without reference to Mr Pyrritt? I don't believe it.'

'Those are his orders,' the General Manager told her.

'I've always had the right to get rid of the unsatisfactory lumps you've foisted on me and I'm not having it taken away from me. I'll go and see him.'

Since Miss Littlejohn was the only person not on the management staff who was allowed to penetrate Matthew Pyrritt's office the General Manager's protest was only half-hearted. Miss Littlejohn marched up to the fourth floor, told the flustered clerk that she was going in and flung open the door of the inner office.

'Now, look here, Mr Matthew, I've worked for you,

and your father and your grandfather before him, and I've come here to tell you to your face . . .'

'Shut the door first,' Matthew said. 'It's bad for my standing in the firm for everyone to hear you giving me a wigging.'

'Much you care! Now, about this girl you're trying to shove off on to me. I'll not have one of your fancy pieces in my department and that's flat.'

'Eliza, you shock me. When did I ever go in for playing the fool with my own employees?'

'Never too late to start. You're at a funny age, Mr Matthew . . .'

'I'm thirty-five!'

'Middle-aged,' Miss Littlejohn said inexorably. 'Three-score years and ten is our lot and you've reached the halfway mark. You should have got married long since and so I've told you more than once, and you would have done if it hadn't been for that Rose Peary, kept like a lady, which she isn't and never will be. I thought when you bought that grand house in the country you meant to settle down, but nothing's come of it. What your father would say, let alone your grandfather, I'm sure I don't know.'

'Not much if you were in the room. Draw breath, Eliza, and listen to me. This is to go no further, mind. I bought Leylands from Miss Kerslake, or from her father's estate, and every penny was swallowed up in his debts. She's got no money and she's none too well placed as far as family is concerned. She wants to try her hand at earning a living and so I'm giving her a chance. Now what I *don't* want is for her to be thrown out for some petty fault without me knowing about it. She's got no more idea of looking after herself than a babe unborn and what she'd do without a roof over her head I tremble to think.'

He met Eliza Littlejohn's searching scrutiny with an impassive face.

'Got a soft spot for her, haven't you?' she asked.

'I'm sorry for the girl, that's all.'

'So I'm to have a lady working for me to salve your conscience because you did a shrewd deal and ended up with what should have belonged to her.'

'It was all above board,' Matthew said quickly.

'Of course! It always is with you, but you're not easy about it, for all that. Very well, I'll look after your fine young lady for you. I'll not spare her, mind, but I won't chuck her into the street without telling you first.'

It was a conversation that lent an added interest to Miss Littlejohn's first meeting with Genevra. She looked her up and down with her searching sideways gaze, and was more suspicious than ever about Matthew's motives. Quite a little beauty, in her way: an air of refinement which would add tone to the Haberdashery Department, if the girl could be taught to sell; pretty, useless, well-cared-for hands; and something else – an appeal which even Eliza Littlejohn's shrivelled old heart recognized. Meeting Genevra's candid eyes she felt a quite unaccustomed shame at having referred to her as a 'fancy piece'. The girl had braced herself to work in a way that went against all her upbringing and there was something gallant about the way she was going about it. More like a brave determined boy than the silly shrinking girl Miss Littlejohn had imagined.

For all that, there was no softening apparent in the way she addressed Genevra.

'Well, Miss Kerslake, you've got a lot to learn and you won't do it by standing around looking helpless. I'll start you off by telling you where everything is. Not that you'll remember, but some of it might soak in.'

By the end of the day Genevra thought that she never

55

wanted to see a length of elastic or a reel of sewing cotton again. Her back ached, her feet were on fire and her legs would hardly support her, but the one attempt she made to ease them got short shrift from Miss Littlejohn.

For a few welcome minutes the department was empty. Genevra had put away the cards of hooks and eyes and rewound the braided trimmings which had littered the counter. She pulled out the bentwood chair which was pushed away in the corner and sat down.

'What do you think you're doing, miss?' Eliza Little-john demanded.

'Everything's tidy, Miss Littlejohn.'

'I'm not saying it's not, but we don't expect our girls to sit down on the job, not at Pyrritt's. Look alert, if you please, ready to serve a customer if one appears.'

'But the chair is here, behind the counter . . .'

'It's not there to be *used*. Now, I've given you a warning; the next time it'll be a sixpenny fine.'

'For sitting down?' Genevra asked disbelievingly.

'If you're not up to the job you don't have to do it. There's plenty ready to take your place.'

But Genevra did have to do the job. She thought the rule inhuman, but she stood up, wincing as the pain shot up her calves.

She was sent to lunch at twelve o'clock and told to be back in twenty minutes, which was manifestly absurd since it took a good five minutes to reach the luncheon room and the same time to return to the Haberdashery Department. The lunch which was provided consisted of soup, which was good and Genevra drank it down thankfully, a bread roll and a generous piece of cheese. There were cups of tea, too, but Genevra looked desperately at the clock and passed up the tea in order to fit in a visit to the lavatory.

'Two minutes late,' Miss Littlejohn said when she returned.

'I didn't know my way,' Genevra protested.

'I'll make allowances this one time, but do remember that if you are late back it cuts into the time I can allow the other girls, which won't make you very popular with them. I'm off myself now. Keep in the background and don't sell anything without referring to Miss Blake.'

Genevra sold nothing at all that first terrible day, but later in the week at a moment when everyone else was occupied she did venture to ask a customer whether she could be of assistance.

'Buttons,' the woman said.

She opened her handbag and brought out a scrap of rich purple velvet.

'To match this.'

Fortunately, buttons were something that Genevra had mastered. She took out the boxes from the correct drawer without hesitating and found an array of purple ones.

'Too pale,' the woman said, discarding the first box. 'Too small. They must be at least half an inch across.'

'Perhaps these?' Genevra suggested, showing her some plain round buttons which seemed to be an exact match.

'Mm . . . n-no, I think not. The buttons are to be rather a feature of this gown. I'll need two and a half dozen. I'd like more of a fancy button.'

Without saying anything Genevra produced a button with an ornamental gold rim.

'That's more the thing. At least . . . I *think* so. They look effective, don't they?'

'I prefer the plain ones,' Genevra said, thinking she was being asked to express an opinion.

'Really? And may I ask why you recommend them above the others?'

'Two and a half dozen purple and gold buttons . . . might it not look rather overdone – even vulgar?'

A small black thundercloud materialized at Genevra's shoulder. Miss Littlejohn directed a tight little smile at the customer, but under cover of the counter she gave Genevra's shin a vicious kick.

'Thank you, Miss Kerslake, I will attend to madam's requirements.'

She picked up the scrap of velvet and felt it with expert fingers.

'With velvet of this quality madam requires something really recherché,' she murmured. 'I wonder if I might recommend this line? The centres cut to resemble real amethysts, you see, and the surround most tastefully ornamented. A *leetle* more expensive, I'm afraid – the amethyst stones have to be imported from Germany – but I venture to suggest nothing could set off a gown better.'

With a little more soothing talk she succeeded in selling the buttons. As soon as the customer had departed she turned on Genevra.

'Nothing we sell at Pyrritt's is vulgar, miss! And never criticize a customer's taste, never! The idea! She can deck herself out like a Christmas tree if she likes. The only thing you have to think about is making a sale, and those ornamental buttons you were running down sell for four pence a dozen more than the plain ones. Just as well I was at hand to put things right. She might have walked out without buying anything, which is something I can't abide.'

Altogether, Genevra could not look back at her first week in the retail trade as a success. Miss Littlejohn was impatient with her and the other girls were condescending, which was galling since they were all younger than Genevra.

She was too tired at first to react to the conditions under which she was living. These were uniformly appalling – far worse than she had expected. The only good point was the friendliness of the girls who shared her hot overcrowded room; but even they laughed at Genevra and told her she was a 'proper lady', which she gathered was not a compliment.

'Haven't you ever heard of putting tops to bottoms?' Sally asked when Genevra pointed out that she had only been given one clean sheet at the beginning of her second week.

'You use your top sheet as your under sheet and put the clean one on top,' she explained patiently, seeing that Genevra looked blank. 'Then next week, obviously, this week's top one goes to the bottom. Didn't you ever do that at home?'

Genevra shook her head, overcome by a memory of fine linen smelling of lavender.

'Your Mum must have been well-off for sheets,' Ruth commented. 'Come on, slow coach, get a move on or you won't get any breakfast.'

Gradually, Genevra adjusted to her new life and began to come out of the stupor of fatigue in which she had lived for the first two or three weeks; and, as she did so, she became aware of a slow swell of indignation that she, or anyone else, should be expected to lead such a life.

She did not rebel until she had endured nearly a month and then it was a small outside occurrence which roused her from her dull acceptance of things as they were. She had a letter from her solicitor.

It was unusual for any of the girls to receive letters and there were curious looks at Genevra when the thick white envelope was handed to her.

The news inside was good, better than she had hoped. Genevra had asked Mr Ryman to sell her lovely mare and he wrote to tell her that he had obtained an excellent price for Marietta. With Genevra's permission, he would invest the money, which would bring her in an income of between ten and twelve pounds a year.

The amount was negligible, it would not have kept Leonora in gloves, but it meant that at a stroke Genevra's yearly income was nearly doubled. More than that, she felt that if ever she should be in dire need she could ask Mr Ryman for her small capital. She was not quite as penniless as she had thought. Indeed, with her eyes opened to the other girls' circumstances, Genevra had come to realize that she had several tangible assets. A few small pieces of jewellery, for instance: a gold fob watch which she was not allowed to wear at work, a fine cameo brooch, a gold locket, a single row of pearls. They could all be sold if necessary.

With this in her mind when she woke up early on the following Sunday morning Genevra began to make plans. Perhaps one day she could have a little shop of her own. She doubted whether she would ever rise very high in Pyrritt's, but if she worked hard and learnt about the trade she might, just possibly, be able to rent tiny premises with a room or two above the shop and set up business on her own account.

All around her on that sunny September morning the other girls sighed and grunted and hunched the bed clothes higher to shut out the light, intent only on getting the rest they so desperately needed. Genevra lay tense and wakeful, her nose wrinkling distastefully at the stuffy atmosphere. Suddenly she sat up, hugging her knees.

I'm letting myself be beaten, she thought. I'm behaving like a downtrodden skivvy. If I want to get up, why shouldn't I? I'll be quiet and not waken the others. If they prefer to spend their free time in bed they can. I'm going to . . . I'm going to have a bath and wash my hair.

Why should I be limited to one bath a week if I'm prepared to pay for the hot water? And I'm going to take the screws out of that window. It's ridiculous for six grown women to be forced to sleep without any fresh air.

She slipped quietly down the stairs in the dressing gown which had made the other girls exclaim over its fine quality; she put a penny in the meter attached to the geyser and ran herself a hot bath. There were four white-enamelled cast-iron baths on legs in the basement bathroom. Each one was divided off by a partition, but there were no doors to the cubicles, which was something else that irritated Genevra.

She dried herself on the one inadequate towel and then bent over the bath to wash her hair. It was not until she had finished that it occurred to her that she would not receive her clean towel until the following day and would be forced to re-use the same one when she washed on Sunday night and Monday morning. Then she remembered that her new wealth would allow her to buy herself a towel to be kept specially for drying her hair, and she felt a glow of pleasure she would not have believed possible in the days when clean dry towels were something to be taken for granted.

Many of the girls went without breakfast on Sundays, preferring to remain in bed. Genevra appeared at the table with her hair still wet and hanging loose.

Mrs Thredgold took immediate exception to that.

'Why are you wearing your hair in that unseemly fashion, Miss Kerslake?' she demanded.

'I washed it and it's still damp,' Genevra replied.

'I thought I heard water running! So it was you! Using the bathroom on a Sunday morning is discouraged because it disturbs people. Please be more considerate in future. Take your bath and wash your hair at the time allotted to you on the rota.'

'Once a fortnight!' Genevra said. 'I'm sorry, but I don't consider that adequate, nor do I like to be restricted to one bath a week. I mean to take a bath every Sunday and to wash my hair at the same time. I think you will find, Mrs Thredgold, that there is nothing in the rules which says I may not.'

Mrs Thredgold's face had turned red.

'I'll have a lock put on the door,' she said.

'Is it worth the trouble? Or the expense? It seems a very small concession, to allow me to use the bathroom at a time when no one else wants it.'

'It will mean extra work for the maid.'

'I left the bath clean – rather cleaner, if I may say so, than it was when I went in. Perhaps I might recommend that you inspect the maid's work rather more closely, Mrs Thredgold. To me, it seems to fall far below what ought to be acceptable.'

There had been a time when Mrs Thredgold had been in the service of a very high-born lady. She recognized the tone of her voice, the habit of command so deeply ingrained that it was taken for granted – and it deprived her of speech. Afterwards she thought of any number of things she might have said to the golden-haired chit; but at the time she was so taken aback that she could only murmur defensively, 'I do my best.'

Genevra's pitying smile hinted that the housekeeper's best was scarcely good enough, but she was quick to see that she had gained a victory and that it would be better not to presume on it.

'I'm sure you do,' she said. 'You have a very difficult task.'

'That I do!' Mrs Thredgold agreed fervently, and while they were still in accord Genevra got herself out of the room.

She did not inform Mrs Thredgold of her intentions

regarding the bedroom window, but she kept to her resolve to unfasten it, using a metal nail-file on the screws which kept it shut.

'You won't half get into trouble if the sash is broken and the window falls down and cracks,' Sally warned her.

'It seems all right,' Genevra commented. 'Stiff, which is only to be expected when it's been shut for so long.'

She banged the frame with her closed fist and the window allowed itself to be pushed down, letting in a welcome gush of air.

'Old Ma Thredgold will go mad,' Ruth said with conviction.

'Does she ever come up here? I doubt it,' Genevra said. 'And the maid certainly won't notice.' She looked contemptuously at her dirty hands. 'She hasn't wiped that window frame or cleaned the window in months. As long as we remember to shut the window every morning when we go out no one will be any the wiser.'

'I don't know that I want the night air coming in on me,' Nelly, who slept nearest the window, protested. 'They say it's not healthy.'

'I'll change places with you,' Genevra offered.

As far as she was concerned it was a highly satisfactory arrangement. She had gained the fresh air she craved, a place near the window, and a few inches more space.

'You'll get the lot of us hung,' Sally said, but not unadmiringly. 'I s'pose I'd better get up. Are you coming to Greenwich for the day with us, Jenny?'

'No, I'm going to church,' Genevra said.

'All right, *be* independent then!'

That was a turning-point for Genevra. She felt that having asserted herself over two small matters she had recovered her personality. She might no longer be Miss Kerslake of Leylands, but neither had she sunk into being an unthinking automaton. She went into work the next morning and for the first time really applied her intelligence to the Haberdashery Department. Instead of letting the dull routine wash over her, while half her mind was given to the way her legs ached and the waste of life it all represented, she began to take an interest in the stock. Thirty-six different types of braid, and every one of them subdivided into different widths and colours: it was a formidable task to keep them all in her mind, but if she was one day going to have a shop of her own it would be as well to know what to order.

'You may be of some use one day,' Miss Littlejohn remarked at the end of the week, which coming from her almost amounted to praise.

The work did not get any easier, nor was Genevra by any means reconciled to the long hours, but she came to realize, almost with disbelief, that Pyrritt's was one of the more enlightened stores. They closed at two o'clock on Saturdays, and that was by no means universal. Ruth spoke with a shudder of the draper's where she had been apprenticed which remained open until midnight every Saturday. Genevra might find the conditions hard, but the other girls were thankful to be working in the bright new store and to be allowed regular breaks for meals, however short. Nor were they particularly sympathetic to her complaints about their lodgings.

'You don't know where you're well off,' Sally told her. 'Some places turn you out all day on Sundays. Last winter my sister took to going to church three times a day regular, walking from one church to another, just to keep from freezing. Honest, Jenny, it may not seem like much to you, but we're lucky to be allowed to sit in our room all day if we feel like it, and to have meals provided. You don't know how hard it is to find somewhere to eat on a Sunday. People get driven into the pubs, and you know what that leads to.'

Genevra had not known, but she was learning. She was woken up one night out of her first exhausted sleep by a persistent tapping at the window by her head. She sat up and pulled back the dingy curtain and was appalled to see Letty, the sixteen-year-old, straddled across the ridge of the roof which ran at right-angles below the window.

Inevitably, everyone else woke up. Genevra raised the bottom of the window and, with Sally's help, seized Letty under the armpits and hauled her into the room.

'Silly little cow! What do you think you're doing?' Sally demanded in a fierce whisper.

Letty was giggling, collapsed on the floor in a helpless heap.

'Only a bit of a spree,' she said.

'We were worried sick when you didn't come in,' Sally told her. 'Where have you been?'

'Went to the Empire with Dick.'

'And somewhere else,' Sally said. She bent over Letty and sniffed. 'You stink of drink.'

'Had a quick one – or two,' Letty admitted. 'Got back and found the door locked. Didn't dare knock. Rotten old Ma Thredgold, she'd get me thrown out.'

'Of course she would! You know we're not supposed to go into pubs.'

'How did you get on to the roof?' Genevra asked.

'Up the fire escape in the Men's Hostel, in one window and out another on to the roof. Dick helped me.'

'You could have been killed!'

'Not me! It was a lark. I nearly died laughing.'

'You won't laugh in the morning when you look out of the window and see where you've been,' Sally told her. 'You're too flown with drink to see the danger tonight. Come on, into bed with you. Look what you've done to your stockings, you silly girl.'

'That's what comes of opening that window,' Nelly

65

pointed out. 'There was a good reason for having it shut after all. If Letty can get in one of the men might do the same.'

'You should be so lucky!' Sally said rudely. 'Oh, come on, Letty! Don't keep flopping about.'

Genevra waited until the next day and then she cornered Letty. The youngster was looking pale and sorry for herself, but Genevra refused to sympathize.

'I'll say this once and I won't say it again,' she said. 'If you ever do that silly trick with the window again I'll report you to Mrs Thredgold.'

'You wouldn't!' Letty stared at her, unable to believe her ears. 'Nobody would do that to another girl – nobody!'

'I would, and you'd better believe that I mean it. The other girls may feel that they are doing the right thing in shielding you, and I'll fall in with that this time: but I was not exaggerating last night when I said you could have been killed. I have no intention of closing that window up again and I refuse to have your death on my conscience.'

She saw that Letty looked sullen, but shaken, and pressed on relentlessly.

'You seem to have become friendly with a very unsuitable young man. No one who really cared for you would encourage you to drink and behave so foolishly.'

'Don't you dare say a word against Dick! I love him!'

'Then behave responsibly. How would he have felt if you'd slipped last night.'

'Too late to warn me about slipping,' Letty said with a giggle. 'I'm a fallen woman, that's what I am!'

Genevra felt her colour rising and regretted it, knowing that Letty had spoken with the intention of embarrassing her and was watching to see whether she had succeeded. Because Mrs Bertram had seen no reason to shield her young mistress from reality, Genevra was well aware that there had been girls in the village, a maid at Leylands even, who had got themselves into trouble with their young men and had been married off with more haste than decorum. Mrs Bertram had explained the situation to Genevra with a frankness which Leonora might have disapproved, but for which Genevra was grateful. As far as Mrs Bertram was concerned, it was one of the more deplorable facts of life that girls were foolish and men took advantage of it. As long as they managed to get themselves respectably married before the baby was born then such sin could be forgiven and forgotten – though not, as she hurriedly pointed out, when it involved a young lady like Genevra, from whom a higher standard of behaviour was expected.

Bearing all this in mind, Genevra said hesitantly to Letty, 'Are you and Dick going to get married?'

'Of course we are – one day.'

'One day,' Genevra said. 'Letty, I don't know what to say to you, but I do think you're making a terrible mistake.'

'It's none of your business, madam. You think you're a cut above the rest of us, but I'm as good as you are any day of the week and I'll not be preached at.'

'I haven't preached,' Genevra pointed out.

She felt quite helpless. It was one thing, she discovered, to hear about lapses in morality secondhand, and quite another to be faced with a defiant Cockney girl, wildly in love and ungovernable. Besides, Letty was right: it was not for Genevra to dictate her rules of conduct. Except that she was so young, and so silly, and so irresponsible about the possible consequences of throwing herself into her young man's arms.

Perhaps, after all, there was some logic behind the tiresome regulations that hedged the girls in the hostel.

Rules – as a necessary substitute, perhaps, for the strict moral code by which Genevra herself had been reared? It was all very difficult, far more difficult than she had realized before she had come out into the ordinary world.

5

As Genevra grew more accustomed to her work she found time to look around her and to appreciate the array of goods and services provided by Pyrritt's Department Store. There were special counters for ribbons, for lace and for shawls, as well as the larger departments for gowns and mantles. Mourning wear had a whole floor to itself devoted to jet and crepe, where specially trained assistants could advise on the exact depth of mourning suitable for all relationships. There were separate departments for children and for outfitting servants. Nor were men neglected. They could purchase a complete outfit and the luggage in which to pack it without having to pass through the fripperies of ladies' millinery or perfumery.

At the rear on the ground floor was the Food Store, full of aromatic smells of tea and coffee, spices and confectionery, warm new bread, exotic fruit and the earthy scent of vegetables, while the Butchery had a cold-room which was the envy of London.

The store was a continual kaleidoscope of shifting movement, with a hum of voices in the background. Lift doors clashed together as the clients were conveyed from floor to floor with the sharp young lift-boys chanting their monotonous recital of departments.

There were carpets on the floors, acres of polished mahogany counters, clear glass cabinets full of artificial flowers, feathers and fans. There were brass fittings and immense chandeliers, all glitteringly reflected in mirrors attached to marble columns.

The young ladies in Model Gowns wore silk, which was forbidden to the other assistants. They were such superior beings in their rustling black gowns that Genevra was surprised that the customers dared to give them orders, but for all their airs and graces they still shared the same mean lodgings she had to endure herself. Only a few privileged old hands, like Miss Littlejohn, lived out.

Mr Pyrritt introduced Christmas decorations at the beginning of December – festoons of coloured paper and tinsel and huge golden bells swinging from the ceiling. The tempo began to increase, every day the store was more crowded, the shuffle of feet became a regular tramp, the hum of voices rose to a roar. The opening hours were extended and the staff worked themselves into a state of speechless fatigue.

What nagged at the back of Genevra's mind all through the long exhausting days was that she had nowhere to go. Christmas Day fell on a Friday that year, which meant a welcome extension of the holiday over Sunday; but unless she humbled herself and appealed to Leonora she could not think where she would spend the three days.

'What are you doing for Christmas?' Sally asked her carelessly.

'I don't know,' Genevra admitted.

She saw from the look of doubt that flitted across Sally's face that the other girl was wondering whether she ought to invite Genevra to go home with her, but she also knew that Sally's home would be bursting at the seams with all the family expected for Christmas. To her enormous relief, she was rescued from her dilemma by an invitation from Mr Ryman, her solicitor.

'It was so very kind and thoughtful of you,' Genevra said gratefully when she arrived at his house on Christmas

Eve. 'I'm sorry to arrive late, but Pyrritt's didn't close until nine o'clcok.'

She looked round the comfortable middle-class villa, and realized that whereas she would once have thought it small and stuffy it now seemed like the very epitome of comfort.

Mrs Ryman, she saw, was nervous of her.

'So brave of you,' she said in a vague twittering way. 'Working, I mean. And in a shop. Not that Pyrritt's . . . but still, quite different from Leylands . . . and your father . . . though of course he was unconventional himself.'

'Papa would have laughed and congratulated me on my independence,' Genevra said firmly. 'Oh, you have a Christmas tree! How pretty!'

'The children . . . grandchildren, that is,' Mrs Ryman said. 'They'll be here for tea tomorrow. Such dears. Two boys and two girls. Do you like children, Miss Kerslake?'

'I haven't had much experience of them,' Genevra admitted. 'I'm sure your grandchildren are delightful.'

'I would have thought . . . perhaps a governess . . . rather than a shop,' Mrs Ryman said doubtfully.

'I didn't think I had the talent for teaching,' Genevra said.

'Church in the morning, of course,' Mrs Ryman ventured. 'But we thought . . . we wondered . . .'

'We usually attend St Luke's at Charleigh,' Mr Ryman intervened. 'I hope that won't distress you, Miss Kerslake?'

'I'll be glad to have the opportunity of wishing some of my old friends a happy Christmas,' Genevra said.

Mrs Ryman's face lost its worried frown. 'So glad! Our nearest church . . . All Saints, you know . . . a little *high* . . . incense . . . quite sickly.'

'I expect Miss Kerslake is tired,' Mr Ryman suggested.

'Indeed I am,' Genevra agreed.

Her room was clean and warm and she had it to herself. Did the Ryman's understand what luxury they were offering her? Genevra grimaced as she pulled the blankets round her shoulders. Taking pleasure in this blissful respite was all very well, but she must remember not to allow herself to enjoy it too much or the contrast would be unbearable when she returned to London.

Genevra had rebelled against wearing for Christmas Day either of the two black gowns she wore on alternate days for work. Instead, she had taken out of her trunk a dress of dark crimson wool. She realized that Mrs Ryman was surprised to see her out of mourning; but Genevra volunteered no explanation. When they left for church she wore the supple sealskin jacket which had been a gift from her father the previous Christmas, and felt that she was once more Miss Kerslake of Leylands.

Her appearance caused a small stir in the church. Genevra kept her eyes lowered until she was seated in the Rymans' pew, then she allowed herself to look round.

St Luke's, in which she had been christened and confirmed, looked just the same – small, grey and holy. It was decorated with holly and branches of pine, and some expensive-looking white chrysanthemums. The flowers had probably been provided by Mr Pyrritt, Genevra decided. They were just the sort of thing he would think proper.

He was there, in the Leylands pew. It was the first time Genevra had set eyes on him for months. There were other people in the pew with him, presumably his guests for Christmas. Rather an odd crew, Genevra thought, and then her attention was caught by the sight of a familiar face. Eliza Littlejohn, a guest at Leylands? It was almost unbelievable. True, everyone knew that she had worked for the Pyrritt family for ever, because she

72

never stopped talking about it; but all the same, Genevra had not realized that she was on such intimate terms with their employer.

In the churchyard after the service Genevra was surrounded by old friends wanting to wish her a happy Christmas. They were curious, she guessed, to find out what they could about her present circumstances, and she was glad that she had made an effort to appear amongst them looking something like the young lady they all remembered.

Mr Pyrritt was talking to Mr and Mrs Ryman, with Miss Littlejohn standing by. Genevra broke away from her wellwishers and went towards them. She was smiling, with more colour than usual in her face and a sparkle in her eye.

Matthew Pyrritt turned his usual sombre look on her, but when Genevra smiled frankly at him his expression softened.

'The compliments of the season to you, Miss Kerslake,' he said. 'I'm pleased to see you here. You're keeping well?'

'Quite well, thank you, and having such a lovely rest. Just think, after breakfast today I sat down for nearly three hours.'

'Is that your idea of a good Christmas?'

'It's my idea of heaven, and would be yours, too, if you served behind a counter, Mr Pyrritt.'

There was a crack of laughter from Miss Littlejohn.

'He's done it in his time, Miss Kerslake,' she said. 'But it doesn't do any harm to remind him what it's like.'

Genevra looked at the older woman curiously. If she was staying at Leylands then she must know Genevra's story and probably had known it all along, and yet she had never given the slightest hint of being aware of it.

Another woman, goodlooking in an over-emphatic

73

way, with a high colour and massed coils of black hair, was hovering on the edge of the group, trying to catch Matthew Pyrritt's eye.

'You and the others go on without me, Rose,' he said impatiently.

The woman pouted in a petulant fashion; but she obeyed him and, after a moment's hesitation, Miss Little-john followed her.

'When are you going back to London?' Mr Pyrritt asked Genevra.

'On Sunday afternoon.'

'Sunday travelling . . . such a pity . . . not what one would wish,' Mrs Ryman fluttered.

'Unavoidable if I'm to be at my post by eight o'clock on Monday morning,' Genevra said.

'My carriage will be taking Miss Littlejohn to the station that afternoon. There'll be room for you if you'd like to be picked up. The two of you can travel back together.'

Genevra glanced at Mr Ryman and then accepted the offer, stammering a little over her thanks. Mr Pyrritt merely nodded and turned away abruptly, catching up his party at the lychgate.

'Extraordinary man!' Genevra murmured, looking after him.

'Most odd,' Mrs Ryman agreed. 'But really quite kind, in his way. Concerned, you know. When he asked about you . . . such a good thought, coming to us . . . delighted, of course . . . and Sir Francis and Lady Hamden being away . . .'

'Mrs Ryman, do you mean it was Mr Pyrritt's idea that I should spend Christmas with you?' Genevra asked.

'Why, yes . . . oh, dear, perhaps I shouldn't . . . but, as I say, *delighted* to have you.'

Since she was obviously embarrassed, Genevra let the

74

subject drop, but that did not mean that she put it out of her mind. Matthew Pyrritt, amongst the multitude of matters he had to deal with, had found time to remember that one of his junior employees would be without a home at Christmas. He had also seen fit to entertain an old colleague from his less affluent days. It almost reconciled Genevra to his shortcomings as an employer. Almost, but not quite. Flashes of benevolence could not make up for the long-term lack of care for the wellbeing of his staff, not in Genevra's estimation.

She could not resist trying to draw out Eliza Littlejohn when they travelled back to London together on Sunday afternoon.

'Do you usually spend Christmas with Mr Pyrritt?' she asked.

'Depends. Sometimes I go to my married sister. This year Carrie – that's my sister – arranged to go and stay with her daughter in Brighton so I was a bit high and dry.'

'And Mr Pyrritt invited you to visit him?'

'That's right.'

'And were the other guests also former employees?'

'A couple of them worked for his grandfather in the old days and there were some neighbours who lived next door when Mr Matthew was growing up. What I didn't expect, and wouldn't have been a party to if I'd known about it beforehand, was that Rose Peary being in the house.'

'Someone you don't like?' Genevra guessed.

Miss Littlejohn had had an ample lunch topped up with just enough of her host's port to loosen her tongue.

'Mr Matthew keeps her and has done this four years past,' she said. 'They kept it quiet over Christmas, I'll say that, and I suppose if she's his fancy then he's as much right to invite her to his house as any lord who's bedding his neighbour's wife. There's some funny goings on in High Society, Miss Kerslake, you can take my word for it. All the same, it's not what *I* approve of, as Mr Matthew well knows, and it's my belief he'd asked her before he knew I was at a loose end and then he couldn't get out of it.'

She settled herself more comfortably in the corner of the railway carriage and yawned.

'What Mr Matthew needs is a wife.'

'Perhaps he'll marry Miss . . . Mrs Peary,' Genevra suggested.

'Mrs she calls herself, though I have my doubts about whether she's entitled. No, Mr Matthew won't marry her. He'll be looking round for a lady to go with that grand house and whatever else she may be Rose Peary is no lady.'

She yawned again, closed her eyes and snoozed for the rest of the journey, leaving Genevra to her own not very happy thoughts. So Matthew Pyrritt had a mistress of several years' standing – that highly-coloured woman who had approached him in the churchyard – and he had seen fit to invite her to stay with him at Leylands. It threw a most unpleasant light on his proposal of marriage to Genevra. She had never believed that he had fallen in love with her; but she had treated the proposal as an honest attempt to secure a wife who would be suitable both for him and for Leylands. Now she felt herself dishonoured by the offer, even to the point of putting Francis's rejection of it in a more reasonable light. Just what sort of marriage had Matthew Pyrritt had in mind? He went to London for three nights of every week. If Genevra had accepted him would he have devoted those nights to his mistress, leaving his wife behind in the country to run his house and be a figurehead for his social pretensions?

Genevra felt both angry and humiliated. The worst thing of all, the thought she did not want to face, was that there had been times during the last few months when she had secretly regretted her decided rejection of Mr Pyrritt's proposal. Not now, though. She would certainly not reconsider her decision in the unlikely event of it being renewed.

Unseen by Eliza Littlejohn Genevra smiled a small rueful smile to herself as she reflected what a long way she had come since the days when she had been the protected daughter of the house at Leylands. A year ago no one would have dreamed of mentioning to her that a man had a mistress. Now she knew all about her father's besotted infatuation for a worthless actress; she knew that a girl was not necessarily safe from unwanted attentions under the roof of a close relative; and she knew that a man could offer marriage to one young woman while keeping another to satisfy his lust. Very carefully, so as not to attract Eliza Littlejohn's attention, Genevra found a handkerchief and touched it to her eyes – but she would have been hard put to it to decide what it was that caused her tears.

Everyone was jaded after the Christmas festivities. The girls were snappy with one another. Genevra, hauling her trunk out from under the bed to stow away her crimson gown and few precious items of jewellery, was accused of taking up more space than she was entitled to and was dismayed to hear the shrillness of her own voice as she replied: 'Do be patient! I'll put everything back in a moment.'

'You're not opening the window tonight, are you?' Letty asked. 'It's freezing outside.'

'I'd still like a breath of fresh air.'

'Don't see why we should catch our death of cold just to please you.'

She picked up the little case which contained Genevra's cameo brooch and opened it. 'Oo, that's a pretty thing! Where did you get that, Jenny?'

'It belonged to my mother. Give it to me, please.'

Genevra stowed away the brooch with her watch and locket, and her pearl necklace, under the black silk evening-gown she had worn at Christmas for the first time since she had left her cousins' house.

'You've got some nice things,' Letty commented, looking over her shoulder. 'Funny, I didn't think you were a particularly dressy person.'

'I'm in mourning,' Genevra replied. 'In a few months' time perhaps I'll start wearing some of my old gowns again.'

She shut the trunk so quickly that Letty only just had time to take her hand away from feeling the black silk.

'No need to be nasty,' she said, aggrieved. 'I was only looking. No harm in that, is there?'

She stretched and sighed voluptuously. 'Oo. I did have a good Christmas! Roll on the New Year, that's what I say. You can leave the window open that night, Jenny. I'm seeing the New Year in with Dick, no matter what.'

'I've told you what will happen if you try to climb through that window again,' Genevra said. 'I mean it, Letty.'

After that it was no great surprise when Letty, in floods of tears, was heard telling Mrs Thredgold on New Year's Eve that her dear old grandmother, who had brought her up, was dying: Letty pleaded for leave to stay out overnight to be with her in her last hours. When permission was granted her tears cleared up miraculously and she gave the other girls a wink and a cheeky grin.

'That girl ought to go on the stage,' Ruth commented.

'But once she's seen the New Year in where will she stay the night?' Genevra asked.

Ruth and Sally looked at one another. 'Better not to ask,' Sally said.

Genevra never heard how Letty spent the first night of 1886. She was left out of the low-voiced confidences Letty shared with some of the other girls, but she gathered from their shocked titters that the tale was highly spiced and lost nothing in the telling.

The Sales started in January, and while they were less demanding in Haberdashery than in some departments it was still a busier time than normal, so that Genevra began to feel that all the benefit of her rest over Christmas was disappearing. And Mr Pyrritt must be making good profits: in her new-found disgust with him, the thought gave Genevra no pleasure.

By early February it seemed as if the winter would never end. Genevra had lost the fight to keep the bedroom window open at night; all the girls had colds; and the news she read in the occasional paper she bought was enough to make anyone cling to the job they had, however distasteful it might be. There was a good deal of unrest in the country. On Monday, 8 February 1886, a meeting of the unemployed was held in Trafalgar Square, to protest about the lack of work and the poverty resulting from it. Trafalgar Square was a long way from Oxford Street and nothing was heard of the rally in Pyrritt's Department Store. Trade was not particularly brisk, but Monday was often quieter than other days. Genevra was rewinding a length of lace edging after a successful sale when a messenger boy paused by her counter and muttered, 'Looks like trouble in Trafalgar Square. They say the men are going on the rampage.'

79

In accordance with custom, the Haberdashery Department at Pyrritt's was situated on the ground floor near the main entrance. A few minutes after the boy had spoken Genevra looked out of the large plate-glass windows and saw an unusual number of people in the street. There were women hurrying along in alarm, even running. Some turned into Pyrritt's, as if taking refuge. One of them, an elderly woman, looked round distractedly, then tottered, putting a hand to her head. Genevra went out from behind the counter, partly out of concern and partly to see what was going on.

She heard a strange sound, like a roar, and realized that it was made by men's voices shouting slogans, and by heavy boots running along the pavement. She heard a crash and someone screamed. Then the running men came in sight and she saw that they were hitting out at the windows with staves of wood.

With an arm round the woman who had seemed about to faint, Genevra flinched as a stone shattered one of the big windows, showering the goods on display with splinters of glass. Horrified and fascinated, she watched as a full-size brick hurtled through the air. It smashed through a glass panel of the front door and Genevra exclaimed in pain as something seared into her cheek.

She put up her hand and took it away covered in blood. There were people all round her, but they seemed more concerned with the customer, who had now fainted in earnest.

Genevra leaned against the counter, feeling sick. Outside, the street was full of shouting, strident men, but she also heard the shrill note of a policeman's whistle.

'Let me through please.' A commanding voice spoke from behind the crowd which jostled round the fallen customer. 'Is someone hurt?'

'Madam fainted, Mr Pyrritt,' Miss Littlejohn said. 'And

I'm sure I don't wonder at it. Your windows are in smithereens.'

'Just a faint? No other damage?' Matthew Pyrritt looked round and his glance fell on Genevra, still propped against the counter. 'What about you?'

'Something hit my cheek.' She touched it gingerly and winced.

'Let me see.' He tilted back her chin. 'There's a sliver of glass in the cut. Keep still.'

There was a stab of pain and then Matthew stepped back. 'There it is. Nasty, but I think the wound's clean now. Come up to my office and I'll get it dressed for you. Here, hold this up to your face.'

He handed her a white handkerchief and Genevra held it over the scratch on her cheek. As he led her away, Mr Pyrritt laid his arm round her shoulders, both to guide and support her. All the way up to the fourth floor she was conscious of that comforting touch; but his manner when they reached his office was prosaic in the extreme.

'I doubt if you'll be permanently marked,' he said when the cut had been washed and covered with a strip of plaster. 'Sit down. I've ordered a cup of tea to be brought up to you.'

'Thank you. I do feel a little shaken,' Genevra admitted. 'It all happened so suddenly, it was so unexpected.'

'Ruffians.'

'I suppose . . . yes, they must have been.'

'I shall sue for damages, of course. We weren't properly protected and someone will have to pay for my broken windows. I doubt whether I can get anything for you.'

'No . . . I wouldn't want . . . it's the merest scratch.' Genevra said.

'Here's your tea. Drink it.'

'I'm afraid I'm interrupting your work,' Genevra said, looking at the piles of paper on his desk.

'You are, of course, but don't let it bother you. Tell me how you're getting on.'

'Reasonably well.'

'Finding it harder than you expected? I thought you were when I saw you at Christmas.'

The reference to Christmas made Genevra stiffen as she remembered that this was the man who had seen fit to invite his mistress to stay in her own old home. Mr Pyrritt appeared oblivious to her reaction.

'It's a fine store, isn't it?' he went on. 'It must make it easier for you, working in such surroundings.'

'The shop is quite magnificent.'

'It was built to my father's plan, but he didn't live to see it finished. I took it over and saw it through, no expense spared, just as he would have wished. The pillars are Purbeck marble, you know. Mahogany counters, carpets on the floors – that was a touch he didn't think of. The electricity was my idea, too. It came in just in time and I think you'll agree it's an improvement on gas. Have you visited the restaurant? No, I don't suppose you have. A pity because the cloakroom alone is worth seeing.'

Listening to this complacent recital, Genevra began to seethe with indignation. Suddenly it was more than she could bear. She put down her cup with a clatter that made Mr Pyrritt look at her in surprise.

'I suppose you spent so much on your wonderful shop that there was nothing left over for the comfort of your staff,' she said. 'The conditions under which we live are atrocious.'

Mr Pyrritt stared at her, his face reddening angrily.

'I always thought you'd be too much of a fine lady to buckle down to the life of a shop girl,' he said. 'It's hardly right to compare your lodgings with Leylands House . . .'

'The *pigs* were better housed at Leylands than we are in Mountfort Street,' Genevra cried.

'You're lodged and fed, everything's provided . . .'

'Our rooms are overcrowded, the washing facilities are inadequate and the food is uneatable. I share a room with five other girls. I wouldn't complain about that if it left room for the maid to clean properly, but it doesn't. The window was screwed shut until I opened it, and I know that was insubordinate and I don't care. There are cockroaches in the kitchen and mice in the pantry. We had rancid butter on our bread for breakfast this morning. Rancid – in February! You can imagine what it was like during the summer months.'

'All the food comes from our own Food Store and it's good,' Mr Pyrritt said with conviction.

'I can hardly believe that it's the same as you supply to the customers,' Genevra retorted. 'If it were, you'd be knee-deep in rotting potatoes, thrown back at you by furious housewives.'

'Have you finished?'

'No, I haven't. Since I've said so much I may as well go the rest of the way. We need more bathrooms and better access to them. And a room in which to sit with a few books in it and perhaps some board games. It's demoralizing to sit in a bedroom all day with nothing to do because it's raining outside.'

'Quite the reformer, aren't you?'

'Am I dismissed?'

'Of course not. You spoke your mind and I'll not penalize anyone for that. You're exaggerating, of course.'

'Oh, am I!'

'You may be overcrowded, I'll admit that. We expanded more rapidly than I'd anticipated, I took on more staff and quarters had to be found for them in a hurry.'

'How long ago was that?' Genevra enquired.

Mr Pyrritt avoided answering the direct question.

'We're on the lookout for another staff house and when it's found there'll be a bit more room. As for the food, it may not suit your dainty stomach, but I'll be bound it's good filling stuff, just the sort of thing the other girls were brought up on.'

'You really believe that, don't you?' Genevra said, marvelling. 'Very well, Mr Pyrritt, I'll challenge you. Come to dinner one evening, without giving warning beforehand. I think you'll get a shock.'

'I'll do it,' Matthew Pyrritt said. 'I'll turn up unexpected and unannounced, without telling you or anyone else when I'm coming.'

'Good. Now can I go back to work?'

'No, you can't. You've been shaken up – must have been or you wouldn't have spoken in the way you have – you'll take the rest of the afternoon off.'

'Will the money be docked from my wages?'

'No!' Matthew Pyrritt almost shouted. 'I'll give orders myself that you're to be paid in full. Now go. You've got me so riled I don't know whether I'm coming or going.'

Genevra collected her hat and coat and left by the back door used by the staff. Time off work during the week was such a novelty that she hardly knew what to do with herself. It occurred to her that she was unacquainted with any of the big London stores apart from Pyrritt's, since she was always working when they were open. A look round one or two of them might be instructive. After all, although she was indebted to Mr Pyrritt for her present employment that did not mean that she had to stay with his firm for the rest of her days. She would like to spy out the land and see what the other stores had to offer.

She decided to go back to the hostel and put on her

84

better hat and then stroll along Oxford Street, perhaps Regent Street as well, and look at the other large stores.

There was a grocery van outside the lodging house. The name on the side was *Dilke's Provision Merchant – High Class Butcher, Grocer and Greengrocer*. So much for Mr Pyrritt's boast that all the food for his employees came from their own store! . . . Except that the goods being loaded into the Dilke's van seemed to be coming out of the house, not going into it . . .

As Genevra reached the front door a man emerged, saying over his shoulder, 'Right, if that's the lot I'll be off, sis. See you Thursday, as usual.'

Mrs Thredgold appeared at the door to close it behind him and saw Genevra waiting to go in.

'What are you doing here at this time of day, Miss Kerslake?' she demanded.

To Genevra's interest she appeared flustered, far more put out than was reasonable because a girl had come home early.

'I had a slight accident.' Genevra said, touching her cheek. 'Mr Pyrritt said I was to take the rest of the afternoon off.'

'Mr Pyrritt himself?' Mrs Thredgold sounded incredulous.

'In person,' Genevra said. 'However, I mean to go out again and get a breath of fresh air so I won't be in your way for long. May I come in?'

Mrs Thredgold stood on one side, still looking put out.

'I was just saying goodbye to my brother,' she said; and again it seemed strange to Genevra that she spoke so defensively, as if the visit of a tradesman required an explanation. 'He's in a very good way of business in provisions,' Mrs Thredgold went on, as if goaded by Genevra's polite but uninterested smile. 'I don't *have* to work at this establishment. Sid would gladly give me a home if I wanted it.'

'How nice for you,' Genevra said with gentle sarcasm.

Baffled by her courtesy, unable to complain of anything tangible and yet sensing that Genevra was not as deferential as she sounded, Mrs Thredgold sniffed and stood to one side, then relieved her feelings by closing the front door with a resounding crash.

Genevra enjoyed her afternoon of window-shopping. It was something of a busman's holiday, spending free time looking round the shops, but it was also interesting to compare the way other popular department stores set out their goods and attracted their customers.

Perhaps of all the shops she visited the one that made the deepest impression was Liberty's. Genevra hesitated before going through the impressive entrance, knowing that she had no intention of buying anything and shrinking from the possibility of her poverty being detected; but she was wearing her better hat and her sealskin jacket and that gave her the courage to walk in as if she were still Miss Kerslake of Leylands House.

Liberty's had been open for ten years and had achieved fame – even notoriety – as the leader of the aesthetic movement. Genevra admired deeply the softly draped gowns and exquisite fabrics on display, the strangely decorated oriental vases, the fans and shawls and embroideries.

She returned to the lodging house more refreshed by this outing than by anything else she had done since Christmas.

'You went round the shops?' Sally asked incredulously when she heard how Genevra had spent the afternoon. 'You must want your head examined.'

'You were ever so brave,' Ruth commented. 'Weren't

you afraid of meeting the mob again? I would have been scared stiff if I'd been cut about the face like you were.'

'The man who threw the brick wanted to damage Mr Pyrritt's property,' Genevra pointed out. 'I don't suppose he meant to hurt me.'

'We didn't see what was going on up in Millinery,' Ruth said, with what sounded like regret. 'They say the men came down Oxford Street like ravening wolves.'

'Oh . . . hardly that,' Genevra protested. 'Just ordinary men who'd got a bit out of hand.'

'Drunk probably,' Sally said.

'Don't you have any sympathy for them?' Genevra asked curiously.

'Not much. True, there's a lot of unemployment, but holding meetings won't make work and there's no call to go round spoiling other people's property. Our front windows at Pyrritt's are a proper mess.'

'Mr Pyrritt took you up to his office, didn't he?' Ruth asked. 'It was all over the shop.'

'*And* he put his arm round you,' Sally added.

'I wasn't aware of it,' Genevra said, knowing that she was not being truthful.

'It's like I told you before,' Ruth put in. 'Our duchess will end up marrying the boss.'

'Oh, no I won't!' Genevra said firmly. 'I don't like the man.'

The man in question took up her challenge to come and share a meal with them at the hostel the following week. Genevra had begun to suspect that he had either forgotten about it or had decided to ignore her complaint. But on the following Tuesday evening, just as they had seated themselves in the basement dining room, the door opened and a flustered little maid came and hissed in Mrs Thredgold's ear, 'If you please, ma'am, Mr Pyrritt's here.'

Looking incredulous Mrs Thredgold began to get up

from her seat at the end of the long table; but before she could rise Matthew Pyrritt had walked in.

'I've come to take potluck with you,' he said.

He looked round the large crowded room. Genevra knew that he had picked her out, but his disinterested gaze merely registered her presence and passed on.

'I'm sure you'd be more comfortable in my own room,' Mrs Thredgold said.

'Perhaps I would, but I'll stay here, I think, if you can find a place for me. Don't you eat with the young ladies?'

'There's so much serving to do, my portion would grow cold before I could eat it,' Mrs Thredgold said. It was the excuse she always offered for taking her meals after the girls had finished.

'We'll serve ourselves first tonight,' Mr Pyrritt said. 'If there's one thing I do hate it's cold food.'

He sat down and since he obviously expected Mrs Thredgold to do the same she joined him, with an expression on her face which Genevra diagnosed as made up of equal parts of disbelief and apprehension.

'What's on the menu tonight?' Mr Pyrritt asked.

'Roast pork followed by bread-and-butter pudding,' Mrs Thredgold said in a faint voice.

'Very nice.'

'I hope he thinks so when he's eaten it,' Sally muttered.

They were all watching him, those who were near enough to have understood what was happening.

'Cooking for a hundred and twenty girls must present problems,' Mr Pyrritt remarked.

'Oh, it does!' Mrs Thredgold agreed fervently.

'Do you think it was a good idea, knocking the two adjoining houses into one and having this large communal dining room?'

'If it was your idea, I'm sure it was right, Mr Pyrritt.'

Matthew grunted, obviously dissatisfied by this answer.

The first plates of fatty pork began to appear on the table. As usual, the slices were cut so thin that they were almost transparent.

'You don't carve the joints at the table?' Mr Pyrritt enquired.

'No, it has to be done in the kitchen to save time,' Mrs Thredgold said. 'I serve the girls and they help themselves to vegetables.'

Mr Pyrritt looked with distaste at the bowl of watery potatoes which had been set in front of him, followed by another dish of wilting cabbage.

'Some nice roast potatoes would have been the thing with a joint of pork,' he said.

'The cost . . .' Mrs Thredgold breathed.

'No more than the cost of boiling up this lot, I would have thought, but you're the expert,' Mr Pyrritt said.

He did eat what was on his plate, but with no appearance of enjoyment, Genevra was pleased to see. The bread-and-butter pudding, however, proved to be more than he could stomach. They were all used to the stale bread inadequately soaked in milk and scattered with a few musty currants. Usually they grumbled, but were too famished to refuse it. Matthew Pyrritt, having had an adequate breakfast and lunch, pushed most of it to one side and sat back, frowning and silent.

No one dared to move until he got up from the table. Genevra had hoped for some immediate comment from him, but the only thing he said was, 'While I'm here I want to take a look at the accommodation. If the young ladies don't mind me looking into their rooms, that is?'

There was a confused murmur of agreement and then, as soon as Mrs Thredgold and her unwelcome guest had left the room, a hubbub of excited chatter.

'That I should ever live to see the day!' Sally exclaimed.

'Mr Matthew Pyrritt sitting at the same table as yours truly!'

'He didn't look as if he enjoyed it much,' Ruth said.

'That was the food – and who can blame him for turning up his nose at that? I say, do you think it might mean an improvement?'

'I sincerely hope so,' Genevra said.

Genevra doubted whether she would hear from Mr Pyrritt at first hand what his reactions were to his visit to Number 92 Mountfort Street. But she under-estimated his ingeniousness. The day after his visit Miss Littlejohn said to her, 'You're to go to Mr Pyrritt's office. He needs a statement from you about what happened when the windows were broken. Something to do with insurance. Look lively.'

When Genevra once again entered the big fourth-floor office she found it was true that Matthew Pyrritt wanted her signature on a statement that had already been prepared – but he had something else to say as well.

'I thought you were exaggerating,' he said in his abrupt way. 'But I have to admit that was as bad a meal as I've had in many a long day. At first I blamed the cook . . .'

'Mrs Thredgold is at fault for allowing anyone so incompetent to continue in your employ,' Genevra said.

'That's true, but the thing that's got me in a puzzle is why the ingredients she was using were so inferior. I've checked up on what was supplied from our own departments and the deliveries for this week bore no relation to what we were eating on Tuesday.'

The uneasy suspicion which had been lurking in Genevra's mind for over a week had to be voiced.

'Mrs Thredgold has a brother who calls himself a provision merchant,' she said. 'I saw his van outside the house last week when I went home early.'

She saw from Mr Pyrritt's quick frown that he had followed her train of thought.

'Cartons with Pyrritt's name on them were being loaded into the van,' she concluded.

'So that's it! She's passing on my quality provisions to him and feeding poor stuff to my girls!'

'What I saw isn't proof,' Genevra said quickly.

'True, but it'll bear investigation. Do you know the brother's name?'

'The name on the van was "Dilke" and Mrs Thredgold called him "Sid". There was an address, too, but I can't quite remember . . . it might have been Hammersmith, but I'm not sure.'

'I'll have it looked into.' He sat back and looked at her with the same intent frown. 'I suppose the least I can say is that I'm obliged to you. It looks as though I've been the victim of a fraud.'

'Your girls as you call them, are the victims,' Genevra retorted. 'You've only had to eat one of those ghastly meals. We've been forcing them down every day. And what about our rooms? You said you were going to look at them, too.'

'You are a bit cramped,' he admitted reluctantly. 'I did tell you I was negotiating for another lodging house, didn't I?'

'You did, but I've also heard that you mean to fill it up with the new girls you will be taking on for the enlarged Drapery Department.'

'You hear a sight too much,' Mr Pyrritt retorted. 'I don't know how these rumour's get around. You've changed, Miss Kerslake.'

'I've discovered the advantages of speaking up for myself, Mr Pyrritt.'

'Mrs Thredgold will get the sack whatever the outcome

of my investigation into her dealings with her brother. Do you want the job?'

It took Genevra wholly by surprise. She could think of no reply, but as Mr Pyrritt patiently waited for her answer she slowly shook her head.

'I could do the housekeeping part,' she said. 'Overseeing the staff, ordering the meals, keeping the cook up to scratch, none of that would be beyond me; but I'm too young to be responsible for the welfare of the girls who would be in my care. The person who would be ideal for the position is Mrs Bertram.'

'My housekeeper? Think again! I've a high opinion of Mrs Bertram; she makes me very comfortable; and I'll not part with her just to keep a parcel of girls in order.'

'She'd bring an authority to the job which I would lack because I'm too close in age to the other girls. Indeed, some are older than I am – and they think I'm soft, which I've come to see is true.'

Mr Pyrritt made no comment on that and Genevra went on, trying to get him to understand her meaning, 'There's a young girl who shares my room who seems determined to spoil her life. I've spoken my mind about it, but she won't listen to me because she thinks I've lived such a sheltered life that I don't understand what drives her to such foolishness. If I can't gain *her* confidence then I don't think I should be put in charge of a whole houseful of girls who might need the advice only a mature woman could give.'

'You've a lot of sense, for all you've been brought up a lady,' Mr Pyrritt said.

'If I have, that's mostly thanks to Mrs Bertram,' Genevra informed him.

'I would have thought you'd have had governesses and things,' Mr Pyrritt said vaguely.

'I did, but Mrs Bertram was of far more use to me,' Genevra assured him.

'How much have you told the girls you work with about your background?'

'Very little,' Genevra admitted. 'Sometimes it seems deceitful, but I couldn't, for instance, bring myself to tell them about our own previous connection.'

She had been thinking about the sale of Leylands, but suddenly the recollection of his proposal of marriage came into her mind and she felt a most unwelcome colour coming up into her cheeks. Fortunately, Mr Pyrritt did not appear to notice it.

'Another thing you'd better keep to yourself is this business about Mrs Thredgold,' he said abruptly.

'Of course.'

'I don't mean for fear of spoiling the investigation. I mean because your part in uncovering her guilt might make you unpopular.'

'But it's for the good of all of us to get rid of her,' Genevra protested.

'All the same, you'd best say nothing.'

'It's not a thing I would want to boast about,' Genevra replied. 'I must go. I've been away from my work too long already.'

'I still think you'd be capable of running the girls' lodging. I'd like you to do it. It would mean more money, your own bedroom and sitting room . . .'

'Oh, don't, please don't, tempt me! I know I'm right to refuse. Besides, I want to stay in the store and learn all I can because my ambition is to have a little shop of my own one day.'

'Setting up as a rival? I'll have to watch my step!' Matthew Pyrritt said, and when Genevra went back to the Haberdashery Department she left him still laughing.

6

Matthew Pyrritt was extremely annoyed about the newly discovered shortcomings in the Ladies' Hostel. At no time did he like to be in the wrong, and he had been forced to admit that he should have kept a better check on the way the lodging houses were run. He also hated to be cheated, and it looked as if Mrs Thredgold had been running a successful fraud for years. Above all, he resented having his faults pointed out to him by Genevra Kerslake.

He was more disgruntled by this than he cared to admit; and because he felt at odds with the world and in need of soothing he went that evening to the discreet little house in St John's Wood where Rose Peary could be counted on to give him a warm welcome.

He opened the front door with his key, as he had a perfect right to do since he owned the house, paid the bills and gave Rose a generous allowance; but to his surprise she called out sharply, 'Who's that? Who's there?'

She came out of the drawing room and was obviously put out to see him in the hall.

'Oh, it's you, Matt! Welcome, stranger.' She glanced over her shoulder in a distracted way.

'Who else would it be?' Matthew asked reasonably. 'I haven't been to see you lately . . .'

'I've scarcely set eyes on you since Christmas. Don't stand there, come on in, but I'd better warn you that I've got company.'

Matthew followed her into the drawing room, not

pleased to discover that she was not alone, but prepared to be polite to some out-of-work actress who had once been in the chorus with Rose.

A young man was standing by the fireplace, poking at the briskly burning fire. He turned as Matthew and Rose entered the room and dropped the poker with a clatter.

'Leave the fire alone, Fred,' Rose said in an irritated way. 'It'll burn well enough without your help.'

In response to Matthew's enquiring look she said, 'This is Fred. Fred, meet a friend of mine – Mr Pyrritt.'

He was a tall young man, ungainly and pallid in an unhealthy way. He held out his hand and Matthew took it; then he glanced down quickly because the touch of it was strange, and saw that the flesh of both Fred's hands was puckered and scarred.

'You've had your tea, Fred, and it's time for you to go,' Rose said. 'I've got things to talk to Mr Pyrritt about.'

From the brisk familiar way she spoke Matthew made a shrewd guess that the boy was a relation. He began to relax, but he stiffened up again at the question Fred directed at him.

'Are you my Dad?' he asked.

'No, certainly not!' Matthew said.

'Fred, I've told you time and time again that your Dad went for a soldier and got himself killed,' Rose said. 'Come along now, time for you to be going. Give my love to Auntie Bea.'

She let him out into the hall and Matthew could hear a low-voiced conversation going on. Rose came back into the room looking annoyed, found her handbag and went out into the hall again. So she was giving him money. Matthew had no objection, except that he had taken a dislike to the pale strange lad.

'Who was that?' he demanded when Rose rejoined him.

She took her time about answering, but in the end she told him the truth and it shook Matthew.

'I suppose you'll have to know now that you've seen him. Fred's my son.'

'Well, I'm damned! I never knew you had a son! How old is he?'

'He's . . . seventeen,' Rose said. 'I had him when I was no more than a baby, much the same age as he is now.'

Matthew made no comment on this. Rose was unaware of it, but he had always known that she had lied to him about her age. She was supposed to be thirty-four, but Matthew was perfectly well aware that she was thirty-eight. As for the young man, he suspected that she had docked at least a couple of years from his age, too.

'What happened to his hands?' he asked.

'An accident when he was at school,' Rose answered shortly.

'And was his father Mr Peary?' Matthew asked, which was unkind since he also knew that there had never been a Mr Peary.

'No, and he wasn't a soldier either,' Rose said. 'It was the only thing I could think of that would satisfy Fred when he was little and I've had to keep it up since.'

'Is he a bit wanting?' Matthew asked.

'No, he's not! He's not clever, that I'll grant. Fred had a setback when he was caught in the fire that scarred his hands, but he's got all his marbles.'

'Why haven't I seen him before?'

'He's been kept in the country, and then he lodged with my Mum down in Margate for a time. Well, you know Mum died last year so I fetched Fred up to London to stay with his Auntie. I don't know what got into him to ask if you was his Dad. I thought he'd got over doing

96

that years ago. I suppose it was the way you walked in as if you owned the place.'

'I do,' Matthew pointed out.

'As you've no need to remind me. What you do need to recall to me is what you look like because, as I was saying when you arrived, I've not set eyes on you this age past.'

She sounded accusing and Matthew had to admit that there was reason for it. He had not been in the mood for visiting Rose recently. The truth was, he had made a mistake in inviting her to Leylands for Christmas. She had not enjoyed it, finding it dull; he had not expected to have Eliza Littlejohn on his hands as well; and there had been something about the atmosphere at Leylands which made him ashamed of entertaining his kept woman under its roof.

His silence began to alarm Rose. Belatedly, she realized that Matthew had reason to be disgruntled at discovering that she had a grown-up illegitimate son whose existence had been concealed from him, and that her welcome had done nothing to endear her to this man who had treated her generously in the past. As soon as she recognized her mistake she set herself to please him once more, perching herself on his knee and winding her arms round his neck.

'I sound like an old crosspatch,' she said. 'But I miss you when you don't visit me, Matt.'

She was as warm and yielding as ever. Getting a bit heavy, Matthew noted dispassionately. She kissed him and her lips were just as inviting, the scent she used had always excited him in the past. He was dismayed by his lack of response to her familiar caresses and at the back of his mind he knew that part of the trouble was that he was haunted by an unwilling memory of a pale graceful girl who had suffered a greater deprivation than he had

97

intended, and all through his own lack of care for his staff.

Matthew's hold on Rose tightened. He kissed her with savage intensity. When he let her go Rose put up a hand to her disordered hair and laughed.

'So that's what's the matter with you! Come on, then. Let's go upstairs for an hour and afterwards I'll give you a nice little supper.'

He left her at midnight. For once, although she knew that he never stayed the whole night, Rose tried to keep him with her. There was something wrong. She was beginning to lose her hold on him and that was something she did not care to think about.

He had never been the same since he bought that damned house in the country. A dead-and-alive hole if Rose had ever seen one. She had gone down there at Christmas prepared to enjoy herself to the hilt. It ought to have been a proper lark, a house full of people, no expense spared and servants to wait on them. Instead, it had been like a morgue. The other guests had been a dreary lot, not to mention Eliza Littlejohn being there and looking down her nose at Rose the whole time. Naturally Rose had believed that Matthew had invited her because he wanted to sleep with her, but he had not visited her room once. She had returned to London in a state of great uneasiness and had not been reassured by his few calls on her since. And now the revelation about Fred had burst on him, just at the time when she had wanted to keep him sweet.

'When will I see you again?' she asked, lying back against the pillows and watching Matthew as he dressed.

It was an unwise question, as she well knew, but she was irritated by his air of preoccupation, considering the effort she had just been making to give him a good time.

'I'm not sure,' Matthew said, as she might have expected. 'I've a lot on my mind at the moment.'

'You always have.' Rose heard the complaining note in her own voice and was alarmed. 'You and your old shop,' she said jokingly. 'You care more about that than you do for any woman.'

'You may be right about that,' Matthew admitted. He bent over her and kissed her, but in a perfunctory way that was more annoying than if he had refrained from caressing her at all. 'I can only say, expect me when you see me. There's nothing new in that. It's the arrangement we've always had.'

Except that she had been able to expect him twice a week at the very least in the early days of their relationship, right up until the time when he had taken to spending three or more nights a week at Leylands. Rose smiled, but her eyes glittered with temper and alarm as she watched him leave the room without a backward glance.

Matthew chose to walk back to his apartment over the shop at Oxford Street. He knew, quite as well as Rose, that their relationship had gone sour. It was nothing he could define and he was aware that it was not Rose's fault. She had aged a little in the four years since he had set her up as his mistress and she had certainly put on more weight, but she was still a bold vigorous lover. She seemed to have become coarser, or perhaps his own tastes were more refined these days. Some of her habits grated on him now in a way they had never done in the past.

The streets were quiet, few people were about on foot and only an occasional carriage went clopping by. In Park Road he passed a policeman on patrol and wished him goodnight. It was shortly after that that Matthew became convinced that he was being followed.

He was wearing a gold watch and chain and there was a wallet full of banknotes in his breast pocket. His hand tightened on the walking-stick he carried in his right hand. If a thief was after him then he was in for a shock. Matthew had grown up in a hard school and he had not forgotten the lessons he had learned in the streets of Bermondsey. He kept himself fit and he was expecting an attack. The truth was, in his present frame of mind he would not be averse to a fight.

The footsteps seemed to come no nearer. Matthew reached Baker Street, turned quickly into a side road and waited. The robber, if he was a robber, hurried after him and then came to a baffled stop. Matthew's hand shot out and he grabbed hold of the man by the front of his jacket.

'Now then, what's your game?' he demanded, but he realized almost immediately that the other man was more frightened than menacing.

'I didn't mean you no harm. Honest, Mr Pyrritt, I just wanted to talk to you.'

'Fred Peary! You were lucky I didn't hit you with my stick.'

Matthew let go of him in disgust. 'What do you want with me at this hour of the night?'

'I know what you've been getting up to with my Mum.'

'I dare say you do, but it's not something I care to discuss in the street at one o'clock in the morning.'

He sniffed and added, 'I can smell you've been drinking. I suppose that's your excuse.'

'I only had a couple of pints, but don't you tell my Mum! She doesn't like me to drink, or to smoke either. She's ever so down on me smoking.'

'How very moral,' Matthew commented, but his sarcasm was wasted on Fred.

'I've been waiting for you to come out of my Mum's house,' he said.

The idea of this unintelligent lout hanging about watching his movements was acutely unwelcome to Matthew.

'You had no right to do that,' he said. 'I don't like being spied on. What was it you wanted to say to me so urgently?'

'My Mum said my Dad was a soldier, but I've got a copy of my birth certificate and it says "Father unknown". I reckon if he'd been a soldier they would have known his name. Stands to reason, doesn't it?'

'Er . . . yes,' Matthew said, finding himself totally unable to go into the explanation for the wording of the birth certificate with Rose's son.

'So if my Dad's name wasn't known it could have been you, couldn't it, no matter what Mum says?'

'Fred, I'm not your father,' Matthew said with all the patience he could muster.

'I reckon you could be.'

'I didn't know your mother at the time you were conceived. I only met her four or five years ago. Until today I never knew you existed.'

'That's what you say,' Fred muttered.

'How old are you?'

'I'll be nineteen next month.'

'And I'm thirty-five. To be your father I would have had to get you when I was sixteen. Do you think that's likely?'

From Fred's dissatisfied silence it appeared he was not convinced by Matthew's arithmetic.

'You won't give me a hundred pound then?' he asked at last.

'No, I will not!'

'If you did give me a hundred pound I'd go to Canada and never come back,' Fred offered.

101

'You can go to Timbuctoo for all I care! This is extortion, Fred. You can go to jail for that.'

'A man's entitled to maintenance from his father,' Fred persisted.

'Once and for all, I am *not* your father. Be off with you before I lose my temper.'

Matthew raised his stick and Fred shrank back.

'If you hit me I'll tell my Mum,' he said.

'She'll hit you herself when she hears what you've been up to,' Matthew retorted.

Fred wrenched himself away from the hold Matthew still retained on his jacket.

'You're a rotter,' he said. 'I hate you. You did ought to give me a hundred pound, you did! I'll get even with you, you wait and see if I don't.'

He ran off into the night leaving Matthew torn between exasperated amusement and real anger. The boy obviously had the fixed notion in his mind that he was the son of a rich man who could afford to give him large sums of money, which was ridiculous. It was also insufferable that Matthew should be accosted in this way. He blamed Rose, but in his heart he knew that it was his own fault for associating with Rose and her like.

Nothing seemed to go right for him after that. He put in hand an investigation into Mrs Thredgold's activities and, as he had expected ever since his conversation with Genevra, had no difficulty in establishing that her brother's shop was being stocked with provisions from Pyrritt's which should have been feeding his shop girls.

'You'll prosecute, of course?' his solicitor said.

'Yes, damn it, I suppose I'll have to.'

'The kitchen staff must have been in the know.'

'I'll sack the cook – her cooking alone would warrant

that. As far as the theft is concerned, I'll be satisfied with pinning it on the Thredgold woman and her brother.'

It got into the newspapers, a sordid little tale of fraud organized at the expense of Pyrritt's employees. This was by no means the sort of publicity Matthew liked. It made him short-tempered and difficult to approach, which was unfortunate at a time when he needed to exercise a certain amount of tact to placate a neighbouring shop-keeper whose premises he was set on acquiring. The man came to his office not, as Matthew had hoped, to negotiate, but to insist that nothing would make him give up his site on the corner of the block that Pyrritt's occupied.

'I'm doing good trade, Mr Pyrritt,' he asserted. 'I'll not budge and that's flat.'

He was only in a small way of business, selling station-ery and office supplies, which was not a line Matthew particularly wanted to take over. It was the site of the stationery shop he coveted.

'It's not essential for you to be in Oxford Street,' Matthew pointed out. 'I'm offering a fair price. Take it and set up somewhere else.'

'Tallent & Sons have been in that shop for the last fifty years. Our customers know where to find us and I'll not deny that being next door to Pyrritt's has done us no harm. Live and let live, Mr Pyrritt. I admit my shop looks old-fashioned, but I'm willing to smarten it up so as not to detract from your frontage.'

'I want to expand as far as the corner.'

Mr Tallent stood up and picked up his hat.

'Well, you'll not do it in my lifetime. I mean to stay where I am.'

Matthew stood up in his turn. 'I'll put the price up a couple of thousand,' he said.

'I'm not interested.'

'Very well. That was my last offer and I won't repeat it. If you change your mind come back and we'll talk terms, but I warn you I'll not be so generous again.'

As soon as Mr Tallent had gone Matthew sent for his General Manager.

'Find a corner in the store where we can set up in the stationery line,' he said. 'Get hold of Tallent's price list and find out what discounts he allows. We'll need a list of his main customers as well.'

'Going to put him out of business?' the General Manager asked, neither approving nor disapproving.

'I'm going to teach Mr Tallent not to hang on to something I want. I offered him a good price – better than the market price, in fact. We'll see if he's as cocky about refusing it in six months' time.'

The General Manager seemed hesitant about leaving the office and Matthew said in surprise, 'Go on, man. You've got your instructions. I'll leave it to you as to how you carry them out. I dare say one of Tallent's large customers will tell you what we need to know, or one of his employees, come to that, if you grease his palm with a few pounds.'

'Oh, I can get the facts,' the General Manager agreed. 'It's just . . . you know, you made yourself very unpopular with the local tradesmen the last time you did something like this – over that butcher's shop, remember?'

'I *needed* that business,' Matthew said. 'And I need Tallent's site. I'm not bothered about what a few envious shopkeepers say behind my back. If they want to oppose me let them fight back on equal terms.'

'Hardly equal,' the General Manager said drily. 'You have the means and they don't. However, if that's how you feel about it, Mr Pyrritt, I will, of course, carry out your instructions.'

Within a month there was a counter on the ground

104

floor of Pyrritt's devoted to fancy stationery and office supplies. A buyer had been engaged and two assistants had been taken on to serve in the new department.

Mr Pyrritt, having been told that the new venture was ready for inspection, walked down one afternoon to have a look at it and was thunderstruck to discover that one of the assistants was Genevra.

'I asked to be transferred,' she said in answer to his question. 'I rather liked the idea of selling stationery and it was a promotion for me.'

'Miss Littlejohn didn't tell me,' Matthew said.

'Why should she? I'm hardly the most important of your employees, Mr Pyrritt. Actually, I didn't tell her I'd applied for the new job until I was sure I had got it. Perhaps I was wrong, but I would have felt foolish if I'd not been selected.'

There was nothing he could do about it without drawing an unwelcome amount of attention to the interest he took in this girl. He felt frustrated and annoyed, all the more so because he knew that his distaste at seeing Genevra behind the stationery counter arose from a realization that she was unwittingly involved in his scheme for bringing a rival concern to heel. He was doing nothing wrong, it was a common enough way of doing business, and yet he would rather not have had her take part in it.

'Are conditions better at your lodgings?' he asked.

'There's been a vast improvement in the food and the new housekeeper seems to be a competent person,' Genevra said. 'But we're still overcrowded.'

'I've told you I'm trying to do something about that.'

She watched him as he walked away. Something about him always seemed to command attention. She noticed the way shoppers glanced up as he passed, even though they might not know who he was.

She was glad that he had not asked any more questions

about the hostel. The situation there as far as Genevra was concerned was not by any means as pleasant as she would have liked.

Genevra had taken Mr Pyrritt's advice and been careful not to reveal the part she had played in unmasking Mrs Thredgold. It was not that she was ashamed of it, just that she felt awkward about admitting that she had complained to Mr Pyrritt and he had listened and taken action because of what she had said.

She might just as well have come out in the open in the first place because the girls who knew her were far too acute not to guess that she had had a part in the drama.

'It was you that told Mr Pyrritt about things being wrong here, wasn't it?' Sally asked.

'What makes you think that?' Genevra countered.

'You had the chance. You were up in his office more than once. And you already knew him, you told us that yourself. It wasn't like one of us, complete strangers to him.'

'He asked me how I was settling down and I said I thought the living conditions could be improved,' Genevra admitted.

It was as much as she was prepared to say, but it did not satisfy Ruth and Sally. Genevra was hard put to it to understand their attitude.

'Surely it's all to the good?' she asked. 'We've got rid of Mrs Thredgold, we're better fed and Mr Pyrritt is no longer being cheated.'

They were forced to agree with all that and yet there was a slight feeling of dissatisfaction in the air.

'Mrs Thredgold's gone to *prison* and so's her brother,' Ruth said.

'Don't you think they deserved that punishment?'

'I suppose so. All the same, I wouldn't have wanted it to happen through anything I'd said.'

'If Mr Pyrritt had looked after the welfare of his staff properly it wouldn't have been necessary for anyone to say anything,' Genevra said.

Sally chuckled suddenly. 'Did you tell him that?' she asked.

'Yes, I did.'

'I'd have given a fiver to have seen his face!'

The awkward moment passed, but there was a subtle change in the relationship between Genevra and the other girls. She had shown herself to be on the side of the bosses, she was someone who took a complaint to the man at the very top of the firm and was listened to: she was different, just as they had always suspected, and it might be better to avoid becoming too intimate with her.

Genevra faced the realization that she was being left more on her own and countered it both by her change of job and by trying to find friends outside the store. She had been remiss in her churchgoing since she had joined Pyrritt's, falling in all too easily with the habit of the other girls of only attending a service when the weather was too bad to do anything else and they were bored with being confined to the house. Now, she began to go regularly to the nearby church, made herself known to the Vicar and offered herself as a Sunday School teacher.

'I must introduce you to Miss Tallent,' the Vicar said. 'I know she'll be glad of your help.'

The young woman to whom he introduced her was about six years older than Genevra. Her head only just reached Genevra's shoulder, though if she had been able to straighten up they would probably have been of equal height. Her face was one of the loveliest Genevra had ever seen – a pale, pure oval, all the features perfectly formed, with wonderful clear grey eyes; but her body was twisted and she walked with a strange crablike motion, dragging her left leg as if it were almost useless.

Genevra looked down at her in helpless pity until Mary Tallent smiled and then she forgot the deformed body in delight at the spirit that shone out from her beautiful eyes.

'Have you taught in a Sunday School before, Miss Kerslake?' Miss Tallent asked.

'When I was at home,' Genevra said. 'Not since I came to work in London.'

'And where do you work?'

'At Pyrritt's Department Store.'

Mary Tallent made a slight, comical grimace.

'Mr Pyrritt is not one of our favourite people at home,' she said. 'However, I mustn't hold that against you. Would you like to visit the Sunday School this afternoon and then perhaps come home with me afterwards for tea?'

Later that afternoon, after helping Mary with her class, Genevra realized with surprise that her new friend lived next door to the shop where she worked herself.

'Will you object to walking up the stairs by yourself?' Mary asked. 'Papa has rigged up a splendid arrangement to hoist me up in a chair and I will be at the top to greet you when you arrive.'

She seated herself in a flying-chair, tugged on a bell pull and was hoisted up the well of the staircase, laughing as if she enjoyed the experience and with no hint of pitying herself for her disability.

Genevra followed more slowly and was received at the top not only by Mary but by her mother and father as well.

'Mary told us she had a new helper with the children,' said Mrs Tallent. 'You're very welcome, Miss Kerslake.'

She was a small round woman with the same fine eyes

as her daughter, but without the beauty that made Mary's twisted body so poignant. It seemed to Genevra that Mrs Tallent watched her anxiously and when she saw that Genevra neither avoided looking at Mary nor went out of her way to give her unwanted assistance she looked satisfied.

Mr Tallent was a tall man in his fifties, with thick grey hair and a ruddy face. To Genevra he looked more like a countryman than shopkeeper. There was something of the same air of sturdy independence about him that she remembered from the yeoman farmers with whom she had mixed at Charleigh. He was more reserved than his wife, but he too appeared pleased with his daughter's new friend.

There was tea served in fine china cups, and cakes which Mrs Tallent admitted to baking herself.

'I do like to get into the kitchen,' she said. 'Keziah – that's our cook – grumbles at me. But even Keziah admits that I've a lighter hand with pastry than she has and it seems to me that if you have a skill and take pleasure in using it then it's a pity to let setting up to be a lady spoil it for you. Do have another bakewell tart, Miss Kerslake.'

'Do you play the piano, Miss Kerslake?' Mr Tallent asked.

'I'm sadly out of practice,' Genevra said.

She looked longingly at the fine grand piano standing in one corner of the drawing room. Mr Tallent went and opened it.

'Our Mary has a splendid voice, but she prefers to have someone else play the accompaniment,' he said. 'We'd be very much obliged if you'd attempt it.'

'If I'd known you expected me to sing I wouldn't have had a second piece of Mama's seed cake,' Mary protested.

She stood to sing, one hand resting on the piano, her twisted body less noticeable than when she was moving.

Her voice was a magnificent contralto, deep and thrilling. When she had finished Genevra had to bend her head over the piano keys to hide her tears. Mr Tallent's hand rested on her shoulder for a moment.

'You play well,' he said. 'I can see we're in for some musical treats – if you'll visit us again and play for us, that is.'

'I'll be glad to,' Genevra said.

It became a regular engagement, to help in the Sunday School, walk home with Mary and have tea, and then to play while she sang. It was several weeks before her employment at Pyrritt's was mentioned.

'Matthew Pyrritt is no friend of mine,' Mr Tallent said. 'It's not your fault that you work for him, Miss Kerslake, don't imagine that I hold it against you. But the man's doing his best to drive me out of business and I haven't a good word to say for him.'

'Remember it's the Lord's Day, George,' Mrs Tallent said mildly.

'I don't forget it, but try as I will I can't think charitably about Matthew Pyrritt.'

'I ought to say that Mr Pyrritt has shown me considerable kindness,' Genevra said.

'You know him personally?' Mr Tallent queried in surprise. 'I thought you just worked in the store.'

'I'm of no importance at all, but I was acquainted with Mr Pyrritt before he took me into his employ. My circumstances were . . . difficult and it was good of him to give work to someone with no experience at all.'

'Well, I'm glad to hear someone speak well of him,' Mr Tallent said.

'No, you're not. You'd just as soon the whole world thought him as wicked as you do,' Mary informed him mischievously.

Her father laughed. 'It goes against the grain to admit that there's any good in him,' he confessed.

'Has he wronged you in some way?' Genevra asked. 'I don't want to pry, but . . .'

'He wants my shop so that he can expand to the corner. I've refused to sell. I should have known that wouldn't be the end of it, not with Matthew Pyrritt! He's set up a Stationery Department and he enticed away one of my best men to run it for him. He's undercutting my prices and it grieves me to know that Albert Bates must be helping him by betraying confidential information. I've lost one or two big customers and I don't doubt I'll lose more.'

'But Mr Tallent, this is terrible!' Genevra exclaimed. 'I work in the new Stationery Department! I had no idea . . . I wanted to get out of Haberdashery and it seemed such a good opportunity.'

'Did Mr Pyrritt put you into the new department?' Mary asked.

'No, it was quite my own idea. In fact, he seemed a little put out when he saw me there.'

'Perhaps he had a bad conscience about involving someone he knows in putting Papa out of business,' Mary suggested.

'I'm not sure he's got a conscience,' her father remarked. 'As for putting me out of business – nonsense! I'm a long way from going under yet.'

7

The more she thought about it the more worried Genevra became about the part she was playing in the business troubles of her new friends. Pyrritt's Stationery Department was thriving; but Genevra could take little satisfaction in being concerned in a successful new venture when she suspected that every new customer was stolen from the next-door shop.

A third assistant was taken on to cope with the increased trade and since she was junior to Genevra that improved Genevra's own position. More than that, Genevra enjoyed handling the books and paper and writing-cases, and took more interest in them than she had in the pins and needles of Haberdashery.

'Are we taking custom away from Tallent's?' she asked the buyer one day.

'Of course we are! We stock the same lines, but we can offer them at a lower price. It doesn't matter to Mr Pyrritt if we make a loss, you see, because he can finance it from another department.'

'But what is the point of doing that?' Genevra asked, testing the man to see how much he knew.

'It's no secret that he'd like the whole of this island site and Tallent's is the last shop standing out against him. I presume his plan is to drive them to a standstill and buy the site up cheaply.'

'You used to work for Tallent's, didn't you?' Genevra persisted.

'That's right.'

'Doesn't it bother you, knowing you're helping to push them out of the shop they've run for so many years?'

'All's fair in love and war, and you can add business to that.'

Genevra bit back a sharp retort. It did not appear to concern him greatly. To her it seemed incredible that anyone who knew the Tallent family could be so unfeeling towards them.

What irked Genevra was that she had ideas for improving the Stationery Department, quite good ideas, she thought. She would have liked to have discussed them with the buyer; but she held back because if she helped to improve their business then it would be at the expense of her friends, the first really congenial people she had met in London.

She might have kept her frustrated ambitions to herself if Mr Pyrritt had not paid them a second visit. He came up to the counter and began a low-voiced conversation with the buyer. Genevra got no more than a curt nod of recognition.

'The first consignment of cash books will be in the warehouse on Monday,' he said at last. 'Shift them as fast as you can, Bates.'

His look of satisfaction aroused Genevra's suspicions – that and the buyer's air of consequence at being singled out by the head of the firm.

'What was that about, Mr Bates.' she asked.

'We're going to increase our involvement in business stationery,' the buyer said.

'Dull stuff!'

'Dull it may be, but it's a profitable line and it'll make Tallent's sit up and take notice.'

Genevra struggled with her conscience and then she said, 'It seems to me that fancy stationery for ladies is the thing that would be most suitable for a department store.'

113

'Your opinion hasn't been asked, Miss Kerslake. I trust I know my trade! There's a customer waiting at the far end of the counter. Go and attend to her at once.'

The following Sunday Genevra asked Mr Tallent if she could speak to him on a matter of business.

'Mrs Tallent will scold us for forgetting that this is the Lord's Day,' he warned her jokingly.

'I have some ideas about the sort of stationery which might sell well if you stocked it in your shop.'

'It's kind of you to take an interest, but I have to remind you, Miss Kerslake, that your ideas belong to your employer.'

'I've tried to make my suggestions to our buyer and he's told me my opinion isn't wanted,' Genevra said, which was true as far as it went, but perhaps not quite on the level of morality Mary Tallent would have approved.

'I won't tell you anything about what we're doing at Pyrritt's. I'll just mention that I think we're neglecting the provision of pretty stationery for the use of ladies and I think you could take advantage of the omission.'

'I already sell good quality writing paper and envelopes, mourning paper, blotters – that sort of thing.'

'I've looked in your window and I think your stock is dull. I've done some designs . . .'

She opened the bag she was carrying and pulled out several sheets of paper.

'Everything matching, you see. Writing cases and blotting books with the same design on the covers; paper inside which tones; letter racks, stands for holding writing paper – everything following through.'

'Your ideas are certainly unusual! Mother, what do you think? Would anyone buy this kind of thing?'

'They're very pretty,' Mrs Tallent said. 'You're a gifted sketcher, Miss Kerslake.'

'I got some of my ideas from looking at Liberty's,'

Genevra admitted. 'Not copying them, of course, but using the same kind of flowing floral decoration.'

'I wonder what the production costs would be,' Mr Tallent said.

'Less than the leather which is used for your better-class goods at the moment,' Genevra said quickly. 'These could be made in less costly materials, such as hardboard for the covers, but you could still charge a high price for the originality of the designs.'

'I might make some enquiries,' Mr Tallent mused.

'I do wish you would.'

'And you say you've already tried out these ideas at Pyrritt's without success?'

'The buyer wouldn't consider them,' Genevra said.

'All the same, I'm not sure it's quite ethical to accept help from someone employed by my rival.'

'I'm not asking for any money,' Genevra pointed out. 'I'm giving you these designs, as a friend. I dare say Mary could do as well now that I've started the idea off.'

'I can't draw a straight line with a ruler,' Mary said. 'I think you should take Genevra's advice, Papa. Quite apart from anything else, it would be such a satisfaction for her to see these pretty things made up.'

'My idea is that you should aim at the middle-class market, Mr Tallent,' Genevra said. 'Ladies with money, but not the sort of money that is spent on tooled leather.'

'The sort of people who shop at Pyrritt's,' he said slowly.

'Exactly. Dress your window up for them and catch them before they get inside our door.'

'Which will be detrimental to your employer's business. Exactly why are you giving me this advice, Miss Kerslake?'

'Because I don't think it's good for Mr Pyrritt to get his

115

own way every time,' Genevra said. 'I wish him no harm, but this is one battle I'd like him to lose.'

Two months later Mr Pyrritt was irritated to find that Mr Tallent was no closer to accepting his offer for the corner site.

'Obstinate man! He must be feeling the pinch,' he grumbled to his General Manager. 'If he's holding out for me to increase my offer then he's made a mistake. I went higher than I intended and I'll not offer a penny more.'

'Have you looked in Tallent's window in the last few days?'

'No, I don't happen to have gone in that direction. Why, is there something in it worth seeing?'

'A new line of fancy goods. Very pretty, and seems to be attracting custom. Different from his dull old stock, and an improvement on what we can offer.'

Mr Pyrritt had no inhibitions about going and staring in his neighbour's window if it was for the good of his own business. He stalked out of the front door of Pyrritt's, turned right, walked past his own glittering plate-glass windows and came to a halt outside Tallent's.

It presented a very different appearance from the former chaste rows of feint-ruled ledgers and discreet penholders. A fall of pale mauve satin was draped across the back of the window. Against it were displayed all the goods Genevra had suggested, every one of them produced in the same dark red and each ornamented with one stylized but flowing mauve iris. The effect was striking and, as his General Manager had said, it was attracting attention.

Two ladies paused to look. 'How elegant,' one of them remarked. 'They'd make charming presents.'

'My dear, Maud's wedding present! I was at my wits' end. I wonder if they have any other designs?'

To Matthew's annoyance they went into Tallent's shop to inspect the stock. Not that one sale would effect the outcome of the struggle, but it was irritating to be frustrated by an enterprise he was forced to admire.

'Why didn't we think of that?' he demanded when he was back in his own store.

'Business supplies were the backbone of Tallent's business so we concentrated on undercutting those prices,' the General Manager said. 'Do you want our buyer to look around for something similar to this new line?'

'We'll look ridiculous if we're seen to copy a tiddly little shop like Tallent's. Let it ride for a while and see how he does. There must be a limited market for these toys.'

The irises remained in Tallent's window for only three days and were succeeded by pale green covers stamped with a flat red rose and set off by green onyx inkstands which proved to be a highly profitable investment.

'Business is certainly looking up, Miss Kerslake,' Mr Tallent reported on Sunday. 'I'm amazed at the way the goods have been moving.'

'I'm delighted to hear it.'

'But you're getting nothing out of it.' Mary said in her gentle way. 'It seems hardly fair when it was all your idea.'

'I supplied nothing but a few sketches. It was your father who had all the knowledge about how they could be translated into the articles I had in mind. He knows about materials and manufacturers, not to mention the all-important pricing. You said it would be a satisfaction to me to see my notions carried out and you were right. I'm perfectly happy with the outcome.'

'What will you do if Mr Pyrritt finds out?'

'Come and ask your father for a job.'

'And you'd get it.' Mr Tallent assured her. 'Just at this moment I couldn't afford to take you on without putting someone else off, which seems hardly right, but if things go on improving I may be able to employ you as my full-time designer.'

They were both of them only half in earnest. Genevra guessed that her friend's father was still far more anxious about his business than he cared to reveal to his family and she had an uneasy conviction that Matthew Pyrritt would not easily be defeated by a few pretty flowers and a possibly ephemeral success dependent on the fickle taste of some idle ladies.

Her idea of her employer was confirmed when Mary confided to her later, 'Papa won't say anything about it, but he's extremely vexed because he's been asked to give evidence to the Select Committee on Shop Hours and he thinks Mr Pyrritt had something to do with it.'

'Surely that can't do him any harm? Your father is such a good man . . .'

'Our assistants work longer hours than you do, for instance. We stay open for an hour later than Pyrritt's and we don't close on Saturday afternoons.'

'I'm all in favour of shorter hours for shop assistants,' Genevra admitted. 'Obviously, I would be!'

'But it would be very hard on the smaller shops not to be able to open as and when they could do business,' Mary pointed out. 'Papa is a good employer and he gives our people reasonable breaks for dinner and tea. If he could afford it he would take on extra staff and let everyone have a half day off in the week, but as things are at present I think it would be out of the question.'

She sighed and said in one of her rare moments of despondency, 'If only I could help!'

118

'You do.' Genevra said quickly. 'I've seen you doing accounts and writing out bills.'

'I wish I could stand behind a counter. I wouldn't ask for wages, you see, and I could free someone else to take a rest.'

Because of this conversation Genevra made a point of following the newspaper accounts of the report of the Select Committee when it appeared in May. To her annoyance, the three hundred and forty foolscap pages of evidence submitted to the Committee confirmed that Pyrritt's conditions of employment, which she had found so arduous, were better than those prevailing in other shops. In this Matthew Pyrritt was in line with the other large department stores. Pyrritt's, Shoolbreds, Marshall & Snelgrove, John Barker's, Debenham's and Whiteley's all closed at two o'clock on Saturdays. None of them stayed open later during the week than seven o'clock in winter, and only John Barker's remained open until eight o'clock in the summer.

Conditions in other areas made shocking reading. In many places the shop assistants worked for eighty-four or eighty-five hours a week. Late opening on Saturdays was common, right up until midnight where sales warranted it.

Genevra's hand shook as she put the newspaper down. Once again she had been forced to acknowledge how much she owed to Matthew Pyrritt, who had saved her from the sort of slavery which some girls had to accept.

Resolutely she forced herself to finish reading the account, searching for Mr Tallent's name. He was a very small fish compared to some of the employers who had been interviewed, but he was mentioned and he did not show up well. No allowance was made for the kindness which made it a natural thing for Mrs Tallent or Mary to visit the home of a sick employee with comforts and

119

reassurance about re-employment when the illness was over. Nothing was said about the good nourishing food they received. Mr Tallent had not been asked about the hours he worked himself; only the shop assistants' hours were mentioned, and they were long.

Had Matthew Pyrritt had any influence on the Committee to ensure that his neighbour would be called and shown in a poor light? Genevra could not help sharing Mr Tallent's conviction that he had.

'Well, Miss Kerslake, you see what a tyrant I am!' Mr Tallent greeted her the following Sunday.

She thought he looked tired and dispirited. Mrs Tallent was indignant and Mary seemed worried. Genevra made light of the newspaper reports, but the recollection of them cast a gloom over what was normally a happy day for her.

It had become so much of a habit for Genevra to join the Tallents every Sunday afternoon that she had become like one of the family. She knew that her preoccupation with the church and Sunday School and her new friends had set her apart from Ruth and Sally and the other girls, and she regretted it; but she had found the Tallent family so congenial that she could not bring herself to go back to her previous habit of spending Saturday afternoons and Sundays with Sally and Ruth.

As for Letty, Genevra was becoming more and more worried about her. Genevra went up to the bedroom one evening when the weather had begun to turn warmer and sank down on her bed for a blessed few minutes' rest. She longed to take off her shoes, but she knew from experience that if she did her feet would start to swell and it would be painful, if not impossible, to force them back into shoes again.

The only other person in the room was Letty, sitting on the side of her bed looking unusually gloomy.

'Had a hard day?' Genevra asked, taking it for granted that the answer would be yes, but wanting to sound friendly.

'Beastly,' Letty said.

She got up and went over to Genevra's bed, standing at the end polishing the knob on the footrail with the flat of her hand, not looking at Genevra.

'Can you lend me ten pounds?' she asked abruptly.

'Ten pounds?' Genevra repeated in disbelief. 'No, of course I can't.'

'I thought . . . you've got more than the rest of us. You try to hide it, but you have. I need the money, Jenny. You could raise it if you tried.'

For a moment Genevra was silent. Mr Ryman had recently been sent the first instalment of interest on the money he had invested for her, the money she had received from the sale of her mare, and Genevra had asked him to bank it for her. It had amounted to just over five pounds. Apart from that she had about two pounds, carefully saved out of her weekly wages, which she was putting to one side for desperately needed new shoes.

'Truly, I haven't got it,' she repeated. 'Why do you need the money, Letty?'

Letty turned away. 'You wouldn't understand,' she said. 'And you wouldn't care. You're hard, Jenny, hard and unfeeling. One of these days you'll be a dried-up old spinster like Miss Littlejohn.'

'I've got a few years to go yet.' Genevra said, but although she tried to turn it off as a joke Letty's taunt hurt. She was not unsympathetic and if she had the money to spare and Letty offered a reasonable explanation for

121

wanting such a large sum Genevra would have been prepared to help.

As for being a spinster, that was all too likely to come true. Genevra had been approached by several of the young men who worked for Pyrritt's and had refused their invitations with a polite firmness that froze them off. She acquired a reputation of being a bit above herself. She knew it, and regretted it, while at the same time quite unable to see herself enjoying a music-hall performance in the company of the young man from Hardware.

She served more male customers in Stationery than she had in Haberdashery, where they were scarcely ever seen, and her fair good looks attracted attention. When one of her customers contrived to give her hand a squeeze as she showed him a range of address books she looked at him in such amazement that he was abashed. But when a bolder man leaned over the counter and murmured, 'What does a pretty little girl like you do in her free time?' Genevra turned away without answering and signalled to the male assistant to take over from her.

'What was that about?' he asked afterwards.

'He was trying to flirt with me,' Genevra said, wrinkling her nose as if at a bad smell.

'Did you have to be so hoity-toity? The gentleman went off in a huff without buying anything.'

'He was *not* a gentleman,' Genevra said.

'He meant no harm. You could have jollied him along a bit and laughed it off if he went too far. It would have put him in a good temper and you might have made a big sale.'

'I see no reason for putting up with that sort of impertinence just for the sake of a few shillings.'

'Oh, very haughty, aren't we? There's no profit in pride, Miss Kerslake.'

Genevra left work that evening in a mood of disenchantment, almost of rebellion, and it did not help to go into the bedroom and find Ruth and Sally holding a low-voiced conversation which they broke off as soon as she entered the room.

The next moment Genevra's awkward feeling of having interrupted something was forgotten as she realized that a seventh bed had been moved into the room, taking up all the space down the middle.

'This is really too bad!' she exclaimed. 'He promised me that we would have more space. I'm going to complain.'

'When you say *he* promised you, do you mean Mr Pyrritt?' Ruth asked.

'Yes, of course I do.'

She saw Ruth and Sally glance at one another and felt compelled to explain.

'I mentioned that we were overcrowded at the same time as I told him our food was uneatable.'

'You've got a nerve,' Sally said admiringly. 'Are you going to march up to his office tomorrow and tell him you won't have another girl in your room?'

'I'll speak to the new housekeeper first,' Genevra said, her first anger beginning to subside. 'Do you know who's moving in with us?'

'Another youngster, a girl of fifteen,' Ruth said gloomily.

'Oh, dear! Not another Letty, I hope.'

There was a brief uncomfortable silence and then Sally seemed to take a decision and said, 'It was Letty we were talking about when you came in. You've possibly noticed . . . no, perhaps you haven't . . .'

'I've seen there's something wrong and she tried to borrow money from me recently and wouldn't tell me why.'

'We think she's in the family way.'

'I was terribly afraid that might be it,' Genevra admitted with a sigh. 'Are you sure, Sally?'

'I'm the eldest of ten, love. I know the signs. How much did she try to touch you for?'

'Ten pounds. I couldn't let her have it.'

The other two girls exchanged a meaningful horrified look.

'Mad little fool,' Ruth murmured. 'Just as well you didn't cough up, Jenny. She probably meant to pay someone to rid her of it.'

With a sick feeling inside her Genevra realized that there had been gaps in the information Mrs Bertram had imparted to her. This was something for which she was quite unprepared.

'I didn't know that was possible,' she admitted.

'Oh, Jenny, sometimes you seem such an innocent! The thing is, what are we going to do about Letty? She'll be found out soon and then she'll be dismissed and where she'll go I really don't know. she's got no family except that old grandmother who was supposed to have died at the New Year – and didn't, of course.'

'Is there any reason why she and Dick shouldn't get married?' Genevra asked, drawing on her knowledge of the way things been handled in her village.

'I don't know what they'd live on,' Ruth said.

'If Dick meant to marry her we'd have heard about it by now,' Sally said bluntly. 'She must be at least three months gone, possibly more. If there'd been a wedding in the offing Letty would have been over the moon, no matter how she'd brought it about. As it is, she's as miserable as sin.'

'You're in with the church people, Jenny,' Ruth said. 'Would they do something to help a girl in need?'

'I'll certainly enquire,' Genevra agreed, and broke off as the door opened and Letty herself came in.

'Get a move on, you lot, or you won't get any dinner,' she said.

She looked cheerful, even excited, with brilliant colour in her cheeks and all her old bounce restored; but now that her own suspicions had been reinforced Genevra looked at her more attentively and saw as Letty turned away that her waistline had started to thicken.

Neither of the other girls spoke, but Genevra was too worried to be tactful.

'Letty, are you expecting a baby?' she blurted out.

'Yes, as a matter of fact, I am,' Letty said with elaborate concern. She glanced round at them and began to laugh. 'Don't look so gloomy! It's not the end of the world!'

'Is Dick going to stand by you?' Sally asked.

'Dick? What's he got to do with it?'

'But surely . . . it *is* Dick's, isn't it?'

'If you must know, it's not.' Their look of shock appeared to amuse her. She laughed again in the same strange excited way.

'No need to worry about me. I'm on my way to making a fortune,' she boasted.

'A fine way to start,' Sally said in disgust. 'You're a little trollop, Letty. The one thing I did think in your favour was that you were desperately in love and carried away. If you've been going with someone else, then I've got no more time for you.'

'I was taken advantage of,' Letty said quickly. 'An older man . . . someone I couldn't say no to.'

'Funny we haven't heard about it before,' Ruth said.

'Naturally he told me I was to keep it quiet.'

'Oh, of course! A secret lover! Come off it, Letty, you don't expect us to believe that, do you?'

For one moment Letty's confidence seemed to waver. Her eyelids flickered and she said uncertainly, 'Why

125

shouldn't you believe me? It happens all the time. I was afraid of losing my job.'

'Lord above, you're not going to tell us it was old Mr Myers, your buyer in China, are you?' Sally demanded.

'Of course not.' The look of creamy complacency came back to Letty's face. 'I can see you won't be satisfied until I give you his name. It was Mr Pyrritt.'

Genevra was both the most shocked and the quickest to find her voice.

'No.' she said. 'It's not true.'

Another of their room-mates burst in. 'The food's on the table,' she said. 'Aren't any of you hungry?'

'I'm not missing my supper, even though Letty has gone raving mad,' Sally said. 'Come on, Ruth, we'll get the truth out of her after we've eaten.'

Genevra felt cold and sick, by no means as anxious as Sally to go and eat. Letty, on the other hand, was triumphant over the sensation she had caused.

'I don't care what anyone says,' she insisted. 'Mr Pyrritt is the father of my baby and I'm going to see that he pays for it.'

8

It took Genevra a long time to make up her mind that she ought to do something about Letty's allegations. Tossing and turning in her bed after an evening in which she and Sally and Ruth had all tried and failed to shake the girl's story, Genevra miserably grappled with her conviction that Matthew Pyrritt ought to be made aware of what was being said about him.

Nothing would make her face him with such a story. The embarrassment would be too acute. Not that she believed it for one moment, not even when she remembered that his morals were not above suspicion. He had been prepared to marry Genevra while keeping a mistress and the thought made her turn over again in her narrow bed as the humiliation bit home once more. But a man who maintained an expensive mistress was not likely to have indulged in even the most passing affair with a girl like Letty.

What could she offer him apart from the fleeting attraction of youth and a certain liveliness of manner? She was neither intelligent nor outstandingly pretty. A brief shaming image of Letty clasped in Mr Pyrritt's arms came into Genevra's mind and was hurriedly dismissed.

She was beginning to despair of ever getting to sleep when she remembered Miss Littlejohn. She was more than employee, she was an old family friend, someone Mr Pyrritt invited to his house. She had known him for so long that she did not hesitate to speak her mind both to him and about him. She would know how to break it to him that one of his younger assistants was accusing him of having fathered her child. With a feeling that a load had been lifted from her mind Genevra turned over once more and fell asleep.

She waited until Saturday afternoon and then went to Miss Littlejohn's small house in Bermondsey, taking a chance of finding her at home. It was a typical artisan's terraced cottage with two rooms upstairs and two down, a scullery tacked on the back and an outside lavatory.

Eliza Littlejohn was surprised to see Genevra, but she did not seem displeased, not until she had listened to the story Genevra had to tell.

'He'll have to be told,' she said when Genevra had finished.

'Not by me,' Genevra said.

She had been invited into the front room of the little house, an honour Eliza Littlejohn did not bestow on everyone. The furniture was old, heavy dark oak blackened by age, but the room was lightened by Eliza's taste for bright flowered chintz.

Miss Littlejohn saw Genevra glancing round and remarked, 'Mr Matthew's grandfather was born in the house next door. This is Mr Matthew's background, for all he's become so grand.'

She spoke abstractedly, making conversation while her mind considered the startling news Genevra had just given her.

'I won't say he's not capable of it,' she said at last, reverting to the subject they were really considering. 'He's a man and no better than the rest of them where women are concerned. What's this girl like? I can't place her.'

'Pretty, lively, silly and very young,' Genevra said. 'She works in China. She's got beautiful hair, really golden yellow, and normally a very high colour in her cheeks.'

128

'I know the one. Sticks her bosom out at every man who passes by. I'm not surprised she's got into trouble. When you say she's young, how young do you mean?'

'Almost seventeen.'

'Old enough to know what she's doing.'

She gave Genevra a long inquisitive look, peering up at her with that curious twist of her head.

'You don't believe her story,' she said. 'Why not?'

'It's not like him,' Genevra said.

Under Miss Littlejohn's continued stare she blushed hotly.

'It's *not*,' she insisted. 'I have no particular admiration for Mr Pyrritt – in fact, in many ways I think he deserves severe criticism – but ruining a sixteen-year-old girl is not something I can believe about him.'

'He's got a weakness for you,' Miss Littlejohn commented. 'And so have you for him, seemingly.'

'Nothing of the sort! I want to see justice done, that's all.'

'These other girls you mentioned, will they keep their mouths shut?'

'For the moment,' Genevra said slowly. 'They were as shocked as I was when Letty first told us her story. The trouble is, she does seem to know a lot about his suite of rooms at the top of the store which is where she says he . . . he used to take her. Sally and Ruth have been shaken and because of that they've started wondering whether it could be true. I don't think they'll talk to anyone at work, but they might bring it out as a choice piece of gossip at home.'

'Even worse. That sort of whispering will do Mr Matthew no good at all.'

'Will you tell him?' Genevra asked.

'Yes, I'm the best person to do it. You were right to come to me. I'll know straight off if he's guilty or not, as soon as I see his face. Matt's never been able to hide anything from me, not since the days when he was pinching apples off my Dad's barrow.'

Eliza Littlehjohn could hardly have broken the news more bluntly when she sidled into Matthew's office on Monday morning.

'There's a yellow-haired flibbertigibbet in China says you've fathered a child on her,' she said. 'Is it true or false?'

'Good God!' Matthew stared at her with a blank astonishment that was wholly convincing. 'Of course I haven't . . . What the devil are you talking about, Eliza?'

'You heard what I said. She's putting it about that you carted her up to those rooms of your upstairs and had your wicked way with her.'

'Do you mean this is common knowledge?'

'She's only told her story to one or two so far, including your Miss Kerslake, who very properly came and told me.'

'It would have to be her,' Matthew said. 'Damn! I can't put a foot right where that girl's concerned.'

'If it's any comfort to you, she doesn't believe it's true.'

'I should hope not! And neither do you, I trust?'

'Not now I've faced you with it and seen how you took it.' Eliza Littlejohn chuckled. 'I've rarely seen a man more confounded.'

A reluctant smile appeared for a moment on Matthew's face.

'It's enough to set any man back on his heels – first thing on a Monday morning, too. What am I to do about it, Eliza?'

'Do you want me to see the girl? I'll scare the living daylights out of her and soon get the truth.'

'No, that wouldn't be wise. No one close to me must

130

see her, especially without a witness. I'd better get my lawyers to deal with it. What sort of a girl is she?'

'Under seventeen and silly as they come. She hasn't thought this up on her own, you know. Someone's put her up to it.'

'Very likely. I suppose they think they'll get money out of me.'

'They don't know you like I do.' Eliza Littlejohn got laboriously to her feet. 'You're not likely to submit to being blackmailed. I could almost feel sorry for the silly little blighter, if I wasn't so peeved with her.'

She glanced at Matthew's frowning face and added, 'It won't damage you in your business, which is all you really care about.'

'No, but it's a nasty thing to have whispered about a man behind his back. If it were true, and I acknowledged the child and behaved generously people would shrug their shoulders and soon forget; but if I deny it there are bound to be some who'll think there's no smoke without fire, and write me off as a skinflint too mean to pay for his bastard.'

'Much *you* care what's said about you!'

'But what you don't know is that I'm being taken up by Society, Eliza! I dined with a duchess last week and I'm invited to Marlborough House on Wednesday.'

From the look of sardonic amusement on Matthew's face it did not appear that he was greatly impressed by his rise in the world.

'Your grand friends should be able to disregard a bit of gossip about you, considering what's said about them, though they might keep their daughters out of your way.'

'Not them! I'm a good catch. In fact, I'm being chased by a couple of matchmaking mothers.'

'Don't let it go to your head.'

'Is it likely? I've been about in the world too long to be taken in by a few smiles and invitations.'

'The man isn't born who can't be made a fool of by a pretty face. That's why I had my doubts about this Letty Jones, though I'm prepared to believe she's lying now that I've talked to you.'

'Is that her name? I can't recollect ever having heard it before, though I think . . . I'm almost sure I know the girl you mean. She came up here once with some samples of dinner services I wanted to look at.'

'Here, to your office, not upstairs?' Miss Littlejohn asked quickly.

'No, never up there, no matter what she may say. What's to become of her, Eliza? I'll have to give her the push and I can't give her any help for fear of it being misconstrued.'

'I understand Miss Kerslake is approaching some of her church friends,' Miss Littlejohn said.

She was watching to see his response to that and she did not miss his look of profound dissatisfaction. Interesting, the way he reacted every time the Kerslake girl was mentioned.

Eliza gave a sudden chuckle. 'I'll be off to my counter,' she said. 'I dare say it's all at sixes and sevens with me being out of the way for a quarter of an hour.'

Genevra was far from easy in her mind about her intervention in Letty's affairs. She was relieved that Mr Pyrritt was going to be warned about her accusation, but she also saw it as a betrayal of Letty's confidence and she knew that the other girls would not have acted as she had done. She tried to redress the balance by asking for Mary Tallent's help.

'Poor silly child,' Mary said. 'No, I'm not shocked. I've

132

seen it happen far too often. I take it the father won't marry her?'

'It seems not,' Genevra said carefully.

'Has she told you his name?'

'Letty was going out regularly with a boy who also works at Pyrritt's, and seemed to be very much in love with him, but she says he's not the one.'

'Oh, dear! That does rather squash one's sympathy for her.'

'I'm not sure she's telling the truth,' Genevra said.

'It sounds like a case for Papa to deal with. He's on the governing board of an association which helps girls like this. I expect a place could be found for your Letty.'

It was not easy to persuade Letty to talk to Mr Tallent.

'Don't see the need for it,' she said with a toss of her head. 'I'll be in the money when Mr Pyrritt pays up what's due to me.'

'Letty, you must stop talking like that. We none of us believe your story.'

'Ruth and Sally do since I told them about the gold-patterned wallpaper and the blue velvet sofa at the end of the bed in his flat upstairs.'

'Anyone could have found out details like that,' Genevra said. 'As soon as your condition is noticed you're going to be without a job. Unless you go home to your grandmother . . .'

'Not likely!'

'You won't have a roof over your head. Now, do be a sensible girl and accept the help these kind people are prepared to give you.'

'Won't do any harm to talk to them, I s'pose,' Letty said. 'Perhaps they can advise me about my rights.'

'No, Letty, you must *not* make any wild accusations about the father of your child. You'll find yourself in terrible trouble if Mr Pyrritt prosecutes you for slander.'

For the first time Letty looked frightened.

'He wouldn't do that,' she said uncertainly.

'I would in his place,' Genevra declared, hardening her heart.

She hoped that she had succeeded in quietening Letty's tongue, but she did not allow for the girl's excitement at telling her story to a new audience, nor for her resentment at being treated with sorrowing pity by a good man dealing with a fallen child. Everything she had told the girls, and more, came spilling out, with the result that Mr Tallent asked Genevra to go and see him at the earliest possible opportunity.

'When you sent her to see me did you know the name of the father of Miss Jones' child?' Mr Tallent asked her incredulously.

'I knew what Letty was saying. I don't believe it's true. In fact, I warned her not to repeat the story to you. Obviously, she disobeyed me.'

'You may not believe her, but I am forced to do so. The details, the obvious knowledge she has of Mr Pyrritt's household, her own distress . . .'

Letty had been playacting to some effect, Genevra thought grimly.

'Doesn't it seem strange to you that Mr Pyrritt was unaware of her condition until I arranged for him to be told? Letty, you will notice, didn't see fit to inform him.'

'Because she is afraid of him, poor child, and who can blame her? I know him to be a ruthless man. I also happen to be aware of certain aspects of his private life which I won't reveal to you, and which make me feel it is all too likely that he would take advantage of this girl's weakness.'

'If you mean his mistress in St John's Wood, I know about her, too,' Genevra said.

'My dear Miss Kerslake! And you *still* defend him?'

134

'Against Letty Jones, I do. She's lying, Mr Tallent.'

Mr Tallent shook his head. 'I think not. The girl is terrified. I've arranged for her to see my solicitors.'

'Then I'm not surprised she's frightened. They'll soon get the truth out of her.'

'I feel it my duty to see that she has proper advice. My own conviction is that they will recommend a suit against Mr Pyrritt.'

Something about the way he spoke sent a chill through Genevra.

'You're pleased,' she said. 'I've given you a weapon against the man you think of as your enemy. What a fool I've been! I thought your charitable feelings would lead you to help Letty, but you're just the same as Matthew Pyrritt. You want to use her to gain an advantage over him.'

'You do me an injustice, Miss Kerslake. Look at it from my point of view. Certainly I can arrange for Miss Jones to be cared for by a suitable organization, but that is something that has to be paid for by charitable people putting their hands in their pockets. Mr Pyrritt is a rich man. He must be made to pay for his own mistakes.'

'But not for other people's! I'm sorry, Mr Tallent, but I feel you've let me down. I thought you'd see through Letty, just as I have. I do beg you not to go on with this absurd idea of legal proceedings. Who is going to pay the bill for that?'

'The guilty party.'

'Meaning Mr Pyrritt?' Genevra shook her head. 'It will end by coming out of *your* pocket, Mr Tallent.'

She saw that she had shaken him by her obstinate conviction that Letty was lying.

'Nothing formal will be done until my solicitor has talked to Miss Jones,' he said. 'If there is a weakness in her story I'm sure he will discover it.'

Letty and Genevra had scarcely spoken to one another since Genevra had refused to believe the younger girl's story; but that evening Letty seized hold of Genevra.

'I s'pose you meant well, sending me to see that Tallent man, and *he* believes me, even if you don't, but I didn't reckon on getting involved with lawyers and such. If you hadn't interfered it would all have been settled quietly.'

'You must be out of your mind to think that!' Genevra exclaimed. 'Did you really think Mr Pyrritt would pay up and let you get away with defrauding him? You should have remembered the line he took over Mrs Thredgold.'

'And that was your doing, too. You're a proper trouble-maker, Jenny.'

'No, I'm not.' Genevra said, really stung. 'Everything that's happened to you is your own silly fault. I've tried to be a friend to you, Letty. I do wish you'd drop this story of yours and accept the help Mr Tallent could give you.'

'No chance of that now. He's properly got the bit between his teeth. Who can blame him? Most people would be glad of a chance to score off Mr Pyrritt.'

'Don't you ever call him by his Christian name?' Genevra asked. 'Considering you are supposed to have been lovers you speak of him very formally.'

'I've had to watch my tongue,' Letty said. 'You don't expect me to go around calling him "darling", do you?'

Genevra was astonished by the anger that question aroused in her.

'I can see you are determined to destroy yourself,' she cried. 'There's nothing more I can do for you.'

'Yes, there is,' Letty said unexpectedly. She looked away and the fact that Letty was embarrassed at something made Genevra instantly suspicious of what she was going to be asked to do.

'Come with me to the lawyer's office,' Letty said.

'Certainly not! Mr Tallent will be with you.'

'I want another girl. He's all right, but I scarcely know him. None of the others will come with me, they're too scared, but you've got more education than the rest of us put together. I know you don't believe me, but when you hear everything I've got to say you'll come round.'

Genevra hesitated, torn between her reluctance to involve herself any further in this sordid affair and a desire, of which she felt obscurely ashamed, to know exactly why Letty was so sure she would triumph in the end.

'I don't like the idea,' she said.

'Please, Jenny. If you really want to do something for me, then do this.'

Her agitated fingers twisted together as she spoke and Genevra suddenly understood the agony of apprehension that lay behind Letty's careless manner. The girl was frightened, really frightened. She had gone into waters that were far too deep for her and now that they threatened to close over her head she was desperate for something to cling to.

'All right, I'll come and support you,' Genevra said.

Mr Tallent was surprised and not particularly pleased when Letty arrived at his solicitor's office accompanied by Genevra. He was also annoyed that the senior partner who normally dealt with his affairs had deputed this matter to his son.

'My father was unable to come in on a Saturday afternoon,' the young lawyer said. 'And as you couldn't arrange the appointment for any other time . . .'

'Not all of us can get off work at the drop of a hat,' Letty intervened and once again Genevra realized that her jaunty words hid an agitation which the two men did not seem to notice.

The girl had dressed for this occasion in her best skirt and jacket, a blouse with a large pink bow at the neck and a straw hat ornamented with a floppy pink rose. The buttons of her jacket were strained across her distending stomach and breasts and Genevra was conscious of a rush of pity for her.

The solicitor was looking enquiringly at Genevra.

'Miss Kerslake works with Miss Jones,' Mr Tallent said. 'I'm surprised to see her here because unless she's had a change of heart since we last spoke she doesn't believe Miss Jones' story.'

To his chagrin the solicitor stood up and held out his hand to Genevra.

'I believe I've seen you in church,' he said. 'I'm Arthur Hendry, you know. I sing in the choir, so I rarely have a chance to meet members of the congregation, but I'm delighted to make your acquaintance, Miss Kerslake.'

His pleasure at meeting her was so obvious that Genevra felt her colour rising.

'Quite a social ocasion, isn't it?' Letty demanded. 'Could I remind everyone that it's me that's here to be talked to.'

'I haven't forgotten it,' Arthur Hendry said. 'I must warn you that there are questions I shall have to ask you that may distress you, Miss Jones.'

He glanced again at Genevra as if her presence embarrassed him.

'Fire away,' Letty said. 'I'm not likely to get upset, not considering what's happened to me already.'

'Quite. You are pregnant, Miss Jones. How many months?'

'Four, going on five, by my reckoning.'

'So your child was conceived towards the end of January?'

'Probably.'

'And Mr Matthew Pyrritt is the father?'

'That's right.'

Letty was beginning to look more cheerful, as if the interview was proving less of an ordeal than she had anticipated.

'How often did you have relations with Mr Pyrritt?'

'He took me up to his rooms four times. As to how often we did it . . . oo! I wouldn't like to say.'

Genevra looked down, her cheeks burning. No wonder Mr Hendry had been embarrassed to have her listening to these replies.

'Can you give me any dates when, as you say, you accompanied Mr Pyrritt to his aprtment?'

'The sixth of January, the thirteenth January, the twenty-first January and the second February.' Letty replied.

The promptness of her answer made Mr Tallent shoot a triumphant look at Genevra, as if he saw it as a vindication of his belief in Letty; but for some reason the young lawyer was frowning.

'Were you a virgin before your association with Mr Pyrritt?' he asked.

Letty hesitated and Genevra guessed that if she had not remembered an unfortunate admission she had once made then Letty would have claimed to have been untouched.

'No, I wasn't,' she said with a touch of defiance. 'I'd been going out with a very nice boy and my feelings carried me away.'

'And what has happened to him since this other affair?'

'I dropped him, didn't I? Me believing I was made for life with Mr Pyrritt taking me up, I hadn't any time for poor Dick.'

'How did it happen that Mr Pyrritt first approached you?'

'He was buying a new dinner service for his house in the country and I took samples up to his office.'

Arthur Hendry took that up sharply.

'To his office, not his apartment?'

'No, I didn't go into his rooms, not that time.'

'Tell me what happened.'

'He was ever so chatty and nice, not a bit frightening like I'd expected. He said he didn't realize they kept such pretty things in the basement – meaning me, not the plates and things. So a few days later I went back to collect the samples and I saw him again and that was when he started making advances to me.'

'You'll have to be more exact than that, Miss Jones. Tell me what happened.'

'Well, he put his arms round me and squeezed me and then he kissed me and, of course, I didn't dare make a fuss and besides I didn't want that lot outside in the office to know what was going on.'

It all sounded horribly plausible, but still Genevra could not rid herself of her conviction that Mr Pyrritt would not have behaved in that way, not with Letty.

'And after that?'

'He asked me if I'd got a young man and I said I had and he wanted to know if we'd ever, you know, made love, so I said yes, we had, and he said in that case how about giving a bit of it to him.'

'Not a very romantic approach,' Mr Hendry commented.

'It was more jokey, like, but I was a bit scared because he wouldn't let go of me.'

The more she heard of this account the more convinced Genevra became that something of this sort had happened to Letty, but not with Matthew Pyrritt, with someone else.

'So then we sparred about a bit,' Letty went on. 'Him

wanting to kiss and cuddle and me trying to keep him off and then he asked me to go and have a nice supper with him upstairs in his apartment that night.'

'And you agreed?'

'Not at first, not until he said he'd have me thrown out in the street unless I gave in.'

'I see. Did you tell your other man friend about this?'

For the first time Letty's fluent tongue hesitated.

'No,' she said.

'Nor anyone else?'

'No.'

'Why not?'

'I was scared of losing my job.'

'Would it have been so very difficult for you to find another job?'

'It would if I hadn't got a reference,' Letty retorted.

Genevra could not help it, she had to intervene. 'If you'd given in your notice to the buyer in China he would have seen that you were given a reference and you could have been gone before Mr Pyrritt was aware of it. He doesn't concern himself with the comings and goings of junior staff.'

'I didn't stop to think of that,' Letty said sulkily.

'Tell me what happened that night,' the solicitor said.

'What, all of it?'

Letty giggled, then saw that her facetiousness was not well received and made herself serious again.

'I went home after work as usual, had a wash and put on a clean blouse . . .'

'Almost as if you were looking forward to your evening out,' Genevra remarked.

'Please, Miss Kerslake,' the solicitor said. 'Let Miss Jones tell her story in her own way.'

'I did myself up because although I was quite frightened

141

I was excited, too, about Mr Pyrritt, of all people, being keen on me.'

'Did you anticipate that you would have sexual relations with him?'

'I'd have been pretty silly not to have expected it after what had happened already, wouldn't I?'

'So you went back to the shop?'

'There's a private entrance at the back and the door was still open. If you go in through the shop there's a lift up to the top, but I walked up the stairs. There are fifty-two stairs – I was puffed by the time I got to the top. They're covered in green linoleum, but outside Mr Pyrritt's front door at the top the last six stairs are carpeted – red Wilton carpet, quite plain.'

'Your memory is most exact, Miss Jones. Perhaps you can also describe the inside of the flat.'

'Red Wilton carpet in the hall and a brownish kind of wallpaper, a sort of mottled all-over pattern. There's a large mirror on the right-hand side as you go in. He's got a small dining room, quite elegant, with a Chinese carpet in pale blue and cream, a sort of sitting room with a lot of books in it, I suppose there's a kitchen, though I never saw it, and one bedroom.'

'We are, of course, particularly interested in the bedroom so perhaps you'd better describe that.'

'Blue patterned Axminster carpet, not so light as the dining room, golden paper on the walls with a pattern that's shiny and matt so that it changes as you move about, blue velvet curtains, a great big bed with a dark blue silk coverlet and a sofa thing at the bottom of the bed. There are small tables on either side at the top of the bed holding lamps with parchment shades with gold fringes. There are photographs on the left-hand table.'

'A remarkably clear description, Miss Jones.'

'Were there any servants?' Genevra asked.

'Not that I saw. There was food laid out in the dining room and we helped ourselves.'

'What did you have to eat?' Mr Hendry asked.

Letty looked aggrieved. 'You can't expect me to remember every little detail,' she complained. 'He gave me a lot of champagne, that's all I can tell you. I scarcely knew what I was doing and so I gave in to him.'

'And went back on three further occasions,' Mr Hendry commented. 'Just give me those dates again, Miss Jones.'

Letty rattled them off without hesitation. 'He stays up in London in the middle of the week,' she explained. 'You'll find he was in the flat, just like I say, on each of those days.'

'I'm sure I will,' the solicitor agreed. 'About Mr Pyrritt, did you see him . . . er, unclothed?'

Genevra wished the floor would open and swallow her up; even Letty gulped before she replied, 'Of course I did.'

'Were there any marks on his body, any distinguishing marks? If you could mention something of that sort, a mole in an intimate position, for instance, it would be most convincing evidence of the truth of your story.'

'I don't remember anything,' Letty said.

She looked grumpy, as if the question had offended her, as well it might, Genevra thought. She would never, never have attended this interview if she had anticipated what it would be like.

'You have to realize that this is the sort of thing you will be asked if the case comes to court,' the solicitor explained.

'I never thought of having to go to court,' Letty said. 'If we face him with it, tell him all I've told you, then surely he'll do the sensible thing and pay up?'

'I'm not too sure about that. I shall approach his

solicitors and see if I can arrange a settlement, but I have to warn you that Mr Pyrritt may well decide to fight.'

The agitation Letty had suppressed while she was answering questions came to the surface once more.

'I didn't ought to be badgered like this in my state of health,' she said. 'It's not fair. I don't feel well. I want to go.'

'Very well. I doubt whether we can do any more today. I'll be in touch with you, Miss Jones.'

'Through me, if you please,' Mr Tallent said. He was looking pale and worried as if he, too, had begun to realize just what he had taken on when he had agreed to help Letty, but for all that he was very solicitous as he ushered her out of the room.

Genevra was following them, but the solicitor called her back.

'I'd just like one word with you before you leave,' he said.

Genevra paused and he motioned her to close the door.

'You don't believe Miss Jones' story?' he asked.

'No, I'm still not convinced, not even after hearing what she had to say this afternoon.' Remembering the details Genevra felt her cheeks burning once again.

'I should have insisted that you left the room,' Arthur Hendry said in a troubled way.

'Letty asked me to stand by her and I couldn't shirk it,' Genevra said simply. 'Does it seem to you that she's telling the truth, Mr Hendry?'

'I'm not sure,' Arthur Hendry admitted. 'Funnily enough, the thing that bothers me is those dates. She had them ready, so pat that she must have rehearsed them beforehand. If she'd said something like "three times in January and once in February" it would have been more natural.'

'It all sounded unnatural to me,' Genevra said. 'Such a mess and a muddle, and her entire life ruined no matter how this case turns out. I feel sorry for her, really I do, Mr Hendry, and I long to help her, but I feel angry too, because I think she's making a fool out of Mr Tallent, who is such a good man. And I suspect that she's maligning Mr Pyrritt.'

'Your feelings do you credit, Miss Kerslake.' Arthur Hendry hesitated, a slight colour creeping into his face. 'In spite of the circumstances, I am very pleased to have made your acquaintance. I wonder, if you are not in too great a hurry to get away after church on Sunday, will you wait and let me walk home with you?'

9

When Arthur Hendry followed up their sedate walk home from church with an invitation to accompany him to the theatre, Genevra hesitated.

'With a party of friends, of course,' he added hastily.

Genevra did not tell him that it was not the propriety of going to a theatre with a man that had given her pause, but doubt as to whether she was doing right in encouraging him.

'I would have to ask permission to be out late,' she said.

'Would there be any difficulty about that?'

'Probably not. The rules have been relaxed a little since I first joined Pyrritt's last year.'

'Then please ask. Is there anything you would particularly like to see?'

'I long to see Henry Irving and Ellen Terry.'

Arthur seemed to hesitate.

'Perhaps you've already been to their present play?' Genevra asked.

'No . . . I just wonder whether you had realized . . . it's *Faust*, you know . . . perhaps not quite what you would wish to see.'

'But surely that's a great classic,' Genevra said, puzzled by his embarrassment.

'Irving's adaptation has not been widely praised, although I understand the settings are remarkable. But that's not what was in my mind. On reflection you may think it not quite suitable.'

'It's been seen by the Royal Family.'

'I've heard that the Queen thought it an undesirable play for Princess May to attend,' Arthur said. 'I thought perhaps . . . *The Mikado*?'

Genevra accepted his suggestion with a gravity which masked both amusement and irritation. But when they went to the Savoy Theatre she discovered the pleasure of being escorted by an attentive young man. Arthur treated her with a respectful courtesy which Genevra thought overdone; but it was undeniably pleasant to travel in a hansom cab, to be helped in and out, to have doors held open for her, an unobtrusive arm to shield her from the press of the crowd, to have good seats at the theatre, a programme bought and presented to her, even a box of chocolates provided.

At the end of the evening Genevra, in a moment of weakness, allowed herself to agree to go to the Italian Opera the following week.

'With my parents,' Arthur said. 'My father is a great opera lover and, of course, as you know, I have a particular interest in singing. Mother means to invite you to dine with us beforehand.'

It was all getting a little out of hand, even though he was a very pleasant young man. Genevra felt worried, as if she were being carried along a stream in a boat over which she had no control.

When Arthur said goodnight to her at the door of her hostel he took her hand in his and held it, respectfully but with an unmistakably warm pressure. Genevra wished him goodnight in an embarrassed rush and was glad when the door opened quickly and she could get away.

There had been no chance to ask for news about Letty's case; but the following week when, punctiliously correct, he called to escort her to his parents' house, Genevra took the opportunity of asking what was happening.

'The more I know you, the more I regret your involvement in that unsavoury matter,' Arthur said.

'It's too late to shield me now,' Genevra replied speaking a little more tartly than usual because she thought his words sentimental. 'Letty has shut up like a clam and I can't get anything out of her. I live in dread of hearing that she's been dismissed. In fact, I can't understand why she's still employed at the store because both Mr Pyrritt and one of his oldest employees know that she is pregnant.'

'Perhaps his conscience is pricking him,' Arthur suggested.

'I doubt it! Have there been any legal developments?'

'I have communicated with Mr Pyrritt's solicitors,' Arthur admitted. 'They sent a formal acknowledgment of my letter, nothing more.'

'No denial?' Genevra asked incredulously.

'Nothing beyond the fact that they had received my letter and were taking instructions. It's quite a normal response.'

It seemed far from normal to Genevra and she was bothered by it.

'It would be better if we didn't discuss the case this evening,' Arthur said.

In front of his mother was what he meant, Genevra decided when she had been presented to Mrs Hendry. Arthur's mother was very polite, but Genevra had caught a flash of surprise in her expression as she inspected this girl her son had brought home. Rather better than she expected, Genevra guessed. Sure enough, she picked up several hints during the meal they shared before leaving for the Opera House that Mrs Hendry was relieved to find the girl in whom Arthur was interested to be perfectly acceptable, even though she worked in a shop.

Genevra was wearing the black silk evening gown

148

which had been new when she went to live with Leonora and Francis. The only time she had worn it since then had been at Christmas. Mrs Hendry was puzzled by everything about her, from her pretty speaking voice to her single strand of good pearls.

'How did it happen that you came to be employed at Pyrritt's, Miss Kerslake?' she asked at last, unable to suppress her curiosity any longer.

'I was left penniless when my father died,' Genevra said. 'My only relatives were a cousin and her husband. I decided I wanted to be independent and going to Pyrritt's was an opportunity that presented itself.'

'You modern girls!'

'There have always been women who needed to earn their own living, Mrs Hendry.'

'But not . . . my dear, you are a lady. There, I've embarrassed you, but I have to speak my mind.'

'Being a lady is singularly poor training for earning an honest crust,' Genevra said drily. 'I am contented with the choice I made.'

She saw that Mrs Hendry was looking both shocked and mildly offended and realized that she had spoken as bluntly as she would have done to one of her workmates. So much the better: it would show Arthur that she was not the delicate flower he seemed to think her.

The opera was *Rigoletto*, which Genevra had never heard before. It crossed her mind to wonder why this tale of seduction and murder should be considered suitable for her to see when *Faust* was not, but she suppressed a mischievous impulse to put the question to Arthur. Presumably the fact that the story was set to music and sung in Italian made it respectable in his eyes.

'You're enjoying it?' Arthur asked in the first interval.

'Immensely! And not just the music . . .' Genevra glanced round the crowded house, meaning to comment on her interest in being at Covent Garden for the first time, on the atmosphere and the fashionable audience. But then she caught sight of the occupants of one of the boxes and her throat went dry.

'What is it?' Arthur asked.

Genevra looked down, trying to hide her face.

'In the box . . . Mr Pyrritt,' she said. But the truth was that it was not the sight of her employer that had taken her breath away, but her unbelieving recognition of one of his companions. It was Leonora.

'So it is,' Arthur agreed.

He was staring openly at the box in a way which Genevra felt was sure to draw attention to them. Mr Pyrritt was lounging by Leonora's side, very much at home it seemed, and looking unusually sleek and well turned out in his evening clothes. Leonora was magnificent in green velvet and old lace, her rich auburn hair gleaming, her colour high as she chatted animatedly with her companions.

'You'd think he was every inch a gentleman, wouldn't you?' Arthur commented. 'I wonder who the other people are?'

'One of them is Lady Hamden,' Genevra said reluctantly.

'Poor little Letty,' Arthur said under his breath. 'What can she expect from him except indifference when he can enjoy the company of ladies like that?'

It was fortunate that the imminent rising of the curtain did away with the need to reply to that question. The second act passed like a dream for Genevra. Only half her attention was given to the drama taking place on the stage. Nothing could stop her stealing a glance every now and again at the box above them. In the dim light she could see only blurred outlines and the occasional flash of

150

diamonds on Leonora's wrist as she raised her opera glasses.

Genevra was on tenterhooks all through the second interval, but even though Leonora's glasses raked the audience in search of acquaintances, Genevra still went undetected. She thought when they were mingling with the crowd as they left the theatre after the performance that she was safe; but Leonora and her party were already in the foyer as Genevra, Arthur and Mr and Mrs Hendry came slowly down the stairs. It was Matthew Pyrritt who caught sight of Genevra. His eyebrows went up in a surprise she thought exaggerated and he bowed slightly. The movement caught Leonora's attention and she turned her head. Genevra was being pressed inexorably forward. For one moment she and Leonora stood silently confronting one another, then Leonora, with all the *savoir-faire* of long social experience, exclaimed, 'Genevra! But what a surprise!'

'Good evening, Leonora,' Genevra said.

She knew that she sounded wooden and that behind her the Hendry family were all eyes and ears.

Mr Pyrritt had gone back to looking inscrutable.

'Your carriage is here, Lady Hamden,' he said.

Leonora was carrying the meeting off a great deal better than she was, Genevra admitted.

'My dear, it's absurd that we don't meet,' she said. 'You must call on me.'

With a smile and a little wave of the hand she was gone, leaving Genevra to reflect grimly that there was nothing more unlikely than that she would drop in at one of her cousin's 'At Homes'.

'I didn't realize you were actually acquainted with Lady Hamden,' Mrs Hendry said.

There was a question behind her remark and Genevra felt bound to answer it.

151

'She is my cousin,' she said.

'The one you didn't want to live with when your father died?' Mrs Hendry asked incredulously.

'As I said before, I preferred to be independent.'

It was obvious that Arthur's mother was far from satisfied. Unspoken questions hung in the air. There was some mystery, and Mrs Hendry did not approve of mysteries, not when they concerned girls in whom her son was taking such a pronounced interest.

As for Leonora, she felt obliged to say something careless to Matthew Pyrritt as they drove away from Covent Garden.

'I'm glad Genevra has acquired some respectable friends,' she remarked. 'Who are they, do you know?'

'I recognized the older man. He's a solicitor with a practice not far from my store. We met on some committee or other. I imagine the younger man was his son. I know he has one who's in partnership with him.'

'A solicitor! Well, as I said – quite respectable, and I suppose suitable for Genevra in her present situation in life.'

What Matthew suppressed was the fact that he was perfectly aware that the Hendry firm was representing the Jones girl. So Genevra Kerslake was on terms of friendship with them, too, as well as the Tallents, was she? Damned impertinence, earning her living at his expense and making friends of all his enemies behind his back. More than friends, unless he had misjudged the protective air young Hendry adopted towards her. As her cousin had quite rightly said, a solicitor would make an entirely suitable husband for her, but it was galling to know that she must be aware of all the details of the case the Jones girl alleged against him. Perhaps they had talked it over between them, damn them.

Leonora touched him on the arm with her fan.

'I've spoken to you twice and you haven't replied,' she said. 'Come, come, Mr Pyrritt, this is not the attention I expect from you.'

Her tone was lightly mocking, but she was annoyed. It was not usual for men to be so *distrait* when Leonora let them see that she found them attractive.

She had chosen to make a friend of Matthew Pyrritt in defiance of all her husband's diatribes against him. They had met in the house of a mutual acquaintance and, as Leonora pointed out, it was quite impossible to turn her back on the man when Maisie Castle had asked him to take Leonora in to dinner. Francis continued to stand aloof, but more and more in recent months Francis and Leonora had gone their separate ways.

Leonora was excited by Matthew's humble origins, which she exaggerated; by his achievements, his wealth, the fact that he did not in the least care whether he was accepted in Society or not. She admired him physically, too, and would not have been averse to a little encounter, just to find out what he was like. It was no more than a thought at the back of her mind, but it lent spice to their meetings.

As for Matthew, he was enigmatic and she had no idea whether or not he thought her attractive. Gazing at herself complacently in the looking glass that evening, admiring her white skin and auburn hair, set off by her dark green velvet gown, she had thought that he would be a fool not to find her desirable.

It would have come as a shock to Leonora to know how accurately Matthew read her thoughts, and she would have been horrified to realize how deeply he despised her. A high-born lady with the instincts of a harlot – that was Matthew's opinion of Leonora. He toyed cynically with the idea of taking advantage of her penchant for him and for the time being put the temptation to one side. She would probably be very good value in bed; he suspected she had had plenty of practice; but he did not really want to get involved in the Society round of well-bred adultery.

All the same, he was sufficiently disturbed that night to take himself off to visit Rose.

She had given up reproaching him for his infrequent visits, but there was little spontaneous pleasure in the welcome she gave him.

'Is that son of yours out of London?' Matthew enquired.

'I sent him off with a flea in his ear after the way you told me he'd bothered you, and he's not supposed to show his face in London,' Rose said. 'What makes you ask?'

'There was someone hanging about over the other side of the road when I came in. I dare say it was nothing.'

He left her in the early hours of the morning, vaguely dissatisfied and depressed, as he usually was when he visited Rose these days. The truth was, he needed a change – but not, if Matthew could help it, Leonora Hamden.

As usual, he chose to walk home, shrugging off Rose's remonstrances and her attempts to get him to stay with her.

'The streets are safe enough,' he said. 'As for staying, you know I prefer to get out of my own bed in the morning.'

'This isn't *your* bed, I suppose?' Rose answered with heavy sarcasm.

Matthew had to walk past the whole length of the back elevation of his store on the way to the entrance to his own apartment. As always, the sight of its size and splendour made him feel better. He gave the entrance to the Food Store a complacent look as he passed by and then his attention was riveted by the realization that one of the big bins of rubbish, placed outside to await collection in a few hours' time, was sending out a cloud of dark smoke.

Without waiting a minute, Matthew went in search of the nightwatchman and together they poured buckets of water over the smouldering rubbish, creating more evil-smelling smoke and, at last, a nasty mush of blackened debris.

'Why wasn't this noticed sooner?' Matthew demanded.

'I've been round the inside of the shop regular as clockwork every hour, sir,' the nightwatchman responded, in a manner that showed he was aggrieved by the question. 'If there'd been flames coming out of the bin I dare say I would have noticed, but this black smoke . . . I'm sorry, sir, but I just didn't see it.'

Matthew ignored this justification. His immaculate white shirt-front was smeared with black smuts and there was a streak of dirt across his cheek.

'I wonder how it started,' he murmured, almost to himself.

'Some fool going by knocked out his pipe on the edge of the bin, as like as not,' the nightwatchman said in disgust. 'Being damp stuff it would have smouldered for an age before catching light properly.'

'Yes . . . I expect you're right,' Matthew said absent-mindedly. 'Well, keep vigilant. We don't want the sort of disaster that's plagued Whiteley's.'

'That we don't,' the man agreed, remembering the other big store's great fires. 'Just as well you happened to pass by, sir,' he added – which Matthew, who knew his workforce too well for their own comfort, perfectly understood to be a dig at his nocturnal wanderings, in retaliation for his remark about the fire not being dis-covered sooner.

It brought an unexpected grin to his face. He smote the older man a companionable blow on the shoulder, handed over a coin which was received with surprised gratitude, and went off to bed feeling, for some obscure reason, better pleased with the world.

The evening at the Opera marked a change in Genevra's friendship with Arthur Hendry. She guessed that his mother had voiced her disquiet that this 'shop girl' should have cut herself off from her influential friends. Certainly, for whatever cause, Genevra saw nothing of Arthur during the following week. She tried to be glad of it, but she could not help feeling indignant that he had appar-ently been influenced against her. She had valued their friendship and she thought poorly of him for not being more independent.

At least it left her free to pursue her other preoccu-pation. Genevra was determined to get to the bottom of Letty's story about her affair with Mr Pyrritt. She did what no one else had apparently thought of doing and tracked down the young man, Dick, who had been Letty's first love.

He was a good-looking youngster – and knew it, too, Genevra decided, resenting the appraising eye he ran over her trim figure.

'I want to talk to you about Letty,' Genevra began.

Dick's face went sullen. Suddenly, he looked much less the practiced ladykiller he aspired to be and much more like a sulky boy.

'I've got nothing to say about that young lady,' he said.

'I thought you and Letty were in love with one another.'

'So did I! Well, I've learnt my lesson. I'll never take a woman seriously again.'

156

'You know she's expecting a baby?' Genevra said hesitantly.

'That I do!'

'Is it yours?'

'Not by my reckoning, it's not! Letty quarrelled with me at the New Year.'

'But she spent it with you!' Genevra exclaimed. 'I remember she boasted about it and made an excuse to stay out all night.'

'We went to a party and the way Letty behaved you wouldn't believe! I was disgusted with her and so I told her.'

'You mean, she made you jealous? With some other man?'

'Half a dozen, more like it! She'd been drinking, of course, and so had they, but there was no call to go kissing everyone in the room, nor for making such a meal of it. What really got my goat was her carrying on with a man old enough to be her father, sitting on his knee and jigging about, *and* he was my uncle, which made it worse.'

'Was he . . . could he be the child's father?'

Dick shrugged, with a look of sullen distaste on his face.

'Don't see how he could be when Letty's so clear in her mind that Mr Pyrritt is responsible.'

'Dick, you know perfectly well that's just one of Letty's fairytales. It's *impossible*!'

'Don't you be so sure! She went up to his office one day and she told me afterwards he'd said things about her and the china both being pretty. She was ever so set up with herself about that.'

'An idle remark,' Genevra said helplessly. 'I'm sure he meant nothing by it.'

'Letty thought he did and she's the one who ought to know.'

'What happened after the New Year? Did you make up your quarrel?'

'I held out for a few weeks, but Letty knows how to get round a man. We made it up, after a fashion, then the next thing I heard was that there was a baby on the way. She tried to make out it was mine, no mention of Mr Pyrritt, oh, no! That only came out when I was suspicious and wouldn't believe I was the father. We had a real bust-up then. She carried on alarming.'

'Was that when she started blaming Mr Pyrritt?'

'N-no,' Dick said. 'We didn't speak to one another for a couple of weeks at least, then like a fool I weakened again and got in touch with her. She was full of bounce by that time, was our Letty! Told me as bold as brass that she'd been Mr Pyrritt's fancy lady and she was going to make him pay for being the baby's father.'

'And you believed her?'

'The way Letty told it, anyone would have believed her.'

'I don't. I think she made up the story to get money because she was frightened when you wouldn't accept that the child was yours.'

'You've got a down on Letty just because she's not been as pure as the driven snow. She's treated me like dirt, but I don't think she could have made up all that story out of her head. She's not . . . not *clever* enough to have thought it all up.'

It came to Genevra in a flash that this was true. Letty had a certain degree of intelligence, but she would not have been capable of fabricating such a sustained and detailed story. Nor, if Letty had ever been in Mr Pyrritt's apartment, would she have been able to report all the minute particulars she had given Arthur Hendry. A vague impression of colour and richness would have been all that Letty would have retained.

'I reckon he's the guilty man,' Dick continued. 'Letty wouldn't be the first girl to be led astray by a rich older man.'

'She'd been led astray by you before that,' Genevra pointed out.

'I meant to marry her. I still would if I was certain in my mind that I was responsible for her condition.'

Dick spoke with an assumption of virtue that irritated Genevra.

'If Letty dropped her story about Mr Pyrritt then you would be certain, wouldn't you?' she asked.

That question seemed to disconcert Dick. He hesitated, floundered and then muttered, 'I s'pose so.'

The suspicion began to form in Genevra's mind that there had indeed been another man, but not Matthew Pyrritt. What about the uncle he had mentioned?

'Was Letty sorry she had made you jealous by flirting with your uncle?' she asked.

'She laughed it off. You know her way.'

'Did you quarrel with him, too?'

'Naturally I did!'

Dick's spontaneous indignation sounded more convincing than the way he went on, as if trying to take back what he had said, 'He meant nothing by it. Uncle Alf's always been a lad for the girls, but I did think it was a bit off when he made a dead set at his own nephew's fiancée. He's as full of fairy tales as Letty. Told her he'd wrap her up in the same carpet as Cleopatra was rolled up in when she smuggled herself in to see Julius Caesar – which wasn't a story Letty had ever heard before.'

'Carpets,' Genevra said slowly. Something stirred at the back of her mind, some memory to do with the story Letty had told. If Dick would stop talking she might recall what it was.

'That's his line,' Dick explained.

159

'Here, at Pyrritt's?'

It was coming back to her, the odd little touch she had noticed when she had listened to Letty's glib account of going to Mr Pyrritt's flat. A Wilton carpet on the stairs, a Chinese carpet in the dining room, an Axminster in the bedroom. How did it happen that Letty could identify them all so accurately?

'Yes, Uncle Alf is in the Carpet Department, like I said,' Dick said.

It was on the tip of Genevra's tongue to ask whether Dick knew whether his uncle had laid the carpets in Mr Pyrritt's apartment, but she refrained. It would be easy enough to find that out later, but first she needed time to think over the new idea that had come to her.

'What is your uncle's surname?' she asked.

'Same as mine, o' course – Cross,' Dick said.

Alfred Cross. Some how Genevra was determined to get a look at Mr Cross, but it was far from easy to make excuses or to find the time to wander around the store.

She managed it by giving up her tea break and darting up to the third floor. The Carpet Department was almost deserted, just two groups of people inspecting the carpets laid out on the floor. One of the groups broke up and the man who had been attending to the customers bowed them to the door. Judging by his obsequious manner he had obtained a satisfactory order.

He came towards Genevra, took in her plain black gown and lack of a hat, coat and gloves and judged correctly that she was a fellow-employee.

'Can I do anything for you, my dear?' he enquired breezily.

If this was Alfred Cross then he was younger than Genevra had expected, but then Dick could be no more than eighteen or nineteen and it was quite reasonable for his uncle to be in his late thirties. When Dick had spoken of him as being old enough to be Letty's father Genevra had formed a vague idea of a man in his fifties, but perhaps Dick had exaggerated.

'I was just passing through and couldn't resist pausing to look at the carpets,' Genevra said in response to his question. 'Are you Mr Cross?'

'That's right. Alf Cross, at your service.' He gave her a bold up and down inspection which reminded Genevra of his nephew's similar technique and added: 'Very much at your service, if there's anything I can do for you.'

Dick would be just like him when he was a few years older. A man sure of his attraction for women and with few scruples about exploiting it. With no difficulty at all Genevra could imagine Letty being excited by his practiced charm and behaving like a little idiot as a result.

'There's nothing you can do for me,' Genevra said with a touch of hauteur that belonged to her old life. 'It was the beautiful colour of that carpet on the wall that made me stop for a closer look.'

'Finest Bokhara, one of the best in the shop. You have an eye for quality, Miss . . . Miss . . ?'

Genevra ignored the implied question. She gave him a slight dismissive smile and walked away.

She was satisfied, even from that brief encounter, that Alf Cross was a man capable of seducing a silly youngster like Letty; but would he also be able to hatch the plot to trap Matthew Pyrritt? Genevra glanced back over her shoulder. Alf Cross was still watching her. He had expected her to look back, he had been waiting for it. Genevra could have hit him for the look of smirking satisfaction on his face.

The question was, what was she to do about her suspicions? She could confront Letty, but that would forewarn the girl that she had been found out and Letty might find some way round it. After all, Genevra had no

161

real evidence. She could do what she had done before and talk to Miss Littlejohn: but Miss Littlejohn was on the other side and Genevra had identified herself with Letty's helpers, even though she did not believe her story. In the end she sent a brief note to Arthur and asked to see him.

This time she went alone to his office. As soon as she went in Genevra saw that he was slightly embarrased by their meeting and guessed that he was wondering whether to make some excuse for not having been in touch with her since their visit to Covent Garden. She thought the better of him when he said nothing.

Very briefly she explained her suspicion that Alf Cross was the father of Letty's child, that he might have had the inside knowledge which would enable her to describe Mr Pyrritt's flat, and that the whole story could be a plot to extract money.

'You're destroying our case,' Arthur exclaimed when she had finished.

'You want to know the truth, don't you?' Genevra asked.

'Letty's story stood up very well. We might have obtained a settlement for her.'

'But not when the whole thing is founded on a falsehood?' Genevra said, puzzled by his attitude.

'No . . . of course my firm couldn't be a party to an attempt to defraud Mr Pyrritt,' Arthur said more firmly. 'But if we hadn't *known*, if no one had found out about your Mr Cross, then I'm just saying that Mr Pyrritt might have been prepared to settle.'

'That would have been monstrously unfair! You're just like Mr Tallent, you want to believe badly of Mr Pyrritt!'

'No, no! Naturally I want justice to be done, but if what you say is true then Letty will get no money and the costs of what we've done so far will fall on Mr Tallent.

Frankly, I would far rather have screwed a little cash out of Mr Pyrritt.'

'You don't blame me for following my intuition?'

'Dear Miss Kerslake – Genevra – you've been remarkably diligent and I know that it is your own strong sense of what is right that has driven you on. I can only admire an integrity that follows the truth even when it is at the expense of a friend, and to the benefit of someone who can hardly be looked on as a benefactor.'

'You're angry,' Genevra said. 'And I'm sure I don't see why.'

Arthur dug viciously at his blotting pad with the nib of his pen.

'I'm not angry,' he said unconvincingly. 'If you must know, I suppose I'm jealous. I don't see why you should go to so much trouble to save that fellow Pyrritt's good name. Would you have got yourself involved in this sordid little case if the man concerned had been a plain Mr Smith?'

'Or Hendry?' Genevra suggested. 'I hope I would. The fact that I happen to know Mr Pyrritt had a bearing on my actions, of course it did, because that was what made me feel that what Letty said he had done was not in accordance with my opinion of him.'

'How did you come to know him so well, that's what I'd like to know!' Arthur burst out.

'Oh, I see! That's what's bothering you! Very well, I'll tell you. The house Mr Pyrritt bought in Surrey belonged to my father – in fact, to me, because I inherited everything that Father left, including his debts.'

She paused, breathing hard, and saw that Arthur was completely confounded.

'My dear Genevra! I had no idea! I realized, after Covent Garden, that you were rather better connected than I had thought. I saw at our first meeting that you were undoubtedly a lady, but I hadn't understood . . .,

'I'm a shop girl,' Genevra interrupted him. 'I chose to be a shop girl. Perhaps you think it eccentric of me, but as I told your mother, I wanted to be independent. Mr Pyrritt behaved generously towards me. I have no wildly exaggerated ideas about his character, but I owe it to *myself* to see that justice is done to him.'

'Yes, of course. Everything is clear to me now.'

Arthur's face was wreathed in smiles. He stood up and held out his hand.

'Come, shake hands with me and be friends. I've been unreasonable, I admit it freely.'

With a certain degree of reluctance Genevra put her hand into his. He held it firmly and even when she gave a tug he maintained his grip.

'I think you must have guessed the way I feel about you,' he said hesitantly.

'Please – no more!' Genevra said in a hurry. 'Not yet. Please . . . I'm not sure . . . I don't know . . .'

To her relief, Arthur let go of her hand. He was smiling, as if her agitation pleased him.

'I'll say no more,' he agreed. 'Not for the present. You will keep it in your mind, I know . . . And I do hope you will come home with me for Sunday lunch after church tomorrow.'

10

The strong hint Arthur had given her about his feelings put Genevra into a dilemma. She liked him, at times she felt quite fond of him, but she was not in love with him and was not sure that she ever would be. How could she know, she wondered doubtfully? He was the first young man who had ever shown such a decided preference for her. She was wholly inexperienced in affairs of the heart. How much of her pleasure in being escorted by Arthur arose from a natural delight in being entertained and how much from just being in his company? He was a very conventional young man, but any tendency towards stuffiness was relieved by his appreciation of music. He had a genuine gift himself and he took a keen interest in the performance of professional artists. His discovery of Genevra's similar tastes had been a turning point in their friendship.

If she encouraged him he would ask her to marry him, Genevra saw that quite clearly. Not yet, that would not be Arthur's way. He would wait a month or two, moving slowly towards the goal he wished to attain, and she must either begin to discourage him soon or else risk dealing him a real hurt.

Could she marry him? Genevra saw with a clear sighted lack of illusion that Arther Hendry probably represented her best chance of becoming respectably established. Well-to-do young solicitors eager to ally themselves to girls with a somewhat dubious background did not grow on trees. Life with him might not be exciting, but it would certainly be comfortable. Arthur would always be good to her and she believed that her growing affection for him might well form the basis of a good marriage. She was sufficiently uncertain of the state of her feelings to allow matters to drift for the time being, yet with an uneasy suspicion at the back of her mind that it would be a mistake to wait too long before either backing away or giving Arthur a more decided encouragement.

With this in mind she refused his invitation to share the Hendry's Sunday lunch. However, because she did not want to sound too unenthusiastic, she made the excuse that she had been neglecting the Tallent family, who had been such good friends to her.

By the middle of the following week disaster had fallen on Letty: she had been dismissed from Pyrritt's.

'What did you expect?' Ruth asked reasonably when Letty was discovered, snivelling miserably as she packed her few belongings into a dilapidated suitcase. 'You're beginning to show what ails you. Anyone with half an eye can see you're carrying. Even if Mr Pyrritt's responsible . . .'

'He is, he is!'

'You can't expect him to keep you in the shop looking like that. What are these legal people of yours doing for you?'

'I've got to go and see Mr Hendry tomorrow,' Letty said, wiping away her tears with the back of her hand. She glanced at Genevra, standing by silently, her face deeply troubled.

'You can't expect Jenny to risk taking time off from work to go with you,' Sally said sharply. 'What are you scared of? They didn't eat you last time, did they?'

'I'd like to be there – if you want me, Letty?' Genevra said. 'I'll pretend to be unwell.'

Her pretence was not far off the truth when the following afternoon arrived. She felt sick and shaky because she suspected that Arthur meant to confront Letty with the possibility that her story had been concocted between her and Alf Cross. Would Letty brazen it out? Genevra doubted it. She thought that Letty's original certainty had already been undermined. It was doubtful whether Alf Cross, if he really were the guilty man, was giving her the support she needed; and Letty was frightened by the enormity of the lie she had told, now that she had been forced to face up to the results.

The two girls scarcely spoke as they walked to the solicitor's office. Letty walked more slowly than she had done in the past, moving a little heavily, and Genevra's heart contracted with pity for the poor silly child.

Arthur was somewhat less compassionate.

'I have a few more questions to put to you, Miss Jones,' he said with a crispness that intimidated Letty. 'What are your relations with Mr Alfred Cross?'

Letty's sharp intake of breath was clearly audible.

'I . . . I know him,' she answered. She made an attempt to pull herself together. 'He's Dick's uncle – my boy that I had before everything went wrong.'

'You quarrelled with Dick Cross because of your . . . flirtation with his uncle, didn't you?'

Letty tossed her head with something of her old self-satisfied jauntiness. 'Dick was ever so jealous. Silly boy, I didn't mean anything by it until . . .'

'Until you found that the – flirtation – had gone too far?'

'If Dick and me hadn't quarrelled I wouldn't have been driven into the arms of another man,' Letty said dramatically.

'But the question is, which other man? Miss Jones, are you quite sure you want to go on with your accusation against Mr Pyrritt?'

''Course I am,' Letty said, but she sounded uncertain.

167

She flicked a pleading look at Genevra, but for once Genevra hardened her heart. Let Arthur deal with this investigation.

'If you persist and your story is shown to be a fabrication you could be in great trouble,' Arthur warned Letty.

'Don't see how anyone could prove it wasn't true, not with me knowing so much about Mr Pyrritt's movements and his flat and everything,' Letty declared.

'You were on terms of considerable intimacy with Mr Cross and he supervised the laying of all the carpets in Mr Pyrritt's apartment only a few months ago,' Arthur said. 'He could have told you everything you needed to know about the furnishing of the flat. I'm sorry, Miss Jones, but that is what the other side are going to say, and they have just as good a chance as we had of finding out about your friendship with this man.'

'How did *you* find out?' Letty demanded.

'I talked to Dick,' Genevra said.

'You traitor! You pretended to be my friend.'

'Letty, you *must* tell the truth! If it's been as easy as this for me to throw a doubt on your story then surely you can see that Mr Pyrritt will be able to do the same? He's a very clever man.'

'*And* rich! It wouldn't hurt him to come down with a little of the ready!'

'Is that what Mr Cross told you?' Arthur asked quietly.

Quite suddenly, and just as Genevra had expected, Letty crumpled. There were tears and sobs and incoherent accusations against Genevra herself, but in the end it all came out: the madness of giving in to Alf Cross, her panic when she realized she was pregnant, Dick's refusal to admit that the child was his – 'Although it *could* be, it could,' Letty insisted passionately; then her frantic

168

appeals to Alf and, finally, his suggestion that she should place the blame on their employer.

'Alf said he'd be bound to pay up, to keep his name out of the papers. He told me what to say and I learnt it off by heart, the dates and the furniture and everything. I never thought it would be like this, people not believing me and friends – so called – going behind my back and finding out things, and getting caught up in the law. I never meant to be a bad girl, I never did! What am I going to do? Oh, what am I going to do?'

Genevra knelt by her side, trying to soothe her, and Letty was so far gone in her bewilderment and desperation that she leaned weakly against the girl she had just called her enemy and sobbed into her shoulder.

'Will Mr Cross support the child?' Arthur asked.

'Not him! He's married with three brats already.'

'If you had him in here and told him that the price of our keeping quiet about his involvement was reasonable maintenance for Letty and the child, he might agree,' Genevra suggested.

'That borders on blackmail,' Arthur said with a slight smile.

'He can't afford it,' Letty said. 'If you'd ever had to bring up three children you'd know why. If this comes out he'll get the sack and he'll blame me and it's the babies who'll suffer. Please don't tell Mr Pyrritt, Jenny, please don't.'

'I have no intention of admitting to Mr Pyrritt's solicitors that I know anything about this man Cross – which isn't to say that they won't find out for themselves,' Arthur said. 'I shall merely intimate to them that Miss Jones withdraws unreservedly her allegation against Mr Pyrritt. I only hope he'll be satisfied with that.'

'Letty's already been dismissed and that's about the worst thing that can happen to her,' Genevra said. 'Now,

Letty, dry your eyes and we'll start thinking what to do with you. The offer of a place in the Home Mr Tallent told you about is still open.'

'I suppose I'll have to take it,' Letty said sullenly. 'But I never thought I'd end up in a Home for Fallen Women!'

Letty's departure cast a gloom over the little group of girls who were still sharing the overcrowded bedroom at 92 Mountfort Road. Her empty bed was a constant reminder of her. Although Genevra was able to tell the other girls that Letty was being looked after they all knew that the worst of her problems was still ahead of her.

What irked Ruth and Sally was that Genevra obviously knew far more than she was prepared to tell them about the dropping of Letty's fantastic story about their employer.

'You're a proper clam,' Sally grumbled. 'I bet you know who was really responsible for Letty's trouble. Come on, tell us – was it Dick?'

When Genevra did not answer, Sally said, 'It wasn't or you would have said yes straight away.'

'You're jumping to conclusions,' Genevra protested, disconcerted by her shrewdness.

'And you're not going to answer me either yes or no, are you?' Sally demanded. 'I'll say one thing for you, Jenny: you're a loyal friend!'

'Let's not talk about it any more,' Ruth put in. 'I'm sick to death of young Letty and her troubles. Drop it, Sal. What are you going to wear to this summer outing Mr Pyrritt's invited us to? I dunno what's come over him. We've never had anything like it before.'

The change of subject was not entirely fortunate as far as Genevra was concerned. Mr Pyrritt was holding a garden party for the entire staff towards the end of June and it was to be at Leylands. Genevra was dismayed, and would have tried to get out of going if she could, but what excuse could she offer? All the girls were agog to see Mr Pyrritt's country house and they would have been incredulous if she had said she would rather not go. As the day drew near she found herself looking forward to the visit to her home with a mixture of anticipation and dread.

The store closed at mid-day on the Saturday when they were invited to Leylands and that, too, was an innovation. Who, Genevra wondered, had made Matthew Pyrritt understand that his staff, men as well as girls, would want to dash back to their lodgings to change out of their drab working clothes into their Sunday best for this outing?

They were expected to make their own way to Victoria Station but, once there, a special train had been reserved for the party and when they arrived at Epsom there were horse-drawn carriages and wagons to carry them to Leylands.

The country lanes were the ones which had been familiar to Genevra since childhood. She knew all the tracks leading up into the Surrey hills, all the little villages, even some of the people they passed who came to their gates to look with curious eyes at this crowd of townspeople noisily enjoying a spree.

Most of the guests were young, all of them were determined to enjoy themselves. The girls wore light summer dresses, many of them far too elaborate for a day in the country, and clutched at flower-trimmed hats which threatened to blow away in the breeze that was created as they bowled along at a smart trot. Genevra, wearing a grey and white striped cambric gown and a plain sailor hat, felt that she looked like a governess by the side of Sally in emerald green and Ruth in embroidered pink muslin.

It was something of a disappointment to the girls to discover that they were to be entertained in a marquee on the lawn.

'I'd like to have seen inside the house, that I would,' Sally said. 'Still, I suppose with a crowd like this you couldn't expect him to let us all go tramping in and out. I say, the ham looks good, and look at those mounds of strawberries! We'll be getting a good feed, that's for certain.'

There was croquet on another stretch of lawn and a cricket match had been arranged for the men; there were the gardens to explore; and some of the more adventurous walked out of the grounds and into the village. Genevra waited until she thought she was unobserved and then slipped quietly round the back of the house and into the stableyard, making for the kitchens, since she was determined not to miss the opportunity of visiting her old friend, Mrs Bertram.

The horses were standing quietly, looking over the half-doors of their stables. Genevra recognized the black horse which had belonged to her father and paused to pass a regretful hand along his silky neck. In the next stall was a brown head which was even more familiar.

'Marietta?' Genevra said, not really believing it.

The beautiful mare tossed her head as if acknowledging her name and Genevra's lips quivered, half smiling and half on the edge of tears, as she greeted the gentle friend who had carried her for so many happy miles.

'I wondered whether you'd find your way round here,' Matthew Pyrritt's voice said behind her.

Genevra turned quickly. He was standing just a yard or two away, watching her with a curious grave look on his face.

'I wanted to say hello to Mrs Bertram,' Genevra said. 'I thought there could be no objection.'

She was annoyed to hear a defensive note in her voice.

'None at all – not for you,' Matthew said. 'I don't want the whole store tramping over my new carpets. And talking of carpets, I hear you've been interfering in my affairs again, and to some purpose.'

Genevra felt herself reddening. 'How did you know?' she asked.

'I employed an investigator and everywhere he went a certain young lady had been before him. I congratulate you, a most perspicacious bit of work. What's happened to the girl?'

'She's been found a place in a home for unfortunates like her.'

Matthew grunted. 'Will she stay there?'

'I hope so,' Genevra said, deeply troubled by the question. 'From what you said about carpets, I gather that you know . . .'

'I believe a certain Mr Alfred Cross is the probable father.'

'What are you going to do to him?'

'I can't go on employing him, you must see that. Fortunately, Mr Cross also realizes it. He gave in his notice the day after your Letty withdrew her allegations against me. I understand he's got the chance of a job with one of my rivals.'

'What about a reference for him?'

When Mr Pyrritt remained silent she added, a little desperately, 'He's got three children.'

'And very nearly four. He should have thought of that before he got the Jones girl into trouble. I'm not going to prosecute either of them, which in the circumstances is generous of me. Frankly, I'd rather not have the publicity, not coming on top of the Thredgold affair.'

When Genevra continued to look at him in a pleading way he added, 'I've not said anything that would stop him being given a reference. How could I, without giving a reason? He was a good salesman, quite an expert in his field. As for his morals, William Whitely can find out about those for himself – and considering his own life I don't think he has any right to quibble at a little by-blow or two.'

'I know nothing about Mr Whiteley's private life,' Genevra said haughtily. 'But I'm glad Mr Cross's children won't suffer as a result of his bad conduct.'

Marietta's chestnut head butted against her arm.

'She thinks you're neglecting her,' Matthew remarked.

'I haven't recovered from the shock of finding her here,' Genevra said, all her attention apparently given to the horse. 'I didn't know you had bought her.'

'I thought it would be a good idea,' Matthew said vaguely.

'But . . . who rides her?'

'One of the lads. Don't worry, I'm not giving her anyone over her weight.'

'That's not what I was thinking. She's so obviously intended for a lady to ride and there's no one . . . But perhaps your guests . . .'

'Over my dead body! No one rides Marietta except her own special lad.'

'You paid a high price for a mare who isn't ridden. Too much, in fact.'

Genevra's head was bent and her voice slightly muffled as she stroked Marietta's nose over and over again.

'I thought I'd like to breed from her. As a matter of fact, she's in foal.'

'Oh . . !' Again Genevra's attention was focused on the mare. 'What a clever girl! Are you going to have a beautiful foal, my angel?'

When she looked up her eyes were wet with tears, and this time she did not attempt to blink them away. She

174

saw Matthew, rather closer than she had realized, his face concerned, almost anxious. He, too, put his hand on the neck of the quiet horse and then he bent towards Genevra as if attracted by an irresistible magnet.

She had no idea what he meant to do, not until she felt his free hand at the back of her head, drawing her closer. Genevra drew in her breath sharply, but before she could protest or move away their lips met. He did not attempt to take hold of her, except for that gentle pressure at the back of her head. His lips were warm and firm. It was nothing like the hot slobbering which Francis had inflicted on her. It ought to have been easy to break away and yet she did not move. Something inside her was responding, whether she willed it or not. A warmth seemed to be spreading from somewhere in the middle of her body, right out to the tips of her fingers and toes, so that they seemed to tingle with new life. It was not Genevra but Matthew who brought the kiss to an end.

She stood looking at him, blinking and confused, her face very pink, her mind totally incapable of rational thought.

'Am I to have my face slapped?' Matthew asked, with a note of deep amusement in his voice.

Genevra shook her head, still unable to find words.

'Well, at least I know for certain now what ails me,' he said obscurely. 'And a confounded nuisance it is, too.'

'It was outrageous,' Genevra said unconvincingly. 'Suppose someone had seen us!'

'Highly compromising,' Matthew agreed solemnly, but Genevra was suspicious of the contrast between his straight face and the way his eyes seemed to be smiling.

'It's not right to laugh at me,' she said with worried dignity. 'If I were more experienced no doubt I would know how to deal with such unwanted attentions, but no one has ever – well, not except Francis, and that was

175

horrible – and so I don't know how to get away when a gentleman forgets himself.'

'I'm not a gentleman,' he pointed out with the same unrepentant cheerfulness. 'Perhaps you'd better take refuge with Mrs Bertram before I forget myself again. Who knows what may happen now that you've aroused my baser instincts?'

'I didn't encourage you,' Genevra said, really put out.

'Well . . . not intentionally perhaps.'

Genevra gathered up her skirt to cross the yard, disgusted to realize that her hands were shaking.

'It must never, never happen again,' she said.

'In our present circumstances it would certainly be unwise,' he agreed.

'I suppose that's as much of an apology as I'm likely to get?'

'Apology? I've no intention of apologizing. I enjoyed it.'

Pursued by his laughter Genevra walked with studied disdain across the cobblestones and into the house, but in the passageway between the outer door and the kitchen she had to pause. It would never do to let Mrs Bertram see her in such a state of confusion. She might guess – and Genevra felt she would die of embarrassment if anyone ever knew that she had submitted, far from unwillingly, to Mr Pyrritt's embrace.

Not that it had been an embrace, just a kiss. Perhaps that made it all the more shocking. He had merely put his lips on hers, exerted a slight, persistent pressure and she had nearly swooned with delight.

That was what had shaken her so profoundly. Matthew Pyrritt had kissed her and she had liked it. No wonder falling in love gave rise to so much trouble if a kiss from someone who meant nothing by it could cause so much havoc in one inexperienced girl.

176

Perhaps she should encourage Arthur to kiss her. It would be easier to make up her mind about him if she knew that he, too, could give her so much pleasure by a simple touch. Arthur was a very proper young man, but Genevra sensed that it would not be difficult to tempt him to cross the conventional divide between them. The trouble was, if Genevra made the first overtures he would feel that she was committed to him and Genevra was by no means sure she was ready to give him a final answer.

Genevra pulled herself up with a rueful little grimace. What was the world coming to when she, Genevra Kerslake, could stand outside the kitchen of her old home plotting to get a young man to make love to her? It was, of course, entirely Mr Pyrritt's fault. Tiresome, unsettling, unpredictable man. Just as well she had not known how easily he dispensed his kisses before exposing Letty's story, because it would have made her considerably less sure of his innocence.

Mrs Bertram was delighted to see her.

'I hoped you would manage to slip away,' she said. 'Dear Miss Jenny, how well you're looking! Such a lovely colour in your cheeks! And you're wearing a pretty frock again. Quite right to come out of your black. I don't like to see a young girl in mourning for more than a year, not even for a father, and dear Mr Kerslake would have been the last one to expect it.'

She bustled around while Genevra had a word with some of the other servants. There were one or two new faces, but it pleased her to see so many familiar old friends still employed at Leylands.

'I made one of my special strawberry shortcakes when Mrs Bertram said she expected you would be here for tea,' the cook said.

'Oh, how tempting it looks! They haven't got that outside in the tea tent.'

'That they haven't! Plenty of strawberries and cream, though. Mr Pyrritt said there was to be an abundance of everything. Very openhanded of him, we thought.'

The mention of Mr Pyrritt brought the colour up into Genevra's face again. She really must control it, she thought helplessly. Her life would be unbearable if she were to blush every time his name came into the coversation.

'I never thought you'd stick that job of yours for nearly a year,' Mrs Bertram said when she had Genevra to herself in her own room.

'Neither did I,' Genevra admitted. 'It's been hard, Bertie. I'm prepared to admit now that I didn't know what I was taking on.'

'And what about the future?'

Mrs Bertram looked shrewdly at the girl who had been both her mistress and her charge.

'Any nice young men, that's what I want to know? Not that I'd like to see you married to a counter clerk, but surely you must see a better class of gentleman sometimes?'

'I have a friend – a solicitor,' Genevra admitted.

'A solicitor!' Mrs Bertram wrinkled her nose. 'It's not what your father would have liked, but I suppose . . . it's a good profession and no doubt he'll always be able to provide for you.'

'Please, Bertie, don't go so fast!' Genevra protested. 'Mr Hendry is a pleasant young man and he likes me. I'm not quite sure . . . I want to wait and see how I feel in a few months' time.'

Mrs Bertram pressed her hand. 'Don't wait too long, dearie,' she said. 'Time goes by quicker than you realize. Sometimes I can't bear to think of you shut away in that shop, not having any sort of life and not meeting the gentlemen it would be proper for you to meet. If he's a nice young man and able to give you a decent establishment and you like him, then don't let him slip through your fingers.'

'What about . . . love?' Genevra asked hesitantly, with all her newly awakened interest in the subject. 'Were you in love with Mr Bertram when you married him?'

'George and I were very comfortable together as long as he lived,' Mrs Bertram said. 'I was fond of the dear man, that I was. As for love, that's a fancy name for something any healthy young couple might come to feel for one another in the days when the blood is still hot. If you marry a decent man and feel a true affection for him then it's up to you, the woman, to make the marriage. Men will stray if they get the chance, even the best of them, but a good wife will keep her man on the right path, especially when the children come.'

'Then you believe I ought to marry Arthur?' Genevra asked.

'You're already thinking of it or you wouldn't have told me about him,' Mrs Bertram said shrewdly. 'Follow your own good sense, Miss Jenny. I wouldn't have talked to you like this before you went away, but you've changed, become more of a woman, in the past year.'

'I've had to,' Genevra said. 'Bertie, one of the girls in my room got into trouble.'

Hesitantly, she told Letty's story, omitting any mention of Mr Pyrritt.

Mrs Bertram shook her head, but her verdict was harsher than Genevra had expected.

'It sounds to me as if that one would have landed in the soup no matter where she found herself,' she said. 'I know the type! I've had maids like that. Sensation, that's what they're mad for. You've done all you can for her, now put her out of your mind.'

'I can't. She may be in good hands for the time being,

179

but what is going to become of her when the baby is born?'

'The baby will be adopted, I dare say. As for your Letty, she'll probably go on the streets.'

'Bertie, no! That's a dreadful thing to say about a girl you've never even met. She's not a bad girl, not at heart.'

'That's what you think,' Mrs Bertram sniffed. 'I hope you haven't got it in mind to suggest I employ her here.'

'No, no!' Genevra said hurriedly, horrified by the idea of Letty working in Mr Pyrritt's house. 'But there must be something I can do to stop her spoiling the rest of her life. I've been thinking of opening a little shop of my own one day. I've got a tiny bit of capital and I could add to it by selling my gold watch, my pearls, my locket . . .'

'Not that beautiful gold locket with your grandmother's portrait on ivory!'

'I could remove the miniature,' Genevra argued. 'The money would be more useful to me than the ornament. I thought perhaps Letty might be able to work for me.'

'Well, Miss Jenny, it's not for me to say,' Mrs Bertram said, with every intention of following up this disclaimer with her own alterable opinion. 'A shop of your own! Scraping for every penny and never a minute when you're not at a customer's beck and call. And that girl with you! You'd never be able to trust her, never! Far better to marry that nice solicitor and settle down with your own family round you.'

Genevra shook her head, not convinced by the picture Mrs Bertram painted; but she saw that her old friend was seriously put out and thought it wiser to change the subject.

The rest of the day passed off pleasantly enough. Genevra escaped to the village and visited one or two cottages. It was heartwarming to find that she was not forgotten, even though the enquiries about her wellbeing

180

were more stilted than they would once have been, before she had challenged all the conventions and gone to work for a wage.

What did worry Genevra was that some of her workmates seemed to be giving her curious glances and several times she saw heads being put together and a whisper going round that broke off when she approached. The dreadful suspicion that she had been seen with Mr Pyrritt in the stableyard began to haunt Genevra: but that was not what was causing the sensation amongst the girls who knew her.

When they were going home in the train Sally suddenly burst out, 'Well, Jenny, you're a dark horse and no mistake!'

'What does that mean?' Genevra asked.

'Some of us walked down to the village and went into the church. It was full of tombstones and memorials to the Kerslakes of Leylands House. Did your family *own* that place?'

'Yes,' Genevra admitted.

'You lived there, you were brought up in that house?'

'Yes, but unfortunately there was not sufficient money to allow me to go on living there.'

'But when Mr Pyrritt bought it? He must have given thousands for it.'

'There were debts,' Genevra said wearily.

'Even so . . . we always knew you were different from the rest of us, but not how different. You ought to be living like a princess. Doesn't it make you angry, spending a day there and seeing what you ought to have and then going back to Mountfort Street?'

'Not angry, not any more.'

'No wonder you thought our bedroom was overcrowded,' Ruth murmured.

181

They did not exactly blame her for keeping her circumstances to herself, but the constraint between them had been reinforced. Genevra, sitting in the corner of the carriage amongst a crowd of people who seemed to have difficulty in talking to her, began to think over her conversation that afternoon with Mrs Bertram. The time was coming when she would have to decide to make another change in her life. Either she must carry out her plan to embark on business for herself or else she must agree to marry Arthur. What ever she decided would take her away from Mr Pyrritt, and that would probably be a very good thing.

They were all tired when they climbed the stairs of their lodging house.

'Quite a day,' Sally remarked, plumping herself down on her bed. 'I enjoyed it, especially the strawberries and cream.'

'And seeing where Mr Pyrritt lives, lucky man,' Ruth added. 'He did us proud, I'll say that for him.'

The trunk which Genevra kept underneath her bed was sticking out in a way that suggested it had been moved. This surprised Genevra because only one young maid had been left behind in the house, and she doubted very much whether Martha would have done any cleaning without being supervised.

She bent down to push it back and saw that the lock had been forced. Genevra pulled out the heavy box and opened the lid.

'What do you want out of that at this time of night?' Ruth asked idly.

'I've been robbed!' Genevra cried. Instinctively she began to smooth out the tumbled clothes under which she had left her few small treasures. 'Someone's taken my watch and locket and pearls.'

Genevra was too dazed by her loss at first to think

coherently. The other girls were all round her exclaiming and peering over her shoulder, but Genevra was hardly aware of them. She was the only girl who said nothing and it was Sally who sent for the housekeeper and the maid who had been left in charge of the house.

It was not until young Martha, nearly hysterical, repeated over and over again, 'It wasn't me! It wasn't me!' that Genevra roused herself to say, 'I believe you, but did you let anyone else into the house today?'

'No, I didn't, except my friend Betty, and she never went out of the kitchen. I had permission to ask her in, didn't I, ma'am?'

The housekeeper was just agreeing when Ruth exclaimed, 'Look! I think someone's climbed in this window.'

The window, which all the girls knew had been shut before they went out, was not quite closed at the bottom. There were signs of something having scraped the windowsill and, now that she looked more closely, a dirty mark on Genevra's counterpane which might have been caused by someone stepping on it.

'We've been burgled!' Ruth asserted. 'I always said no good would come of opening that window, Jenny.'

'We'd better check that nothing else is missing,' Sally said.

'*We've* got nothing worth taking,' Ruth said, with a certain emphasis that reminded everyone of the discoveries they had made about Genevra's past life that day.

They all went through their scanty belongings, but only Genevra had lost anything. The thing that puzzled her, once she was able to think again, was who could have known that she had something worth stealing concealed in her trunk. Any of her roommates might have known, but they had all been with her at Leylands when the robbery had taken place. The only person she could actually remember having seen the inside of her trunk was Letty – and surely even Letty would not take the appalling risk of climbing along the roof to get in the window when she was over five months pregnant?

All she could think was that someone had seen her stowing away her possessions and had talked about it unwarily; but that was not something she cared to say aloud. Let the police, fetched by the housekeeper, follow up ideas of that nature. Genevra answered all their questions carefully, gave them a detailed description of the missing jewellery and in her heart resigned herself to never seeing it again. Nothing remained to her now but the cameo brooch which she had worn at the neck of her gown that day.

She shed a few unhappy tears after she had gone to bed. It had been an exhausting, unsettling day. Seeing Leylands, talking to Mrs Bertram, hearing her pessimistic description of Genevra's life if she did not take her chance to marry, and that extraordinary encounter with Mr Pyrritt. Genevra told herself she would prefer not to remember that. But strangely, it was the memory of the warmth that had swept over at the touch of his lips that comforted her and eventually allowed her to drift off to sleep.

11

Matthew Pyrritt was not the man to let grass grow under his feet once he had decided on a course of action. He had delayed too long over terminating his relationship with Rose Peary; but once he had made up his mind that it must be ended he went straight to her and told her.

'We've had some good times and I'm grateful, but as far as I'm concerned it's over,' he said.

'Found someone younger?' Rose asked. She was deeply mortified, even though she had seen this coming for months past.

'I've no plans for replacing you,' Matthew said.

Rose's eyes narrowed as she weighed up that reply.

'What's going to happen to this house?' she asked.

'I've only got it on a yearly lease. I'll let it lapse. I'll do the right thing by you, Rose . . .'

'I should hope so, after all we've been to one another!'

'I'll buy you a house and settle five thousand pounds on you.'

'Make it ten,' Rose said automatically.

'All right, ten thousand pounds,' Matthew replied with a promptness that made her look at him suspiciously.

'Damn you, Matt, that was what you always meant to give me,' she said.

'I thought you'd try to bargain with me,' he admitted cheerfully. 'Ten thousand is what you've asked for and what you'll get, so I hope there'll be no hard feelings between us. You've not done badly out of our arrangement over the last four years. If you haven't made any savings then you're not the woman I took you for.'

From the complacent look that showed for a moment on Rose's face he guessed that she had managed to amass a sizeable nest-egg.

'You've never been particularly generous with presents,' she complained.

'That's not my way, I paid for what I had and saw no reason to load you with jewels into the bargain.'

'You're a hard man, Matt. What about my feelings? You don't take them into account.'

'We had a fondness for one another and we were both excited by what we could do together in bed; but it was always a business arrangement, on your side as much as on mine.'

'What's to become of me when you've turned me out of my home and given me up?'

'You could settle down and become respectable,' Matthew suggested.

'I haven't put a foot wrong for the last four years. I don't know what could be more respectable than that.'

'If you want my advice, I'd say leave London. Go somewhere where you're not known. A well-to-do attractive widow, still in your thirties, you won't be alone for long. The men will be queueing up to ask for your hand in marriage.'

'Marriage! Well, that'd be something new,' Rose said, forgetting that she had always maintained that there had once been a Mr Peary.

'You could have your son to live with you,' Matthew suggested.

'I could, but I don't know that I want to,' Rose admitted. 'It won't do much for my respectable image if Fred goes round asking every man he meets if he's his Dad. Besides, Fred's been a nuisance lately, insisting on living in London, which I don't think is good for him.'

In the end she admitted to a hankering for a villa in Margate, where she had family connections.

'Going to turn yourself into a seaside landlady?' Matthew asked with a grin.

'No, thank you! Too much like hard work. Mind you, it can be made to pay and I'm not saying I might not set someone else up in a nice little boarding-house with part of my . . .'

'Ill-gotten gains?' Matthew suggested.

'Oh, you take it very lightly, don't you?' Rose exclaimed. 'You walk in here and turn my life upside down – and don't tell me it isn't because you've got a fancy for some other woman because I won't believe you – and then you make a joke of it.'

Because she pulled out a handkerchief and dabbed at her eyes and looked really upset, Matthew went and put his arm round her.

'I'm sorry. I didn't mean to be heartless,' he said.

'You don't care,' Rose accused him.

He tilted up her face and kissed her, but she was too shrewd not to realize that it was a perfunctory gesture. With an effort she held back her rancour. Tears and reproaches did no good once a man had tired of you. Better to part with a smile and as much profit as you could lay your hands on.

'What about the furniture in this house?' she asked.

'Take anything you fancy and sell the rest,' Matthew said.

Rose settled back in a more satisfied way. That would add a nice little sum to what he had already promised her; and there would be the house in Margate, too, which could be sold if she found someone else to set her up in style. Or she might do what he said and turn respectable. Every day brought her nearer to forty and there was no denying that she had passed the peak of her beauty. It might be quite satisfying to please herself for a change instead of spending interminable hours sitting around waiting for a man who might or might not pay her a visit. The trouble with being a mistress, once the first desire had worn off, was that it was bloody boring.

When he left Rose, having refused her offer of one last fling in bed, Matthew felt satisfied that he had done the right thing. It was still quite early and, as usual, he walked home. It had been a warm day and some of the heat still lingered. The air seemed flat, not like it had been when he had left Leylands that morning. The more he saw of Leylands the better pleased he was with it. The staff outing there had been a success and it had given him satisfaction to let all his workforce see the fine house he had acquired through his own efforts. The more he thought about it, the more ashamed he was of having had Rose to stay there. It had been a mistake of the kind that Matthew did not often make. Leylands was a house for a lady, which Rose had never been. It needed a mistress – but not of her sort.

That late June evening was not the first time that Matthew had had the uncanny feeling that he was being followed. He remembered the time when Fred Peary had come after him and his hand clenched on his stick, but when he looked round he realized that there were several people in the street behind him and it was impossible to say that any one of them was deliberately tailing him. He shrugged off the suspicion and finished his walk without being molested in any way.

The next thing he wanted to get settled was the extension of his shop to the corner site. Mr Tallent showed no signs of giving way to the pressure that had been applied to him and he must be made to do so. Matthew reflected with a certain grim satisfaction that Mr Tallent must be smarting at the way Letty Jones had fooled him. Matthew had no qualms about taking advantage of his discomfort-ure. The very next day, without announcing his visit beforehand, he walked into the Tallents' shop and asked to see Mr Tallent.

He was kept waiting, which he had expected, and he spent the time looking round the shop. It was not a bad place, quite well arranged and doing a reasonable amount of business. A look of dissatisfaction crossed Matthew Pyrritt's face as he saw that a large proportion of the customers were fashionable women buying the fancy stationery for which Tallent's had recently become known.

Mr Tallent's office was on the second floor and it looked rather too much like a gentleman's study for Mr Pyrritt's taste. Padded chairs and a leather-topped desk were not, in his opinion, conducive to a strictly business-like atmosphere. Mr Tallent, as he had expected, was extremely stiff and obviously embarrassed at having to talk to him.

'We may as well clear up one thing straight away,' Mr Pyrritt said. 'I don't hold it against you that you took up the case of the girl who was trying to extort money from me. I might have done the same in your case, though not without investigating a bit more thoroughly first. You were had, Tallent, by a plausible little liar.'

'I have to admit to an error of judgment,' Mr Tallent admitted with difficulty. 'She was a pretty child . . .'

'Yes, I remember that,' Matthew said reflectively. 'Yellow hair and blue eyes. One shouldn't let it influence one's judgment, but it does, Tallent, it does.'

'I never suspected that she was capable of such lies. And now, as you no doubt know, she's disappeared.'

'I thought you had her in your keeping – in a strictly respectable sense, of course.'

'No, Letty has gone, and so has the young lad who was her . . . her . . .'

'Paramour?' Matthew suggested with what Mr Tallent thought quite unseemly levity. He ignored the intervention and pressed on with what he was going to say.

'And poor Miss Kerslake has been robbed . . .'

'The devil she has!'

'You didn't know that either? Oh, yes, several precious possessions were stolen from her trunk while the staff were visiting your house in Surrey and naturally the disappearance of Letty Jones and Dick Cross throws suspicion on them. I'm surprised the matter hasn't been reported to you.'

'I don't concern myself with every trifling misdemeanour amongst my staff,' Matthew said impatiently. 'Though in this case . . . yes, I'll look into it.'

'I imagine we're wandering from the subject on which you wished to speak to me,' Mr Tallent suggested.

'I want to know whether you've had any second thoughts about letting me have your premises,' Matthew agreed.

'No. My refusal stands.'

The door opened and a girl came in, moving with difficulty, her twisting, lurching walk totally at variance with the astonishing beauty of her face. Mr Pyrritt, with a courtesy that amazed Mr Tallent, got to his feet.

'Papa, may I disturb you for a moment?' Mary said, before she realized that her father was not alone. 'Oh, I'm sorry! I thought you had no appointments this afternoon.'

'Mr Pyrritt called without prior notice,' Mr Tallent said heavily. 'Mr Pyrritt, my daughter Mary.'

Mr Pyrritt held out his hand and to her own surprise Mary found herself shaking hands with the man she regarded as her father's enemy.

In her confusion she dropped several of the sheets of

190

paper she had been carrying and, with the same surprising politeness, Matthew Pyrritt bent and picked them up. He glanced at them as he straightened up, then stood looking through the sheets without handing them over.

'I see you are the artist behind your father's resurgence of business,' he remarked 'I must make you my compliments, Miss Tallent. Your first designs for the new stationery were excellent and these are just as good.'

'Oh, no! I'm not responsible . . . I'm afraid I'm not artistic at all,' Mary stammered, her confusion heightened by the realization that this was Genevra's employer holding the new designs her friend had passed on to her only the evening before.

'I suppose I'm not to be told who the designer is?' Matthew asked.

'That is our secret,' Mr Tallent said.

They were on tenterhooks for him to hand the designs back, Matthew could sense that, and it made him take a perverse pleasure in examining the drawings more closely. They were good, he saw, possibly even more striking than the first batch. Suddenly he stiffened and shot a look at Mr Tallent's rigid face. Scribbled on the corner of the designs Genevra had written, 'Mary, do you think this background should be blue?' and had added her Christian name.

Without a word Matthew Pyrritt handed the designs back to Mary. She took them thankfully and made for the door, covered in confusion once more as he moved in a leisurely way to hold it open for her. When he turned back to her father, Mr Pyrritt's face was inscrutable.

'To go back to what we were saying,' he said. 'I have a very accurate idea of what your turnover was for the last quarter and it wasn't enough to cover your overheads, no matter how much fancy stationery you may be selling. You won't sell out to me – which I think is very misguided of you – but how about a straight exchange for alternative premises? I'm now in a position to offer you excellent accommodation only a short distance away and I'll pay the expenses of your move. Be a sensible man and accept before you go bankrupt.'

It was hardly the language of diplomacy and Mr Tallent reddened angrily.

'I hardly see how you can be conversant with my affairs in such detail,' he retorted. 'You've had my answer – I won't be driven out by you and that's my final word.'

Matthew shook his head. 'You're a very obstinate man,' he said.

He left without another word and that abrupt departure and something almost regretful about the way he had spoken sent a chill over Mr Tallent.

As for Matthew Pyrritt, he clattered down Mr Tallent's stairs in a mood which defied analysis. Mr Tallent's obstinacy was annoying; but most of his mind was given over to the discovery that it was Genevra who was responsible for the attractive stationery which he had admired and envied in his rival's window. That wretched girl, that thorn in his flesh. He could cheerfully throttle her for the way she had upset his well-organized life. Why couldn't she have married him when he'd asked her? That would have settled everything in a way which, if she could only have seen it, would have been as satisfactory for her as it would have been for him.

And she'd been robbed. That made him angry. Something would have to be done about that. The tiresome Jones girl and her accomplice would have to be traced, which was a great nuisance just when he had thought he was shot of the affair. Prosecution? Genevra would dislike that. She had probably already decided to forgive the girl, which was a weak and irresponsible way to deal with a crime, however minor.

192

As for her misdemeanour in aiding his rival, Matthew decided to meet that head-on. As soon as he reached his office he sent a message downstairs that he wanted to see Miss Kerslake . . . immediately.

It was the end of a long hot day and Genevra was tired. She had been helping to set up a new display on the counter and a few strands of hair had escaped from the smooth bands in which she wore it in the shop. Her feet and legs ached: they never seemed to stop aching no matter how accustomed she grew to long hours of standing. Her face was pale and there were dark smudges beneath her eyes. Matthew Pyrritt saw the signs of strain and frowned.

'You'd better sit down,' he said.

As their eyes met a flood of colour rose in Genevra's face and then receded.

'I've just been visiting the Tallent's next door,' Matthew said. 'Friends of yours, aren't they?'

'Yes. I help Mary Tallent in her Sunday School.'

'Very worthy. And you help her father in his business.'

'Did Mr Tallent tell you so?' Genevra countered.

'I saw some of your drawings. You'd been unwise enough to put your name to one of them. I congratulate you. Excellent designs. Why haven't you put them at the disposal of your employer?'

'I did tell Mr Bates that I had some ideas for improving the stationery department here and he wasn't interested,' Genevra said.

'But did you actually show him your drawings?'

'No.'

'Come, come, Genevra. This quibbling isn't up to your usual standard of truthfulness. If Mr Bates had really known what you had in mind he would have been a fool to dismiss your ideas so summarily. You squared your conscience by mentioning something to your superior, and then you gave the designs to my rival. Why?'

'Because I wanted to help the Tallents. And please call me Miss Kerslake. I have never given you permission to use my Christian name.'

'I've half a mind to tell you that I'll call you exactly what I like, but I don't want to give you that handle against me. Why do you want to help the Tallents at my expense?'

'Because it isn't good for you to be forever getting your own way. Why can't you admit defeat and let Mr Tallent go on trading from the shop where his family has been established for generations?'

'How many generations does fifty years constitute? An alternative site would be just as suitable for him, whereas that corner is the only possible place for me to extend.'

'Pyrritt's is big enough already.'

'I want the whole island site.'

'You want – you want – that's the only thing that matters!'

Genevra caught herself up, frightened by the anger that had exploded in her. Making an effort she said stiffly, 'I'm sorry, that was not a suitable way for me to talk to you.'

'Speak your mind. My shoulders are broad enough to take a little criticism, even when it's ill-informed and misguided. Come over here.'

Reluctantly, Genevra followed him to the other side of his office, to where some plans and a large drawing were laid out on a table.

'This is my father's original design for the store he never lived to see completed. He meant it to take up the entire island site. I've tried for years to get Mr Tallent to see reason . . .'

'And not only Mr Tallent,' Genevra said with deceptive

sweetness. 'I've heard that there was a butcher who went out of business because you took away his customers; and a drapery which sold out to you at a knock-down price, not to mention the small hotel which used to stand on the far corner.'

'I dealt fairly with them. I may have driven a hard bargain, but that's business.'

'Your idea of business, not mine.'

'And that, dear Miss Kerslake, is why I'm a success and you are in my employment.'

'Am I still in your employment?' Genevra asked. 'I thought you were probably about to dismiss me.'

'What would you do with yourself then? Go and work for Tallent?'

'I doubt if he could afford to pay me, though I'm sure he would try if he considered that my dismissal was his fault. Mr Tallent is a good man.'

'And easily deceived. He should never have got involved with Letty Jones.'

'He acted out of the kindness of his heart,' Genevra answered, even though she was not entirely convinced of that herself.

'*And* to get back at me. We're none of us saints, Miss Kerslake, not even your friends the Tallents. I repeat, what will you do if I throw you out?'

'I had an idea of setting up my own little shop, but even my small capital from the sale of Marietta I owe to you and I don't know that I care to take advantage of your . . . your charity. I ought to pay the money back.'

'Over my dead body! No one is going to deprive me of that mare after the expense I've been put to in getting her served by a top stallion.'

It amused him that Genevra took this speech entirely in her stride; while Genevra – accustomed all her life to hearing the breeding of horses freely discussed – was at a

195

loss to account for the way he was looking at her with the corners of his mouth tucked in as if he were trying to suppress a laugh. He disconcerted her even more the next minute when he said abruptly, 'I hear you've been robbed. Was Letty Jones responsible?'

'I'm afraid so.'

She turned her head away, trying not to let him see how much the thought of it hurt her.

'Tell me what you lost,' Matthew Pyrritt said, and the gentleness in his voice unnerved Genevra even further.

'My pearl necklace, a gold fob watch and a gold locket on a chain. That's the thing I really regret. It held a miniature of my grandmother as a young girl, and my mother treasured it greatly.'

'What possessed you to keep them in your room? You should have left them with Ryman or put them in the bank.'

'I never thought of it,' Genevra said. 'They're things I've always had with me. I packed them with my clothes as a matter of course. I didn't know I wouldn't be allowed to wear jewellery in the shop.'

That was a dig at him, as Matthew very well knew.

'I can't have my girls decking themselves out like Christmas trees,' he retorted. 'A simple gold locket for you is one thing, but think how some of the girls would bedizen themselves, given the chance.'

Genevra recognized the truth of that, but she was not going to say so. She kept her face averted and gave a tiny sniff.

'I'll try to get them back for you,' Matthew said in a goaded voice. 'Here, take this handkerchief and wipe your eyes. I can't bear women crying around the office.'

'I don't want Letty to go to prison,' Genevra whispered.

'I knew you'd say that. What a nuisance that stupid girl has been.'

196

'She didn't have the benefit of a good upbringing,' Genevra said earnestly.

'Dragged up in the gutter and that's where she'll stay to the end of her days,' Matthew Pyrritt said. 'Oh, don't cry any more! I could have prosecuted her for that extortion attempt she made on me and I didn't. I thought that would please you.'

'I suppose it was quite generous of you,' Genevra admitted.

'Good of you to say so! If I'd had the little slut clapped in prison you wouldn't have lost your precious possessions, have you thought of that?'

'It can hardly have been Letty herself who climbed along the roof and got in our window,' Genevra said. 'I think it must have been Dick. I suppose they made up their quarrel.'

'Do you think she persuaded him the brat might be his after all?'

'It seems the most likely explanation. It looks as if they've run away together. Mr Tallent is most upset about it after the trouble he went to to get Letty into the Home.'

'Which brings us back to our other difficulty. I can't have you selling your work to him, you know.'

'I didn't sell it, I gave it freely,' Genevra protested.

Matthew closed his eyes. 'Heaven preserve me!' he murmured. 'You have no commercial acumen at all. Those designs were worth money.'

'It was a matter of friendship. Have you ever had a friend, Mr Pyrritt?'

'You say that as if you were convinced that the answer must be no,' Matthew said. 'Yes, I do have friends, Miss Kerslake, and I suppose from time to time I might do one of them a favour. All right, I accept that your motives were of the best, but it must stop now that I know about it.'

'And what will happen if I refuse to give up helping my friends?'

'We're back to the question of dismissal, aren't we? You seem determined to provoke me into giving you the sack, but I shan't let you go that easily. Let me see, what can I do? How about this – every new design that appears in Tallent's window will be reproduced exactly in Pyrritt's stationery department at half the price.'

'You'll lose money.'

'Revenge is sweet.'

'It's despicable!'

'So is suborning one of my employees to do work on the sly that cuts into my profit.'

'It wasn't like that! I *offered* . . .'

'That kind heart of yours is for ever getting you into trouble.'

'You're laughing at me!' Genevra said in sudden suspicion. 'I think I'll save you the trouble of sacking me. I'll resign!'

'And what then?'

'I might get married.'

'The devil you might! Who's the lucky man?'

'It's none of your business. He's a very respectable young man and he likes me . . .'

'It's that young solicitor. A dull dog if ever I saw one. Don't marry him, Genevra. You'll be suffocated with boredom.'

'Better to be bored – which I wouldn't be – than to be bullied and . . . and mocked

'I'm not mocking you. I'm giving you very good advice. Are you in love with the lawyer?'

Genevra was silent.

'You're not. What's become of your high ideals? You

wouldn't marry me because you didn't love me, but you're prepared to consider taking him on.'

'It's different,' Genevra said helplessly. She struggled with herself to understand why it was easier to think of entering into marriage with Arthur Hendry than with Matthew Pyrritt. 'I have an affection for him, which I didn't have for you because I didn't know you.'

She thought again while Matthew waited and at last she said, with the honesty which had usually characterized her dealings with him, 'Arthur's expectations are lower than yours would have been. If I marry him I shall be able to measure up to what he wants.'

'You're condemning yourself to a life of mediocrity, my dear.'

'The alternative seems to be to remain a spinster and continue working for you.'

'I can think of at least two other options. One of them is to patch up your misunderstanding with your cousin, go back to living with her and take up the life you ought to be leading.'

'As a dependent parasite? No thank you.'

'And, of course, there's still the problem of Sir Francis. You let that cat out of the bag when I – er, forgot myself.'

Genevra's face reddened once more, but she said in a determinedly offhand way, 'Then you'll understand why I will not return to Leonora.'

She waited for him to tell her the other option, but he remained silent.

'What are you going to do with me?' she asked, when his frowning silence began to seem oppressive.

'If I forbid you to supply any more of your charming designs to Tallent, will you take any notice?'

'If you give me an order I suppose, as one of your employees, I'll have to obey you.'

'Grudgingly, and holding it against me! I don't want that. Very well, I won't ask you to stop helping the Tallent family; but in return, and in justice to me, I want you to come with me to look at the premises I'm suggesting for Tallent. I think you'll be surprised at what he's refusing to consider.'

'I can't run about London with you,' Genevra said, trying to find a way out of doing what he wanted. 'What will everyone think?'

'That's something that bothers you a great deal too much. I think it's the least you can do considering the concession I'm making over your drawings.'

There seemed to be no way she could refuse him. He was being far more forebearing than she had expected over something which, uneasily, Genevra had always felt was somewhat underhanded. He was hard, unfeeling, immoral – but he did have some redeeming features, and it was only right that she should, as he had said, do him justice. Besides, there were times when he had been extraordinarily kind to her and it was possible that Mr Tallent was misjudging him after all.

12

The inspection of the premises Mr Pyrritt wanted Mr Tallent to occupy took place on the following Saturday afternoon. Genevra, already on the defensive because of what her workmates saw as her friendship with their employer, had insisted that she would not be seen walking out of the store with him. She went back to her lodgings after the morning's work, changed into one of the light-weight cotton gowns which belonged to her previous life and slipped out with a vague murmur about going for a walk with Mary Tallent, which was perfectly true because Genevra had taken the precaution of including her friend in the expedition.

When they met Mr Pyrritt she saw the quick twitch of his thick eyebrows and the way his mouth turned down in a sardonic line and hurried into speech.

'You do know Miss Tallent, don't you? Mary has never seen the place you want her father to take and so I suggested she should come with us.'

'A chaperone,' Matthew murmured. 'How very prudent!' But he raised his hat to Mary and proffered her his arm with exemplary courtesy.

'I get along better on my own,' Mary said with cheerful directness. 'Poor Genevra has been on her feet all the morning and probably needs your arm more than I do, Mr Pyrritt.'

'Ah, but will she take it? In fact, the distance is very small. Just round the corner and down the road.'

'Not fronting Oxford Street,' Genevra pointed out.

'Unfortunately not, but that means that the overheads will be lower.'

They were reduced to a slow saunter by Mary's inability to walk any faster. Genevra lifted the skirt of her gown with the tips of her fingers to keep the delicate fabric from dragging in the dust. It was quite the prettiest of her summer gowns, a cotton voile sprigged with violets, moulded fashionably close to her figure, with the skirt looped back to a large bow of purple ribbon. Because it was two years old it had been made without the extreme bustle which was beginning to jut out from the back of the newer gowns and the line was all the more charming for that. On top of her head she wore a tiny hat of mauve straw with a bunch of violets peeping out from under the little brim. She had even discovered the parasol which had been ordered to match her gown and used it now to shield her face not only from the sun but also from Mr Pyrritt's too searching eyes.

Since Genevra was being aloof he directed his conversation towards Mary. 'I believe you do a great deal of charitable work, Miss Tallent?'

'I try to be of use,' Mary agreed. 'I hope before we part I shall be able to sell you a ticket for the concert we are organizing in aid of the Home for Mothers and Children . . .' She broke off, realizing that this was perhaps an unfortunate reminder.

'The one where young Letty Jones was housed for a time?' Mr Pyrritt said with cheerful unconcern. 'Yes, I should certainly support that.'

'I'm singing a solo and Genevra has agreed to accompany me both for that and the duet I am to sing with Mr Hendry.'

'I'll take ten tickets.'

Genevra tilted her parasol so that she could see his face.

'To buy ten tickets and then not to attend may seem charitable, but your empty seats will be a great discouragement to the performers,' she said.

'I'll get up a party and come in style.'

The parasol went back to an angle at which he could only see the tip of her chin, but even that small glimpse of her face was enough to reveal that Genevra did not want him at her concert.

The premises they were to inspect were soon reached, even with the handicap of Mary's dragging walk. The building was, as even Genevra had to admit, not only as good as the Tallent's present premises, but possibly even better. Certainly the shop area was equally spacious. It was also more modern and better lit.

'A suite of rooms upstairs for living quarters, just as you have at present,' Mr Pyrritt pointed out. 'Do you feel equal to tackling the stairs, Miss Tallent?'

'You go ahead and I'll come after you,' Mary said. 'No, I'd rather not have any help. I'll cling to the banister and get myself up.'

Since she obviously did not want to be watched, Genevra and Mr Pyrritt obeyed her and walked ahead up the stairs. Even though they took them slowly they had reached the first floor while Mary was still labouring over the first half dozen stairs.

'One can only admire her courage,' Mr Pyrritt said under his breath. 'To preserve a cheerful spirit in such a body . . . I don't think I could do it.'

'She suffers a great deal of pain, but she never complains,' Genevra said quietly.

'I suppose they've had first-class medical advice?'

'One of the reasons Mr Tallent is a poor man is that he has expended large sums of money trying to obtain help for Mary.'

'Such beauty, too! I never saw a lovelier face.'

He turned his eyes towards Genevra and added, with a jeering note in his voice which she realized stemmed from his reluctance to admit to the softened feelings Mary aroused in him, 'Not even yours, my dear, and I must tell you that you look quite delightful in that pretty outfit.'

Mary arrived, breathless and with a line of pain between her eyebrows, and he went towards her saying, as if he did not notice her distress. 'I've complimented Miss Kerslake on her appearance and now she's embarrassed and won't speak to me. I rely on you, Miss Tallent, to admit that this is a most charming room. There's a low windowsill here where you can sit for a moment to admire it. Now, don't you agree that this would make a fine drawing room?'

'Yes . . . I have to admit that it would,' Mary said, subsiding thankfully on to the wide ledge he indicated. 'As for Genevra, I never saw her looking better.'

She smiled at her friend with warm affection, as if no thought had ever crossed her mind about the contrast between them, and for once in his life Matthew Pyrritt was humbled by simple goodness.

'I wish you could persuade your father to move to these premises,' he said with a troubled look on his face.

'He's very attached to the place where he was brought up,' Mary explained. 'We've been in Oxford Street a long time, Mr Pyrritt.'

'Who owns this building?' Genevra asked.

'I do,' Mr Pyrritt said in surprise. 'I'm prepared to make it over to Mr Tallent in exchange for the site I covet. It would be a good bargain for him if he could only be brought to see it. I tried to buy him out, but that didn't answer: so this is my alternative offer – and a generous one, though I say it myself.'

'Now that I've seen this building I'm prepared to tell

him that I think it would suit us,' Mary said. 'Whether that will sway him or not I can't say.'

'That's more than I'd hoped for, since I didn't know you would be coming along this afternoon,' Mr Pyrritt said. 'I merely wanted to persuade Miss Kerslake to do me justice.'

'And indirectly to get me to influence Mr Tallent,' Genevra suggested.

'That wasn't part of our bargain, but I did hope a kind word from you might help to change his mind.' He turned to Mary. 'You know I've given permission for Miss Kerslake to carry on designing your notepaper and knick-knacks? Mind you, I think she ought to be paid, but that's between her and your father.'

'You've been generous,' Mary said. 'But are you still going to close my father down if he refuses to fall in with your plans?'

Mr Pyrritt's reply was unexpectedly gallant, but Genevra at least noticed that he avoided a direct answer.

'I'll find it more difficult now that I know you, Miss Tallent. Talk him round – please. Now, young ladies, will you give me the pleasure of buying you an ice at Gunter's?'

'It's a little far for me to walk,' Mary answered regretfully.

'I ordered my carriage to be outside here at four o'clock.' He glanced out of the window. 'And it's just drawing up. Icecream at Gunter's and a drive round the Park?'

Glancing at Mary, Genevra saw that she wanted to accept and for the life of her she could not deny her friend the small pleaure that was offered to her.

Altogether it was an unsatisfactory afternoon from Genevra's point of view. Mr Pyrritt had shown himself in a good light: he had made Mary like him, which was peculiarly annoying, the building he wanted to make over to Mr Tallent was unexceptionable, and the little treat of ices in a fashionable tearoom followed by a drive under the trees in a luxurious carriage was undeniably pleasant. She could not have said why the whole thing made her feel out of temper, and yet it did.

Genevra asked to be set down with Mary when Mr Pyrritt eventually took them home.

'Still afraid of being seen with me?' he asked softly as he handed her out.

'If you had any understanding of the sensation it would cause if I were seen driving up to the hostel in your carriage you wouldn't ask that question,' Genevra replied. 'Thank you for your hospitality, Mr Pyrritt.'

'You are more than welcome, Miss Kerslake. And you, too, Miss Tallent. Good afternoon to you.'

'Well! And I thought he was such an ogre!' Mary said, watching the carriage drive away.

'So he is,' Genevra said crossly. 'Well . . . he has some good points, I suppose. He irritates me unbearably because I always have the feeling that under the surface he's laughing at me.'

'He admires you.'

'Nonsense!'

'No, truly, Genevra. There's something about the way he looks at you, as if he can't help smiling.'

'That's exactly what I said – he laughs at me,' – Genevra said with heightened colour.

Mary shook her head, unconvinced by Genevra's denial; but she let it drop, turning her mind instead towards the problem of convincing her father that perhaps after all they should move.

Mr Tallent was not pleased by his daughter's expedition. But he was influenced in spite of himself by her conviction that the new premises might suit them very well, even to the point of admitting that he had never been to look at the building and ought to do so before renewing his obstinate refusal to consider it.

'So Mr Pyrritt has attained his object,' Genevra said. 'Yes, I know he wasn't aware that I had asked you along this afternoon, Mary, but having got hold of you didn't he take advantage of it! He's an . . . an opportunist!'

Genevra walked back to her lodgings still feeling disgruntled. It was not far, but the walk through the hot dusty streets was a sharp contrast to the drive earlier in the afternoon, bowling along in a well-sprung carriage with a pleasant breeze created by their motion. In her pretty dress, with her parasol carried at just the right angle, she had felt like a young lady of fashion; and now she was ashamed of having given in to a moment of regret for what she had put behind her.

'There's a package been delivered for you, Miss,' the little maid said as Genevra entered the house.

Genevra looked in surprise at the small parcel, wrapped in brown paper, tied with string and copiously sealed with red wax, wondering what it could be. It had obviously been delivered by hand, since only her name appeared on the outside. She carried it upstairs to her room and wrestled for several minutes with the wrappings, which seemed to have been designed to prevent her opening the parcel.

Sally wandered in and sat down heavily on her bed.

'What have you got there?' she asked.

'I wish I knew,' Genevra said. 'I'll have to use my nail scissors on these knots.'

At last the packet was open. There was a brown cardboard box under the paper, again sealed with red wax.

'They don't mean you to get at it in a hurry, do they?' Sally commented.

Genevra lifted the wax seal with the blade of her scissors and raised the lid of the box. Inside were her gold watch, her pearls and her precious locket.

'I can't believe it,' she said in a whisper. 'I can't believe it!'

'Well, there's a turn-up for the book,' Sally said. 'Did our Letty have a conscience after all?'

'Oh, I do hope so! It's wonderful to get my things back, but best of all is the thought that Letty – if it was Letty, or rather Dick, who stole them – has thought better of it and returned them. And it must mean that they're all right for money, mustn't it?'

'Probably pinched something else to get them out of pawn,' Sally suggested.

'No, no! don't say that,' Genevra pleaded. 'Dick has got a job, I'm convinced of it. He's able to provide for them. Oh, I do wish Letty had included a note, just a word to say how she is.'

Sally looked at her curiously, taking in her excited flush, the smile that trembled on the verge of tears.

'You're a good sort, Jenny,' she said. 'Still worrying over that worthless little slut, aren't you?'

'I feel responsible for her being found out,' Genevra admitted. 'Sally, this afternoon I went with Mary Tallent and Mr Pyrritt to look at the shop he wants her father to take, and afterwards he gave us ices at Gunter's and took us for a drive in the Park.'

'I thought you were dressed up to the nines! Did you enjoy it?'

'Very much, except for feeling all the time that someone from the shop was sure to see me and misunderstand.'

'Is that why you told me?'

'I suppose so. I don't like secrets, concealing things. I kept quiet about my background and now I feel you all distrust me.'

'It's not distrust exactly,' Sally said. 'More a feeling that you're different. Not just because your family are Kerslakes of Leylands House – much I care for that! – but because of the way you behave and the way Mr Pyrritt takes notice of what you say. He does, you know. Have you heard the latest? The new hostel is ready for use and we're down on the list to move.'

The move took place the following week. Sally, Ruth and Genevra found themselves occupying a newly-decorated room, with a bathroom and lavatory on the same floor which they had to share with only three other girls.

'Luxury!' Ruth gloated. 'And the beds are much more comfortable than at Mountfort Street.'

'Plenty of hanging space,' Sally said. 'You'll be able to take your dresses out of your trunk, Jenny.'

'It's clean,' Genevra said with satisfaction. 'And we can actually see some trees out of the window.'

'Have you seen downstairs? A recreation room! Books and some board games for rainy days. And armchairs! I can't remember when I last sat in an armchair. Even at home our armchair is Dad's and no one else ever sits in it.'

'It was you told Mr Pyrritt we were overcrowded, Jenny,' Sally pointed out. 'You see, he *does* take note of what you say.'

Because of these pleasant changes and the satisfaction of having her stolen jewellery returned, Genevra prepared for the charity concert in a happier state of mind than she had known for some time. She wore her black silk evening gown and her pearls, and felt a renewed delight as she fastened the strand around her neck.

'Very distinguished,' Sally said. 'You do us credit, Jenny.'

'A bit sombre for my taste,' Ruth commented.

209

'I'm only the accompanist, so I have to keep in the background,' Genevra explained.

'Fancy getting permission to stay out all night,' Sally said.

'The concert will be over late and there's to be a reception for the musicians afterwards,' Genevra explained. 'It was very kind of Mrs Tallent to ask me to stay with them. I shall spend tomorrow there, too, as it's Sunday.'

'Church in the morning, Sunday School in the afternoon – you're getting proper pious,' Ruth remarked. 'Has that young man who sometimes walks you home got anything to do with it?'

'Of course not,' Genevra said, but her heightened colour made the other girls suspicious.

'He's a solicitor,' Sally informed Ruth. 'And very nice, too, if you like the quiet kind. We'll see our Jenny married off yet. Can we both be bridesmaids, Jenny?'

'You do talk nonsense,' Genevra said. 'Mr Hendry is just a friend.'

She ran down the stairs followed by their disbelieving laughter and could not help smiling. Arthur Hendry was more than a friend, as she very well knew, and the rehearsals for the concert had drawn them even closer together than they had been before. He was such a dear, she liked him so much. She would probably marry him. It was almost certain. She was on the verge of committing herself.

Genevra could tell that the concert was a success from the solid hum of conversation in the hall beforehand, from the pleasure of the performers at the applause they received and from Mr Tallent's beaming face as he totted up the takings. Some of the more sophisticated people might have been condescending about the dramatic sketch and the comic recitation, but every rustle in the hall was stilled by the glory of Mary's voice.

It had been Genevra's suggestion that the concert should conclude with a group of songs and that the curtain should be lowered and raised again to reveal the stage arranged as if it were a drawing room, with Mary and Arthur already in place, the other performers grouped round them in chairs, and herself at the piano. She had guessed, although Mary had said nothing, that it would be an ordeal for her to have to make her painful way across the stage in full view of the audience, in spite of her normal cheerful disregard of her disability.

Mary sang her solo, then Arthur came forward to sing his; finally they sang a duet and all the cast rose to join in a rousing chorus. The applause was tumultuous. Arthur looked round with a smile and held out his hand, insisting that Genevra should come forward to take her share of the acclaim. As she stood between him and Mary, with one of her hands in each of theirs, Genevra saw Mr Pyrritt and his party. In their silks and jewels they made a striking contrast to the rest of the audience. And to Genevra's fury, the woman sitting next to Mr Pyrritt was Leonora, and beyond her was Francis.

Since Mr Pyrritt had not only bought a block of tickets but had also made a generous donation to the charity, he was naturally invited to the party for the performers after the concert; and he had insisted that all his party of fashionables should join him.

'Do you really expect me to consume lemonade and iced cakes at this hour?' Leonora drawled.

'I do – though I'll top it up with champagne in my apartment afterwards, if you care to join me. You and Sir Francis, of course.'

'If you knew what an achievement it was to get him to

come with me this evening you wouldn't ask for anything more,' Leonora complained.

'I do know and I'm grateful, but I want more than that from you.'

From the languishing glance she gave him Matthew knew that she had read into his words a significance he had not intended. With a smoothness that concealed his contempt for her he went on, 'Make up the quarrel with Miss Kerslake.'

If Leonora was disappointed she concealed it very well. Her eyes opened wide and she said, 'But, my dear Mr Pyrritt, there has been no quarrel!'

'Not with you perhaps, though you can hardly have approved of her taking a job with me; but between Miss Kerslake and Sir Francis, I think there is still some . . . misunderstanding. If he makes an overture in this public place she will accept it.'

'Why should you care whether Genevra and Francis are on speaking terms or not?'

Matthew weighed his words carefully before he spoke. 'I believe Miss Kerslake may be married soon, but the man concerned has an eye to his position. It might ease the way if she were married from your house.'

'You *do* take an interest in her! You would be right, of course, if she were going to take her place in the county. But if it's the young man who held her hand on the stage I can hardly see that it matters whether we acknowledge her or not.'

Matthew took her hand and smiled into her eyes.

'A whim,' he said. 'Do it to please me, Lady Hamden.'

'Why should I put myself to any trouble on your account?'

'Because I'm a coming man, Lady Hamden, and you do like to be in the swim.'

'Oh, you impossible man!'

Leonora had chosen to wear apricot-coloured satin to grace this strange occasion. It swirled round her as she moved towards her husband, standing alone and looking sulky, and as she walked the close-fitting skirt of the gown revealed the long line of her thigh. A luscious piece, Matthew thought dispassionately; but he had put temptations like that behind him.

'Francis, we are faced with a social dilemma,' Leonora said in her most conciliatory tone. 'We can hardly ignore Genevra. She's known to be our cousin. It will look so strange if we don't speak. Will you come with me and say something complimentary about her performance?'

'She cut herself off from us,' Francis pointed out. 'I don't see why we should put ourselves out to be nice to her.'

Leonora put her hand on his arm and moved closer.

'I'm told on very good authority that she's likely to be married soon, and a reconciliation with us would help matters along. So much more satisfactory than this eccentric job in Mr Pyrritt's store! My dear, I've been asked more than once what has become of Uncle Ludo's young daughter and I'm hard put to it to know how to answer. If I could reply that she had married – no matter *who* she married – it would dispose of the matter for good and all.'

Francis, too, had been embarrassed by enquiries about Ludo Kerslake's only child, and because of that he allowed himself to be led towards the group of people gathered round Genevra.

Leonora swooped on Genevra and kissed her on the cheek.

'My dear, such a delightful evening! You all did so well. Miss . . . Miss Tallent has a wonderful voice and Mr . . .' Her voice tailed away as she looked enquiringly at Arthur.

'May I present Mr Arthur Hendry,' Genevra said. 'Mr Hendry, my cousin, Lady Hamden.' She looked beyond Leonora and added in a colourless voice, 'And Sir Francis Hamden.'

Arthur was given Leonora's hand and a bewitching smile, but Francis contented himself with a curt nod.

'You play as well as ever,' Leonora told Genevra. 'I was disappointed that you merely accompanied and didn't play on your own.'

'I no longer have sufficient time to practice.'

'Silly girl! When will this notion of earning your own living come to an end? You must take a holiday and visit us, mustn't she, Francis?'

'Pleased to see you,' Francis said, resentment struggling with the knowledge that Leonora was a great deal more acute than he was when it came to social questions.

'And now we must leave,' Leonora said. 'I'd simply love to stay and meet all those divine performers, but we have another engagement – you know how full my life is!'

'You must have many calls on your time. It was good of you to give us your support this evening,' Arthur said in a respectful way that grated on Genevra.

Leonora smiled again with vague sweetness and led her taciturn husband away.

'Whatever your differences in the past, Lady Hamden seems prepared to forgive them,' Arthur remarked.

'*She* had nothing to forgive,' Genevra said.

For a few moments the two of them were isolated in the middle of the chattering crowd. When Arthur spoke again it was in a low confidential tone.

'Dear Miss Kerslake – Genevra – it's wrong to harbour resentment. I thought Lady Hamden was most gracious. Don't refuse the hand of friendship when she holds it out

214

to you. You must know how deeply concerned I am with your future . . .'

'You mean well,' Genevra said; and the way she spoke was enough to discourage a more ardent spirit than Arthur Hendry's. Without allowing him to say anything more she moved away and was engulfed in the group surrounding Mary.

It had not been kind to speak in such a quelling manner to Arthur. Genevra knew it and regretted that she had allowed her irritation to vent itself on him; but it had been very trying to have Leonora patronizing her and Francis grunting out meaningless invitations. She felt thoroughly put out and would have welcomed an opportunity of complaining to the man she held responsible for their presence. But Mr Pyrritt had gone off without so much as a word to her. Of course, her role that evening had been a minor one; she had deliberately kept in the background; she was of no importance at all. All the same, he might have spoken to her.

Genevra was subdued for the rest of the evening. When Mary suggested that she was tired she admitted that she did feel fatigued. That was what must be the cause of the dragging feeling of disappointment that sapped her energy and made her glad when Mr Tallent said it was time to leave.

They were escorted to the door by Arthur. He did not say anything, but Genevra knew from the warm clasp of his hand that he felt he had offended her and was asking for forgiveness. She smiled at him and returned the secret pressure, wanting him to know that she, too, regretted the fleeting cloud that had passed over their friendship. His face brightened and he would have kept hold of her hand, but Genevra shook her head with a smile of reproof and he let her go.

It was well after midnight before the two girls retired

to bed. Genevra looked round the comfortable, over-furnished room she was to share with Mary, slightly bemused by the very feminine style of decoration. The bed was draped with white broderie anglaise threaded with pink ribbons; similar hangings concealed the bottom of the dressing table; the carpet was a mass of pink roses, and the pink silk curtains at the windows were elaborately draped and tied back by golden cords. Then Genevra's amusement faded as she realized that this was Mary's sanctuary, the place where she could forget that she was not the same as other women, perhaps the place where she dreamed of the love and marriage that would almost certainly be denied her.

'What a pretty room!' Genevra said valiantly.

'Do you like it? Papa gave me a free hand as a present for my last birthday.'

'And did you give the order to Pyrritt's?'

'No! There was already bad feeling between Papa and Mr Pyrritt, even then. Mama and I took our custom to John Barker's.'

'Mary! Such treachery to Oxford Street.'

'I know, but the prices were extremely reasonable.' Mary sighed. 'I did hope that this evening Papa and Mr Pyrritt might become better friends, but they scarcely spoke to one another.'

'Mr Pyrritt hardly spoke to *anyone*,' Genevra said. 'I do think it was unkind of him to bring Leonora and Francis without a word of warning to me.'

'But they seemed to be so friendly towards you,' Mary said in surprise. 'And his party certainly added style to our little gathering. Lady Hamden's gown! It was quite, quite lovely.'

'Oh, Leonora dresses well,' Genevra agreed. 'And she was in good looks,' she admitted, struggling to be fair.

A nasty little suspicion crossed her mind that Leonora's

216

looks might have something to do with Mr Pyrritt's interest in her, but Genevra hurriedly dismissed it. Such thoughts were not to be indulged in, especially not in Mary's company. The lovely candour of her friend's conduct was a reproach to meaner spirits. In a sudden rush of affection Genevra bent and kissed Mary on the cheek.

'Goodnight, dear, sleep well,' she said.

It seemed that Mary was able to do just that. She dropped off to sleep almost immediately, while Genevra lay wakeful. Try as she might she could not help her thoughts turning towards the dilemma that faced her. Should she marry Arthur Hendry? It appeared that if she did he would expect her to be on terms of friendship with her cousins. Why? Did he want it for Genevra's sake or because he saw their social standing as enhancing his own position? He would be swiftly disillusioned if he thought that Leonora would include an obscure lawyer in any of her invitations. Would he mind? Would he be disappointed? Would it affect his feelings for Genevra? Genevra tried to tell herself that he had taken an interest in her long before their first meeting with Leonora; yet she could not help feeling that the relationship had increased her value in Arthur's eyes, and it was galling beyond words to know that he attached importance to a connection which Genevra would rather have discarded.

She turned over cautiously, not wanting to disturb Mary, and then sat up. She could smell smoke. Genevra sniffed again, telling herself that she must be mistaken. Mr Tallent had indulged in one of his rare cigars, the scent of it must have wafted up the stairs. But it was hours since Mr Tallent had finished his cigar and the acrid smell in the air had nothing to do with the aroma of tobacco.

Moving carefully, Genevra slipped out of bed, felt her

way across the room and opened the door. A wave of grey smoke billowed towards her like some evil phantom escaping from its hiding-place.

Genevra caught up her dressing gown as she hurried back to the bed to shake Mary urgently by the shoulder.

'Mary, Mary, wake up! We're on fire!'

13

Someone was pounding insistently on the front door of Mr Pyrritt's suite of rooms above the store, so that the noise eventually penetrated to his bedroom and roused him from sleep. He felt his way to the door and turned on the light, shielding his eyes against the sudden brightness. Electric light was a great boon, but it nearly blinded a man still half asleep.

On the landing outside he found one of the night-watchmen from the store, out of breath and in an agitated state.

'Oh, Mr Pyrritt, sir, there's a fire!'

'In the store?' Matthew demanded, instantly awake.

'Yes, sir. It looks bad, sir.'

'Have you sent for the Fire Brigade?'

'Jim's doing it, sir, but I thought of you up here and I came to warn you. Not that it's this end, but it's spreading so fast there's no telling where it may go.'

'Don't stand there, man. Get back and start fighting it. I'll throw on some clothes and be down in a minute.'

He seized trousers, a jacket and shoes at random and was dressed and running down the stairs almost before the slow-moving watchman had returned to the scene of the fire.

From the outside of the building it was obvious that the main conflagration was on the first floor. As the watchman had said, it was confined to the end of the building furthest away from Matthew's apartment. He had also been right in saying that it was burning fiercely.

'Don't just stand there!' Mr Pyrritt said, finding his

219

employee on the pavement, apparently hypnotized by the flames. 'Rouse some of the men in the hostel, start a bucket chain – and what about those fire hoses we fitted?'

'I'm thinking the first thing we ought to do is warn anyone who may be in Tallent's building,' the man said. 'The flames are running that way.'

'You're right. And the wind's in that direction, too. They may well be alight already.'

'No sign of life. They can't have woken up.'

'Where the devil's that fire engine?'

Matthew cast a look down the almost deserted street. It was after two o'clock in the morning and only one or two loiterers had drifted up to see the excitement. A policeman came hurrying up, feeling for his whistle to summon assistance.

'Has the fire service been called?' he asked.

'One of my men is seeing to it. Officer, lend me your truncheon. I'm going to break into the place next door to make sure they are aware of the danger.'

'Best leave it to the firemen, sir.'

Above them a window cracked, showering the pavement with fragments of glass. The flames seemed to take fresh life, leaping out of the empty panes.

'I dare not wait,' Matthew said. 'There are at least half a dozen people in there – a couple of servants, Mr and Mrs Tallent, their daughter – who is crippled and will need assistance . . .' His voice faltered as he remembered something he had heard that evening. 'And one of my own employees,' he finished in a flat unemotional voice.

Between them they managed to break the window in which Genevra's pretty stationery was displayed. Inside, the shop was in darkness, no electricity here, and they had to feel their way towards the stairs. There was a little smoke, filtering down from higher up, but on the ground floor little signs of the fire that was raging on the floor above in the store next door. Perhaps after all it had not penetrated the dividing wall.

There were sounds of activity on the stairs.

'Tallent, is that you there?' Mr Pyrritt called out. 'Get the women down. The fire's bad next door.'

'Is that you, Pyrritt? Take my wife. Genevra is helping Mary. I must go up and get the maids. They don't seem to have woken up.'

Matthew ran up to the first floor and took hold of Mrs Tallent.

'There's a policeman here who'll help you,' he said. 'Mary needs more assistance than you do.'

He stood aside to let her pass and jumped away from the wall in a hurry as he felt it hot against his back. Above him he could just make out the dim white figures of Mary and Genevra.

'Don't you worry about me, I'll manage,' Mary said, but her voice was a shaky whisper.

They could hear Mr Tallent shouting and banging on the door above and then frightened exclamations followed by the sound of the cook and maid hurrying down the stairs.

'Get down as quick as you can without falling,' Mr Pyrritt said when they reached the little group which had arrived at the turn of the stairs. 'Mary, I'm going to carry you.'

'I'll carry my daughter,' Mr Tallent said.

'Don't argue, man! I'm younger and fitter than you are. You go ahead with Genevra.'

Mr Tallent seemed to hesitate and then he obeyed and began to descend the stairs. Genevra was just behind him, but she paused and looked back to see Matthew sweep Mary up in his arms. There was only a space of three or four stairs between herself and Mr Tallent when a section of the wall between the two shops buckled and collapsed inwards. A great tongue of flame leaped through the gap, Mr Tallent gave a cry and they heard him fall; but they could see nothing through the curtain of fire and smoke.

Even though he had Mary in his arms Matthew managed to get a hand free to seize Genevra by the shoulder. She turned and clung to his arm. Without that support she thought that she must have fallen down through the hole in the stairs which the tumbling wall had created.

'Get back upstairs,' Matthew said in a hoarse voice.

They retreated to the landing and he put Mary down.

'It looks as if we'll have to wait for the firemen to rescue us, after all,' he said with a calm cheerfulness which was more reassuring to Mary than to Genevra, who detected the uneasiness behind his words. 'They'll be able to get a ladder up to the back windows.'

'All the first-floor windows have bars across them,' Mary said.

Matthew hesitated for only a second. 'Then we'll retreat to the second floor. Come along, Miss Tallent, let me help you.'

'I think we're too late,' Genevra said, with her horrified gaze on the stairs above them.

With a perversity that seemed deliberately malign the fire had leapt past the first-floor landing and the flames were licking eagerly at the stairs they had hoped to climb.

None of them spoke for a moment as they watched the encroachment of the fire on their way of escape; then Matthew said, 'If we can't go up then we'll *have* to go down. Is there any water up here?'

'A bathroom,' Mary said.

'Thank God for that. Come along, Genevra, you'll have to help me. I want the mattress off your bed and I want it soaking wet.'

Almost at once she saw his intention to attempt to

block off the wall for long enough to allow them to get down the stairs.

'We'll never get over the gap,' Genevra said.

'Yes, we will. Or, if we don't, the firemen will bridge it with their ladders – when they eventually get here, damn them.'

'How long is it since the alarm was given?'

'Less time than I like to think about,' he said grimly; and Genevra knew that he was telling her in an obscure way that he doubted whether they could afford to wait for the fire engine to arrive.

The mattress was unwieldy, but between them they hauled it to the bathroom. Heavy with water, it was even more difficult to handle, but Matthew levered it against the part of the wall that was still standing and began to slide it down the stairs. He reached the gap and the charred wood of the stairs cracked ominously beneath his feet. Genevra held her breath. The fire seemed to be reaching towards him, but he steadied the mattress and held it like a shield between himself and the worst of the flames.

It slid downwards, and there was a hissing noise as the flames encountered the water. For one moment the mattress teetered and then it lodged against a lower stair and held. Matthew turned his head.

'Start coming down,' he said.

It was only a few stairs, but to Genevra it seemed an eternity before they managed to creep down them.

'I'm going to lower myself to the part of the stair that's still intact and lift you over the gap,' Matthew said.

By the shifting light of the flames above them he looked from one to the other of the two girls.

'Mary first,' he instructed. 'Because it will be more difficult for her and she'll need your help, Genevra.'

'No . . .' Mary whispered.

'Don't argue,' Matthew snapped.

Genevra could feel the fierce heat through her thin nightclothes. It seemed as if it must sear her skin. The mattress shifted and she put out her hand to it; it was still wet, but getting hot.

'That's right, hold it in place,' Matthew said.

He swung himself down to a point at which the stairs would bear his weight and looked up.

'You'll have to lean right out,' he told Mary. 'Genevra, put your weight on her legs until I tell you I've got her safely.'

Genevra could feel Mary trembling all over. It appeared for one moment that she would not have the courage to reach out to Matthew's upraised arms; but then with a sob of fear she launched herself forward and he seized her under her arms, staggering as he took her weight.

'All right, let her go,' he ordered Genevra.

The smoke was bad again. The mattress had begun to catch and was sending out acrid fumes. Genevra could scarcely see what was happening below her. Her eyes were smarting, she was choking and coughing.

'When I put you down you'll have to make your own way to the front door,' Matthew said to Mary. 'There are people there ready to help you.'

'Papa . . .'

'We can't worry about him now. I must see to Genevra.'

'Yes, of course.'

She began to crawl away and Matthew turned back to the girl still crouching on the stairs above him.

'Do the same as Mary did,' he ordered. 'Lean out and I'll catch you. Come along, my treasure. Trust yourself to me.'

Genevra gave a choke, half sob and half laugh, and then coughed harshly as the smoke caught in her throat.

She did as she was told, reaching out towards him and Matthew took hold of her, a lighter weight than Mary had been, but just at the moment when his arms closed round her the charred mattress collapsed towards them.

Matthew staggered, lost his balance, and with Genevra clinging tightly to him fell through the gap in the stairs, as the burning mattress toppled on to them.

It was not a great fall, but it was a painful and dangerous one. Genevra fought her way out from under the smothering mattress, desperate for air. Her impact on whatever lay beneath them had been cushioned by Matthew's body, but he was lying ominously still. Around them the flames from the mattress and the fallen debris had begun to lick at the wooden shop-fittings, and the fire that had been released from the temporary plug provided by the mattress was roaring up the stairs.

Outside, at last, came the clamour of the fire engine as it raced up Oxford Street. Help was on the way, but Genevra could not leave Matthew in this dangerous position. She staggered to her feet, seized him under the shoulders and began dragging him in the direction of the window. Why did no one come and help her, she thought, not realizing how quickly everything had happened.

Matthew groaned and stirred. Genevra abandoned her attempt to move him and knelt down by his side.

'Mr Pyrritt! Matthew! Please, please try to hear me! We must get out!'

By the light of the flames she saw him open his eyes, then he raised himself on his elbow.

'God, my head! No, I'm all right. Only stunned for a moment.'

'Can you stand?'

'Have to.'

He got to his feet unsteadily, but apparently unharmed apart from the blow to his head.

225

'Lean on me,' Genevra said anxiously.

The ghost of a chuckle came wheezing out of him.

'I'm supposed to be rescuing *you*,' he said; and then they were suddenly surrounded by people, the men who had carried Mr Tallent to safety and gone to his daughter's aid, firemen playing hoses on the flames, policemen with solicitous hands to lead them out into the street.

So many people, so much noise, everything was in confusion. Genevra saw Mary at last and was thankful that she seemed unhurt; she had her arm round her mother, who was crying quietly. But Mr Tallent, blackened, bruised and bleeding freely from a cut on the head, appeared to be beside himself with fear and rage. With his eyes wild and his voice hoarse he turned on Mr Pyrritt.

'You murdering swine,' he said. 'You've ruined me. You've burnt out my business and nearly killed my wife and daughter. You can have the building you wanted. I've no further use for it.'

This can't be happening, Genevra thought. Mr Tallent is out of his mind. I'm going to faint. I've never fainted before in my life, but I'm going to do it now.

They were surrounded by a crowd of people – young men from Pyrritt's hostel who were no longer needed now that the firemen were in control; local residents who had been roused by the excitement, all avid for sensation. Unbelievably, someone laughed; Genevra heard it distinctly, a strange high chuckle, overstrung and hysterical. Matthew heard it, too. She saw him turn his head sharply towards the sound, momentarily distracted even from Mr Tallent's terrible outburst.

Someone pushed his way through the circle and seized hold of Genevra.

'My dearest girl, are you all right?' Arthur demanded. 'We heard the commotion and I came out to see what was happening, never dreaming . . . Thank God, you're safe! But you're hurt! I must get you to shelter, some clothes, a doctor!'

'I'm not hurt,' Genevra said, but as she spoke her overwrought nerves gave way. She burst into tears and collapsed into his arms.

14

Genevra woke up the next morning feeling rather worse than she had done the night before. Her head ached, her eyes were sore and her throat and chest felt as if they had been scraped. She was covered in scratches and bruises; she had burns which were of minor importance but extremely painful. It needed no great persuasion on Mrs Hendry's part for her to agree to remain in bed for the rest of the day.

Quite apart from giving her time to recover, the extra day also saved her from an interview with Arthur which Genevra was by no means sure she wanted. Mrs Hendry did not think it proper for a young man to visit a girl in her bedroom, even when she was unwell. So Arthur was only allowed to come to the door to make his anxious enquiries about the way Genevra was feeling, with his mother smiling indulgently in the background but with no intention of leaving the young people alone.

Genevra had been too dazed to consider the consequences when Arthur had insisted on taking her to his own home after the fire; but now she realized from the way Mrs Hendry spoke to her and from Arthur's solicitude that they both considered her as good as engaged to him. She felt trapped, as if a decision had been taken out of her hands and her future arranged without anyone consulting her.

She was kept very quiet that first day and only told that there had been many enquiries about her. The Tallents, she gathered, had found refuge with the Vicar of their church; but nothing was said to Genevra about Mr

Tallent's strange outburst, and Mrs Hendry was vague about what had happened to Mr Pyrritt.

It was not until the following day, when Genevra went downstairs in spite of Mrs Hendry's protests, that she saw the lurid accounts of the fire in the newspapers. They made it sound a great deal worse than she had thought it at the time, and that had been bad enough.

'Foul play suspected,' the headlines said, which caused Genevra to put down the paper with a troubled face. Mr Pyrritt was quoted as saying that the severity of the fire would not stop him from carrying on business; the damaged wing would be closed off and trade would continue in the remainder of the shop. The cause of the outbreak was only conjecture, but all the accounts agreed that it had started in storage space adjacent to Men's Wear.

'Mr Tallent is under medical care,' Mrs Hendry said when she realized that nothing would stop Genevra from discussing the fire. 'He was more badly hurt than anyone else and remained on his feet without attention for far too long. Mary and Mrs Tallent suffered, of course, but not to the same extent.'

'I'd like to see Mr Pyrritt,' Genevra said.

'Well, dear, we'll have to speak to Arthur, won't we, and see whether he thinks it advisable?'

'He did save my life,' Genevra pointed out.

'Arthur says it was a quite unnecessary piece of heroics. If you had waited quietly upstairs the firemen would have taken all of you out of the window.'

'Arthur obviously doesn't know all the circumstances.'

'Yes, dear. You're still a little overwrought. You mustn't get excited. Arthur will scold me if I let you upset yourself.'

Genevra said no more, but she was not in the mood to be dictated to by Arthur's mother. She wrote a brief note and asked the Hendry's maid to deliver it to Mr Pyrritt at the store.

It brought him round to visit her that afternoon. Mrs Hendry was flustered, neither particularly pleased to see him nor sure how to deny him access to Genevra. When she showed every sign of remaining with them in the drawing room Genevra said, 'I wish to speak to Mr Pyrritt on business, Mrs Hendry. He is my employer and I want to talk to him alone.'

'But, Genevra, my dear, what will Arthur say . . .'

'That is between me and Arthur,' Genevra said; and before she well knew what was happening Mrs Hendry found herself outside her own drawing room door. It revived all her former misgivings about Arthur's wish to marry this unconventional girl.

'You treat your future mother-in-law in a very high-handed way,' Mr Pyrritt commented.

'I am not engaged to Arthur Hendry,' Genevra said. 'Not yet, anyway. I'll make up my mind whether to marry him if and when he asks me.'

'He must think the question superfluous after the way you threw yourself into his arms on the night of the fire.'

'I was in a very shocked state. We all behaved strangely that night. What is happening about Mr Tallent's allegation that you started the fire?'

Mr Pyrritt shrugged his shoulders, as if he placed no great importance on Mr Tallent's outburst.

'The man was raving. He's been kept under opiates for the last two days. When he recovers he'll probably remember nothing of what he said.'

He studied Genevra's troubled face and added softly, 'I did *not* set light to my own extremely expensive and beautifully decorated shop in order to gain the run-down premises next door.'

'Of course not. Did you imagine I thought it was true?'

'You might have done, especially after reading the hints the newspapers are throwing out. Why did you want to see me?'

'To thank you for saving my life,' Genevra said carefully. 'To enquire about your own injuries. To find out how the fire started. They *coddle* me here. I want to know the truth.'

'The fire was started deliberately. Remains of oily rags have been found in a cupboard where the blaze caught hold.'

'Who would do such a thing?'

'There's plenty of choice. I don't lack for enemies. A business rival, a disgruntled worker who'd been given the sack, a supplier whose goods didn't come up to scratch. Mrs Thredgold and her brother are out of prison and their movements are being investigated.'

'I'm glad you don't mention Letty and Dick.'

'No, it couldn't have been them,' Mr Pyrritt said absentmindedly.

'I forgot to tell you, such a lovely thing happened! My stolen jewellery was returned. It made me so happy.'

'I'm glad about that. I haven't asked how you're feeling. You look very pale, and what's happened to your hair?'

'It got singed. And you?' Genevra studied him carefully. She thought he looked tired, with lines on his face she had never seen before. There was a livid bruise on his temple and both his hands were bandaged.

'You don't look at all well,' she said abruptly. 'I suppose you've gone back to work?'

'Naturally. There were decisions to be made.'

'And of course no one could make them but you.'

'That's right. Now, I daresay that anxious little woman will be back in a moment so we'd better make up our minds what's to be done with you. Do you want to escape from this place?'

231

It was exactly what Genevra did want, but she was reluctant to admit as much to Mr Pyrritt. While she was hesitating he went on, 'What I'd really like to do is to send you down to Leylands for a week or two.'

'That's out of the question!' Genevra protested.

'It might make Arthur Hendry think twice about proposing to you,' Mr Pyrritt agreed. 'In my opinion that would be no bad thing, but while you're still dithering about it I suppose it would be unwise to scare him off. The Hamdens are at Perry Court. You'd better go to them. In fact, I've already written to Lady Hamden.'

'You had no right to do that. If you can go back to work then so can I.'

'You'll be all the better for some country air first. Besides, I'm not at all sure that I shall take you back.'

'But you must! I've done nothing wrong. What am I to do if you dismiss me?'

'Go back to living with your cousins. Or marry Hendry. Or you can marry me. I always meant to renew my offer once you'd realized what a good thing you turned down.'

'I can marry *you*?'

Genevra felt as if she had been dealt a blow in the midriff which had deprived her of all breath.

'What a way to fling it at me! You were more respectful the first time you made me an offer, but of course that was before I became a mere shop girl.'

'I value you even more highly now than I did then.'

'And I've found out things about you that make me even more reluctant to accept you,' Genevra retorted. 'I'm certainly not going to tie myself to a man who intends keeping his wife in the country and his mistress in town.'

'Someone told you about Rose, did they? That's all over. I sent her away some weeks ago.'

'Poor woman! What's to become of her now?'

'She did very well out of the arrangement.'

'The arrangement!' Genevra exclaimed. 'You didn't care for her, any more than you do for me.'

'I was fond of Rose, in a way which I can see you may find difficulty in understanding,' Mr Pyrritt said slowly. 'She excited me, I desired her, and the only way I could have her was to buy her favours. The way I feel about you is completely different, though I do find you desirable, too.'

'Mr Pyrritt, this is a *shocking* conversation!'

'It is, isn't it? The thing is, I can only think of one way of convincing you that I do care for you and if Mrs Hendry comes back and finds me kissing you then that will put paid to your hopes of joining the Hendry establishment.'

'Please leave immediately.'

'Very well, but do keep my offer in mind. Go and stay with Lady Hamden and get your strength back. Think sensibly about your future. Hendry is a worthy young man, of course, and I'm a self-made rogue, but all the same you'll do better with me than you will with him.'

Genevra's obvious agitation after her talk with Mr Pyrritt put Mrs Hendry in a twitter and gave Genevra the excuse to retire to her room for the rest of the day. Arthur spoke anxiously about sending for the doctor once more, but Genevra insisted that it was unnecessary. She was glad to have some time alone to think.

Mr Pyrritt had told her to keep his offer in mind. Did he imagine she would be able to think about anything else? How dared he address her in such terms! Did he imagine she would marry him because he had said that he . . . that he *desired* her? No gentleman would say such a thing to a lady. She was shocked to the core.

Or was she? The more she thought about it the more Genevra realized that what really consumed her was a strong wish to know exactly what Mr Pyrritt had meant. He had not said that he loved her. Was love something different from the emotions he talked about? On the night of the fire he had called her his treasure. She had liked that. Even at that fraught moment she had experienced something of the warmth that had swept over her when he had kissed her. He was an outrageous man. She must put him out of her mind and, of course, she could not go on working for him. That was what she ought to be concentrating on: what she was going to do if she did not marry Arthur and did not return to her job at Pyrritt's. In the meantime, Genevra could see no better path to take than to go and visit Leonora and Francis.

She tried very hard to stave off a formal proposal from Arthur before she left, but that was not possible. The stage was set for them, they were left alone in the drawing room after dinner and it was obvious to Genevra that Arthur had already taken his mother and father into his confidence. Mrs Hendry's congratulatory smile as she got herself out of the room seemed to imply that she had no doubt of the outcome. Genevra felt harassed.

Arthur sat down beside her on the sofa and took one of her hands in his. Genevra let it lie limply in his grasp, but she kept her eyes lowered and Arthur evidently found this entirely natural.

'Dearest Genevra,' he said. 'You must allow me to call you that because you *are* the dearest girl in the world to me. I love you devotedly. I can only offer you a modest establishment, but my prospects are good. Will you be my wife?'

'Oh, Arthur . . .' Genevra said helplessly.

Glancing up, she saw from the satisfied smile on Arthur's face that he took this inadequate response as encouragement. She must try to put that right immediately.

234

'I am very attached to you,' she said. 'I honour you and I know that in many ways we are well suited to one another.'

'In every way,' Arthur said eagerly.

'Not quite. Our feelings are unequal. You care for me more than I do for you.'

'But once we are married, dearest . . . I know I can make you love me as I love you.'

'It's a risk I can't take,' Genevra said slowly. 'Not until I'm more sure of my . . . my regard for you. Let me leave my answer open until my visit to Leonora and Francis is over.'

'I'm afraid that once you're back in that life of luxury and fashion you'll forget me.'

'I shan't do that. I don't like Leonora's world.'

'Then share mine! Say yes, Genevra, please!'

'If you press me I shall have to say no, out of fairness to you. Give me time to think about it.'

'I've already been very patient. I thought you'd had sufficient time to reach a decision.'

'It should have been long enough,' Genevra agreed. 'It's because I'm still undecided that I'm worried in case my feeling for you doesn't go deep enough.'

She could see that Arthur did not fully understand her, but she was determined not to give in to his wish to have her fully committed to him before she went off to the country.

She leaned towards him. 'Will you kiss me, Arthur?' she asked.

Arthur was very much in love. Her words surprised him, but he had been longing for weeks to do just what she was asking and so he took her in his arms and kissed her on the lips. Genevra clung to him in a way that raised his highest expectations; but Arthur did not know that she was waiting for something to happen that did not happen.

'You see,' he said in an exultant whisper when they separated. 'You do love me!'

He was a little angry with her when he still could not shake her resolve and his parents could not believe that their son had been, if not rejected, then asked to wait on the whim of a girl who should, in Mrs Hendry's opinion, have been grateful to marry him.

It was a trying situation and Genevra was thankful to escape when the expected invitation from Leonora arrived. It was also a relief when Leonora made it clear that she did not intend altering her engagements for Genevra's sake.

'Delighted to see you back again, of course,' Leonora drawled. 'But at this time of year my life is just one long round of visits and I don't think I need put them off, do you? It's not as if you were ill.'

'I shall be perfectly happy on my own,' Genevra agreed. 'Except . . . will Francis be here at Perry Court?'

'My dear, are you afraid he'll pounce on you again? No. Francis is heavily involved elsewhere, dancing attendance on Maisie Castle. One cannot admire his taste! I suppose I shouldn't tell you such things, but you seem to have grown up in the last year. Are you staying with us indefinitely or are you going back to Mr Pyrritt?'

'I've had an offer of marriage and I'm going to decide about it while I'm here.'

'Congratulations! Much the best solution, of course.'

'I don't think I love him.'

'Oh, my dear, don't be romantic,' Leonora begged. 'If he can offer you a respectable establishment, take it.'

'You sound like Mrs Bertram,' Genevra retorted, which puzzled Leonora because the only Mrs Bertram she could think of was the housekeeper at Leylands.

236

Left to herself Genevra passed her days in much the same way as she had when she first went to live at Perry Court, except that now she did not have Marietta to ride and was confined to walks to places she could reach on foot.

Three weeks passed in growing boredom. She received two letters from Arthur, respectful notes saying how much he missed her but little else. She also heard from Mary and gathered that Mr Tallent had been restored to health and, Genevra hoped, his right mind. She did not receive any communication from Mr Pyrritt and although he was at Leylands from Friday to Monday each week he made no attempt to get in touch with her.

Genevra found herself resenting that long silence. He had asked her to marry him. Was he so sure that she would come round to the idea that he thought it unnecessary to do anything to fix his interest?

She had been nearly a month at Perry Court and had made up her mind that the following week would determine the course she intended to take, when a letter arrived for her from a most unexpected source – America.

Genevra looked at the envelope in bewilderment. The large, uneducated writing meant nothing to her. She slit open the envelope and removed the two sheets of rough lined paper. When she turned to the signature she discovered that it was from Letty.

Genevra was astonished by the pleasure it gave her to find that Letty had taken the trouble to write, but the contents of the letter came as a shock.

'Dear Jenny,' Letty had written. 'You will see from this that Dick and me are in America. Mr Pyrritt said I was not to write to you to tell you what he had done, but you know me never one to do what I was told. Jenny, I am very sorry about taking your things. I would not have

237

let Dick do it if we hadn't been desperate. They was not sold, only pawned, and always meant to get them back if possible. Dick believes now that the baby is his, which I always said it could be, and when Mr Pyrritt found us and said he would pay our passage to America we got married. The voyage was horrible I thought my last hour had come, but the baby survived alright and yours truly as well. It is due late October early November but I hope November as that will convince Dick it is his. Well, Jenny, I have to say that Mr Pyrritt was good to us in the end and I am sorry about what I said blackening his good name but it was a great temptation which I was led into by an older man that should have known better. I hope you received everything back safely and have forgiven me. Dick has got a job in a hardware store which suits him very well and we have two rooms in an apartment block and hope for better things later. No more for now, Jenny. Hoping this finds you well which Dick joins me in. Your esteemed friend, Letty Cross.'

Genevra read the letter through twice. Mr Pyrritt had found Letty and Dick; he had packed them off to America – just like him to find such a drastic solution; and he had rescued Genevra's stolen jewellery and returned it to her without a word. Why? What had made him go to such elaborate lengths to locate the two delinquents, redeem her locket, watch and pearls, and give Letty and Dick money, which must have gone against the grain with him?

As she sat thinking about it Genevra began to remember all his other strange acts of generosity. He had bought Marietta, at what she had always thought an inflated price; and no matter what he said about the mare's breeding value, Genevra was now convinced that he had done it so that she should have a little money of her own. He had, as the other girls pointed out, listened to her complaints about their living quarters and done something to improve them. He had thought of her at Christmas. He had allowed her to go on designing stationery for the Tallents.

His treatment of other people, too, was by no means inhumane. He had not behaved as harshly towards Mr Tallent as she had at first believed, since the proposed new premises were perfectly adequate. He had not prosecuted Alfred Cross, although he would have been perfectly entitled to do so, nor had he pressed the case against Letty. Instead, he had helped her and Dick.

Above all, he had watched over Genevra in a way which was quite different from his attitude towards his other employees. He loved her.

The more she thought about it, the more convinced Genevra became that this was the clue to Matthew's behaviour. He had been attracted to her when they first met and had thought that she would make him a suitable wife, and then as their knowledge of one another had deepened he had fallen in love with her. She saw, quite clearly, that he could not quite bring himself to say so, not without being sure of having engaged her own deepest feelings in return; and so he had been offhand about it, dropping hints which she could decipher if she pleased, preserving his pride, waiting for her to turn to him.

But was she going to turn to him? It seemed to Genevra that, like a traveller in an unknown land, she had to make a choice between two diverging streams: one progressing towards a gentle shallow river, meandering through a placid landscape; the other full of rocks and rough water, dangerous but exhilarating and – if she could steer her course successfully – ultimately leading to grander country than the safer stream.

A year earlier she would have been fearful of committing herself to the shoals and rapids of life with Matthew: now she knew that a conventional marriage to Arthur

239

would not satisfy her. She had been spoiled for the easy way by a glimpse of the joy of companionship with a man who would expect her to share his problems, especially the ones which were of his own making; a man full of faults, who might not always make her happy, but who would never let her sink into a dull acceptance of life. A large-hearted man who belittled his own generosity for fear of appearing soft. A hard man with a seam of tenderness which could be brought to the surface by the right touch. A man of quick sympathies and a rough manner. A man who could be ruthless and yet had principles from which he did not stray. A man who perceived his goal so clearly that he swept over obstacles in a way that seemed unscrupulous, but who was prepared to stop and make amends for the havoc he wrought. A proud man who could humble himself to admit his faults. A mass of contradictions. A man she could love in a way Arthur would neither expect nor understand.

Why was she telling herself that she 'could' love him? She did love him. It was already too late to consider marriage to Arthur.

Genevra sat so long that when she eventually moved she found that she was stiff in all her limbs. She went to her desk and wrote two letters. The first was to Arthur telling him, as gently as she could, that she could not marry him. The other was to Matthew, asking him to call on her when he was next at Leylands House.

15

Matthew did not flatter himself that he had handled his last talk with Genevra well. As always, she had thrown him off balance and he had found himself renewing his offer of marriage, which he had not intended to do – not there, not then.

It was a matter that occupied his mind more than was convenient at a time when he needed all his business acumen to rescue his enterprise from the disaster of the fire. He studied his rival, William Whiteley's tactics. Whiteley had had three disastrous fires and had not done too badly out of them. The thing to do was to announce a sale of damaged goods and buy in from a warehouse plenty of stuff which could be sold at a profit.

With this exhilarating prospect before him Matthew was able to dismiss Genevra from his thoughts, sometimes for as long as an hour at a time. She haunted him in the evenings, though, when he was alone and wishing he were not. It was the most difficult thing in the world not to rush over to see her when they were in the same county, within a few miles of one another; but still he held off.

He was in his office, surrounded by letters which needed urgent replies, when Eliza Littlejohn demanded to see him.

'Come in,' Matthew said with resignation. 'But keep it short. I'm up to my ears in work.'

'Work! Pushing a pen over paper. And not even doing that yourself,' Eliza said. 'I want to talk to you about the fire.'

'I suppose you know something the rest of us have missed? Why didn't I think of sending the Fire Brigade to ask your advice?'

'No need to be sarky. I hear you've packed Rose Peary off to Margate.'

'How do you get to know these things, Eliza?'

'Daft question. We all grew up in the same streets, didn't we? Your family got grand and moved to Holborn, but I've still got the old contacts. I knew Rose's Mum and Dad before she was born – if he *was* her father, which I take leave to doubt. Rose's Mum was just such a fly-by-night as her daughter grew up to be.'

'Never mind the family history. What's all this got to do with the fire?'

'Do you know Rose's son, Fred?'

'I only found out about him recently.'

'I expect she told you he'd grown up in the country? There was more to it than that. He lived with his Granny when he was a little lad, that's how I came to know about him. There were two fires in his school before he was ten, but no one ever found out what caused them. Mr Smith at the corner shop caught Fred pinching lollipops and gave him a clip round the earhole, and Mr Smith's garden shed burnt down. His Gran wouldn't let him keep rabbits in the yard and woke up one night to find the kitchen alight. They knew Fred was responsible that time, but they still thought it was a bit of childish naughtiness. Then he was caught setting fire to some stables, for no reason except to see the flames run through the straw, and after that he was put away.'

'He had an absurd idea that I was his father and he asked me for a hundred pounds to go to Canada,' Matthew said slowly.

'And you refused him. Pity, it would have been a good investment,' Eliza said with one of her sardonic chuckles.

'It's going to cost me a lot more than that to put the shop right,' Matthew agreed. 'I'm grateful to you for telling me this, Eliza, but it gets us no further. There's no proof that Fred was responsible.'

'I've not finished,' Eliza said. 'Fred's been employed here at Pyrritt's as a porter for the last couple of months, but he hasn't been seen since the fire.'

'That looks bad! Where will he have gone?'

'Back to his Mum or his Auntie Bea. If you can get hold of him and get the truth it'll put paid to these rumours about you setting the fire yourself.'

'No one really believes that!' Matthew protested.

'Mr Tallent seems to. Accused you to your face, didn't he? You'll have to clear it up, Matt, for the sake of your good name.'

'Tallent may take back what he said. I can't do anything while he's still incapacitated. And if it *was* Fred . . . I don't want my connection with his mother plastered all over the newspapers.'

He had a sudden thought and demanded, 'That reminds me, was it you who told Genevra Kerslake about Rose?'

'I might have let something slip,' Eliza admitted cautiously.

'You're a gossiping old woman. I didn't think you'd do that to me, Eliza.'

'You shouldn't have had us both to stay under the same roof at Christmas.'

Eliza Littlejohn took herself off, totally unrepentant, leaving Matthew in a dilemma about his next move.

It was a relief when he received Mr Tallent's card a few days later and was told that his former neighbour was waiting in the outer office.

Matthew stood up when the older man came in, but he did not offer his hand.

'I've come to apologize,' Mr Tallent said. 'I understand

that while I was not myself I said things which you may find unforgivable. I can only say that I have no recollection of it, only of something like a dream in which I blamed you for all my misfortunes. I didn't know I had spoken out loud.'

'You'd had a knock on the head. No man in his senses would have believed I'd do myself so much damage just to get hold of your premises. I've got something to say to you about that. There's nothing like nearly losing your life, let alone someone else's life, for putting things in perspective. If you want to hang on to that corner site you can keep it.'

'I was going to say almost exactly the same thing,' Mr Tallent said in astonishment. 'That night I thought I'd lost the dearest thing in the world to me, next to my wife – my daughter, Mary. It made my obstinacy over moving seem petty.'

'The dearest thing in the world . . .' Matthew said. 'Yes, precisely. Well, we seem to have changed places. Are we going to quarrel now about your wish to move and mine to prevent you?'

'I hope not. I can't carry on trade with the shop in its present state. I'd rather hand it over to you and make a fresh start.'

'You'll be short of stock. I'll be closing down my own stationery department and you can take what you want from me at cost price.'

'Good of you.'

There seemed to be nothing more to say, but Mr Tallent was reluctant to let the interview close as abruptly as that.

'Have you had any more news about the cause of the fire?' he asked.

'It was set deliberately. Someone with a grudge against

me, or an imagined grudge. I doubt whether we shall ever get to the bottom of it.'

After Mr Tallent had gone Matthew dwelt with satisfaction on the outcome of their talk. He had got the corner site he coveted and could complete his father's plan, provided he could raise the money, which might be a problem when he already needed a loan to restore the damage to the existing shop. He would have to apply his mind seriously to screwing as much as possible out of his insurance brokers, but first he needed to make a visit to Margate.

Mr Pyrritt took no one into his confidence about his trip to the seaside. He took a cab to the station and travelled by train after having informed his office staff that he would be in the City all day discussing his financial affairs.

He located without difficulty the house he had bought for Rose. She did not seem at all pleased to see him, something which he noted with interest.

'I thought we'd made a clean break,' she said.

'Found someone else already?' Matthew enquired.

'No, I haven't! And if I had, what's it to do with you? I'm known around here as a widow and I don't want anyone guessing different, that's all.'

'Is Fred living with you?'

'No, he's with his aunt.'

'But he's been on the loose in London, hasn't he? Was that wise?'

'He's old enough to look after himself.'

'I don't think he is, Rose. I doubt whether he ever will be. I've found out how – and why – you kept him hidden for so long. He'd been put into some sort of mental home, hadn't he? Your son is a fire-raiser, Rose.'

'I suppose Eliza Littlejohn told you that? Much she knows about it! There's nothing serious the matter with

Fred. He's like a child who plays with matches, that's all.'

'More dangerous than that, I think. Fred had a grudge against me – completely imaginary because I couldn't possibly have been his father, and there was no reason why I should give him a hundred pounds to go to Canada.'

'Is that what he asked?' Rose demanded incredulously. 'As if I'd have let him go, all on his own.'

'Why not? He's a grown man.'

Rose stayed silent and Matthew supplied his own answer.

'Because he's a danger to other people and to himself. Has he told you that he tried to burn down my shop?'

'There've been hints in the newspapers that you did it yourself,' Rose retorted with a flash of her old spirit.

'The man who said that has taken it back. When did you last see Fred?'

'He came here the day after the fire,' Rose admitted. Her shoulders sagged and she suddenly looked years older. 'I couldn't make out what was the matter with him at first. He was wild with excitement. I guessed when he told me there'd been a wonderful fire. He'd enjoyed it, you see, as if it had been a firework display. It means no more than that to him. Matt, what are you going to do to him?'

'He'll have to be put under restraint. People came close to dying because of Fred's liking for fireworks.'

'Not prison! It'd kill him and me, too, just when I've got myself settled.'

'A private clinic. Somewhere he can be watched and given a certain amount of freedom, perhaps even be allowed to do some work around the place.'

'He likes gardening,' Rose said, suddenly hopeful. 'But then there's the bonfires . . . that's how we first found out about his craze for lighting fires. Piles of leaves going

246

up all over the place and he always found the matches no matter where we hid them.'

'As I said, he'd have to be watched.'

'And who's to pay for this fancy clinic?'

'Considering what you've had out of me I should have thought you could have afforded it,' Matthew said.

'You're the one who's chosen the place and from what you say I don't doubt it's expensive. If you want my help in placing Fred there then you'll have to help with the cost.'

Looking at Matthew's grim face Rose thought that he was going to refuse.

'You'll not want stories in the newspapers about Fred being my son, with hints about our connection,' she suggested.

'You're right about that! Especially at the moment when I'm raising money for repairs and an extension.'

Matthew was still frowning, but he said, as if suddenly making up his mind, 'Very well, I'll bear the cost of the clinic, but I'll have to make it a condition that the doctors don't let Fred leave without my permission.'

'Fair enough,' Rose said. 'Fred's promised to come home this weekend.'

'Keep him with you. I'll get the doctor from the clinic to come and see him as if he were someone offering him a job.'

'I suppose I should be grateful for the way you've taken it,' Rose muttered. 'It's been a nightmare, not knowing where he was or what he was up to. I couldn't believe it when the first place he was in let him out. Too old, they said, they only looked after children. What is he but a child?'

She got to her feet, moving heavily. 'You don't want to see him yourself?'

'There's no point in facing him with what he's done. I

doubt if he's capable of understanding it. Besides, I don't want to revive the idea in his mind that I'm his father. And I don't want him dogging my footsteps all round London any more. I began to get quite unnerved.'

'You! You've got the nerve of the devil,' Rose said. 'Give us a kiss before you go, Matt.'

She was in tears as he kissed her, but Matthew hardened his heart and left. Comforting Rose was a complication he did not intend to add to his existing troubles.

On the whole he thought he had done well. Rose had broken down and admitted Fred's weakness more easily then he had expected and she had fallen in with the suggestion of a clinic with a speed which made Matthew realize how anxious she had been. He had been right to put up a show of resistance to bearing the cost, although he had always expected it to fall on him in the end. In her anxiety to avoid paying the fees herself Rose had agreed without a murmur to making the doctors responsible to Matthew so that at least he would get fair warning if the tiresome lout ever broke out again.

When Matthew arrived back in London he found Genevra's letter waiting for him. It was a stiff, formal note asking him to call on her and giving no hint of whatever decision she might have reached about her future. Damn the girl, was she going to marry Arthur Hendry after all, when he'd been so sure that if she had time to think about it she would realize what a mistake it would be?

The following Saturday Genevra received him in the library at Perry Court, surrounded by heavy leather tomes, a setting which made Matthew feel uneasy. The September weather had turned chilly and she was wearing a crimson gown he thought he had seen before. She had lost her pallor and her bruises and her hair had regained its customary smoothness.

'I was right to recommend country air,' Matthew said. 'You look like your old self.'

'I'm fully restored,' Genevra said. 'Please sit down, Mr Pyrritt. You make me nervous looming over me like that.'

He subsided into a chair, scowling at the coolness in her voice.

'If I want to come back to work next week will you take me?' Genevra asked.

'No, I won't. That tomfoolery has gone on long enough.'

'It was silly of me not to see that you were only playing at letting me earn my own living. However, I expected that reply and so I've made other arrangements.'

'Are you going to marry Hendry?'

'No, I've written to poor Arthur and refused him.'

'Good. I knew you'd see sense over that.'

'I've asked Mr Ryman to realize such assets as I have, and to look at the possibility of buying the goodwill of a small fancywork shop in Epsom. Knitting wool and embroidery silks and things of that sort, you know.'

'The devil you have!'

'Please don't swear.'

'That's not swearing,' Matthew said in surprise. 'Not compared with what I've got it in my mind to say. You can't do this, you idiot girl.'

'I think I can. But what concerns me, and the reason why I want to speak to you, is that I've heard from Letty.'

Genevra was pleased to see that he looked disconcerted.

'What did she have to say for herself?' he demanded.

'She told me about your remarkable generosity. I gather that you paid for her and Dick to go to America. What is more, you redeemed my jewellery from pawn and what bothers me is that now I have it in mind to sell it I really ought to offer to repay you.'

'Don't you dare try to give me money! I'll . . . I'll . . .'

'Choke me with it?' Genevra suggested.

'Something of the sort. You were my employee and I felt responsible for your loss. I'm glad to have been able to restore it to you.'

'Good. Then I can sell it with a clear conscience.'

'No!' Matthew almost shouted.

He forgot her injunction to him to sit down and got up and began walking about the room.

'What about my own offer?' he asked with his back to her.

'Oh, yes. A marriage of convenience to provide you with a housekeeper and hostess and me with a roof over my head. No, thank you.'

'It's *not* a marriage of convenience,' Matthew said. Goaded beyond endurance, he muttered, 'I love you.'

'Speak louder, please. I can't hear you.'

There was a faint tremor of laughter behind her words and Matthew was quick to catch it.

'I believe you're pulling my leg,' he said suspiciously. 'You've got no more idea of setting yourself up as a fancy-goods lady than you have of flying to the moon.'

'You can ask Mr Ryman if you don't believe me. I did ask him about the shop in Epsom, but I only mean to fall back on it if this talk with you doesn't go as I hope. For instance, if you can't bring yourself to tell me that you love me in a voice that I can hear.'

'I love you,' Matthew said experimentally.

He pulled her up out of her chair and stood holding her hands and looking down into her face.

'You know I do, Jenny. I've been in love with you ever since you came to my shop and started answering me back.'

'But that was *after* you'd asked me to marry you,' Genevra murmured.

'Oh, well. I liked the look of you before that and I did think it would be a highly convenient arrangement if you took me on and ran Leylands House. How was I to know that you would turn out to be quite different from the meek-and-mild young lady you seemed to be then?'

'We have got to know one another a great deal better over the past year. I certainly never imagined that I would come to admire you for your moral qualities.'

'Admire? Can't you say "love", Jenny? Do you mind me calling you Jenny? It's the way I always think of you.'

'I love it. I love you. I have every intention of marrying you.'

She had hardly got the words out before he began kissing her. It was just as wonderful as she had hoped it would be – even better than the time in the stableyard because now she was not shy of holding back, but eager to return the love that poured out of him.

'Oh, Jenny, Jenny, my dearest darling,' Matthew said, with a foolishness he would never have believed himself capable of. 'I'll be a good husband to you, I promise you, my treasure.'

'No, you won't, you'll be a terrible husband,' Genevra said, freeing herself from his embrace. 'I'll take second place to your business, you'll go up to London and forget about me, you'll leave me to deal with all the problems at Leylands and you'll ride roughshod over my ideas and bully me into agreeing with everything you want.'

'It sounds like a fairly good reading of my character,' Matthew agreed. 'Does the prospect daunt you?'

'It would if I hadn't come to recognize the other side of you, the thoughtful, caring, compassionate man you keep hidden. I want to cultivate that man.'

251

'That's only a very small part of me, but perhaps I can improve with your help.'

'I don't intend to be a passive little woman you can keep in the country to run your house. I need to have more of a purpose to my life than that. For instance, I'd like to help the girls like myself who have to earn their living and have no friends to assist them.'

'Spending my money?'

'More than that. I want your time – and I know how precious that is – and the prestige of your name behind my schemes.'

'So I'm marrying a social reformer?'

'Do you dislike the idea?'

'I'll try to adjust my mind to it,' Matthew said. 'I know you're not easily turned aside when you've made up your mind to do something.'

'I won't neglect you,' Genevra promised with a smile.

'That's what's worrying me, of course,' Matthew agreed, not entirely jokingly.

He leaned his cheek against the soft fair hair above her forehead and said in a low voice, 'I . . . I need you, too, Jenny. Just as much as your friendless girls, perhaps more.'

'I know, dear, and I'm glad you've said it,' Genevra said. 'Promise me you won't shut me out of your troubles. If I don't know what's worrying you I won't be able to help you.'

She smoothed back the hair from his brow and looked at him searchingly.

'You've had a hard time since the fire,' she said. 'I read the insinuations in the newspapers and they made my blood boil. Is Mr Tallent still under the impression that you were to blame?'

'No, we've sorted that out. He's agreed to move and we're better friends than we've ever been. And I know

252

who did start the fire. Sit down with me and I'll tell you about it.'

He made a brief story of it and at the end Genevra said, 'You're going to help her with him. That's good.'

'It means keeping in touch,' Matthew said. 'But there's nothing between us, you needn't fear . . .'

'I know. I'm glad you broke with her when you did. I wouldn't want to feel I'd been sharing you with anyone else since you started to love me.'

'The way I feel about you means that there's no room in my life for any other woman. It's a great surprise to me, let me tell you. I had no idea I was capable of loving like this. The night of the fire . . . the hardest thing I've ever done was to take Mary out first.'

'But it was right and so you did it. Do you wonder that I love you?'

She held up her face, mutely offering her lips, and Matthew kissed her until she had to protest.

'What a sight I must look,' she murmured, putting up her hands to her hair. 'You're a very rough lover, Matthew.'

'Not half as rough as I'm going to be, my girl. Which brings me to the subject of the wedding. We'll get married next month. Your wedding gown can be made in our own department – it'll be a good advertisement. I can only manage a week for the honeymoon. Where would you like to go?'

He paused as he realized that Genevra was helpless with laughter.

'I'll leave the choice to you,' she said. 'You seem to have settled everything else. A month is very short notice, but I suppose I shall have to give in to you.'

'Six weeks?' Matthew offered. 'I don't want to begin by dictating to you.'

'Next m-month will be very suitable,' Genevra said.

'Oh, Matthew, you are funny! You know perfectly well that if I said I needed six weeks to get ready you'd immediately start trying to whittle the time down to what you really want. I've learnt a thing or two about your tactics while I've been working for you.'

'I drive a good bargain,' Matthew agreed. 'And when it's something I want as much as I want to be married to you then I don't have any scruples about how I get my way. Shall I kiss you into submission, baggage?'

'That would be lovely,' Genevra said. 'Oh, what a dreadful life I'm going to have! And how I'm going to enjoy it!'